The Big Ask

Also by Shane Maloney

The Brush-Off
Stiff
Nice Try

The Big Ask

A Murray Whelan Mystery

SHANE MALONEY

ARCADE PUBLISHING • NEW YORK

Originally published in Australia by Text Publishing

This is a work of fiction. Names, characters, places, and incidents are either the product of the author's imagination or used fictitiously.

Arcade Publishing books may be purchased in bulk at special discounts for sales promotion, corporate gifts, fund-raising, or educational purposes. Special editions can also be created to specifications. For details, contact the Special Sales Department, Arcade Publishing, 307 West 36th Street, 11th Floor, New York, NY 10018 or arcade@skyhorsepublishing.com.

Arcade Publishing® is a registered trademark of Skyhorse Publishing, Inc.®, a Delaware corporation.

Visit our website at www.arcadepub.com.

10 9 8 7 6 5 4 3 2 1

Library of Congress Cataloging-in-Publication Data is available on file.

ISBN: 978-1-62872-416-5

Printed in the United States of America

This project was assisted by the City of Melbourne.

The author gratefully acknowledges the support of the Clarisse Ghirardelli Writers Centre.

This book is dedicated
to Christine, Wally and May.
I have no choice—
they know where I live.

The author of this book, its setting and its characters are entirely fictitious. There is no such place as Melbourne. The Australian Labor Party exists only in the imagination of its members.

The Big Ask

1

THE SMART MONEY was home in bed.

It was 4:30 A.M., a Monday morning at the arse-end of winter, and I should have been there too, clocking up a few hours' sleep before the eight o'clock flight to Sydney. My son Red was somewhere in Sin City, missing and possibly in danger.

Instead, I was sitting in a greasy spoon cafe at the Melbourne Wholesale Fruit and Vegetable Market, nursing a bruised forehead, drinking over-brewed coffee and talking to a truck driver named Donny Maitland about his campaign to unseat the leadership of the United Haulage Workers.

Dawn was still two hours away and a frigid wind was sweeping off Port Phillip Bay, one of those bone-chilling breezes that descend on Melbourne in late winter and make us wonder why we bother to live here. Vendors were standing in front of their stalls, stamping their feet and rubbing their hands together. Beyond them, past rampaging forklifts and crates of vegetables, the tower blocks of the central city were etched against the sky above the railway switching yards, dark on dark.

Donny had just arrived, five hours from Nar Nar Goon with a load of spuds. He breezed through the door in a gust of arctic air, a craggy, cleft-chinned, stout-featured bloke in a woolen pea-jacket.

One of those men, you knew if he was ever hit, wouldn't fall down. Not that I could imagine anyone trying it on. Donny wasn't that type. His body was a fact, not an assertion. Something he lugged around to do the work.

He spotted me straight up, plonked his frame onto the stool beside me and laid a hefty hand on my shoulder. A flush of good cheer rose across his cheekbones like old sunburn, almost managing to conceal the fatigue in his amiable brown eyes. He must have been shagged, a night behind the wheel, but he wore it well. Donny was a stayer, all right. More than once over the years, he'd drunk me under the table while the women came and went, talking of Michelangelo. Or Solzhenitsyn. Or Sinatra.

"Sorry to keep you waiting, Murray," he declared. "I stopped to help some bloke who'd lost his load on the South Gippsland Highway. Hope the bastard votes for me."

"It'll take more than random acts of kindness to win control of the Haulers," I said.

Donny jerked his thumb over his shoulder. "Don't worry, comrade. The rest of the crew are on the case, spreading the word among the cabbages. And the kings, too, if they find any. For the time has come, as the walrus said."

I glanced through the glass wall of the eatery and caught sight of one of Donny's running mates, a scarecrow of a bloke called Roscoe, as he disappeared into the hurly-burly of the market, distributing handbills. Donny extracted a sheaf of flyers from his peajacket and thrust one into my hand. "Vote UHW Reform Ticket," it was headed. "Fight for a Union that Fights for Its Members."

As I read, Donny squinted at my forehead. "Where'd you get the bump? You look like you've gone three rounds with a revolving door."

I touched my hairline and winced. "Must be this all-male environment."

"You've been brawling, haven't you?" Donny tilted his chin up and stared at me with astonishment. "In the twenty years we've known each other, I've never once heard of you swinging a punch."

"The other bloke swung first and swung harder," I said morosely. "Name of Darren Stuhl."

"Bob Stuhl's son?" Donny puffed his cheeks and exhaled. "Runs the Stuhl Holdings depot down here for his old man. Did he realize he was taking a poke at a senior advisor to the Minister for Transport?"

"This was personal, not professional," I said. "We had a run-in a couple of nights ago. I never expected to see him again. Then, five minutes after I arrive here at the market, he turns up and decides to go for a repeat performance."

Donny grinned and shook his head. "You're a wild man, Murray Whelan. What's Angelo Agnelli going to say when he finds out his trusty lieutenant has been trading punches with the heir to the biggest private trucking company in the country?"

"What the boss doesn't know won't hurt him." My gaze extended over Donny's shoulder, out to where a dark-haired man in a gray leather jacket was leaning against a crate of oranges. He had a face like a cop in a French movie and his thousand-yard stare was turned in our direction. "And right now we've got a more pressing problem than some bad-tempered rich kid," I said. "You know a Haulers' organizer by the name of Frank Farrell?"

Donny looked at me over the rim of his cardboard cup. "I do indeed," he said. "He's an all-purpose goon. Ex-shearer, ex-army. Works both sides of the street. A head-kicker for the union who does freelance favors for Bob Stuhl."

"Well, he's spotted us," I said. "And right now he's putting two and two together and concluding that you and I didn't just happen to bump into each other. Come office hours, he'll be on his mobile phone reporting to Hauler headquarters that a member of the minister's staff was cooking something up with a rank-and-file activist in the market cafe. And I don't mean toasted sandwiches."

Government interference in the internal affairs of a union was the dish Angelo Agnelli had in mind. A little stirring of the industrial pot. But the success of the recipe would depend on whether Donny could stand the heat of the kitchen.

He turned to look, but I clamped my hand on his forearm. "Farrell told me he was here to deal with some sort of irritation," I warned.

"That'd be us." Donny looked pleased. "Word must've got back that the natives are restless."

"And Farrell's not alone. He's got a bunch of roughnecks with him, lurking around the Stuhl Holdings depot."

"Told you they consider us a threat," said Donny. "I'd better warn the others to expect trouble. We can't ask anybody to vote for us if we can't hold our ground, so we should put on a bit of a show." He checked his watch. "It's 4:40 now. We'll rustle up a campaign rally in the parking lot in thirty minutes, show the flag before the place closes for the day."

"I can't stay that long," I said. "Something's come up. You remember Red, lives in Sydney with his mother, Wendy?"

"Never understood what you saw in that woman," nodded Donny.

"One of the eternal mysteries," I agreed. "The thing is, Red's done a bunk. Disappeared. I'm on a flight at eight. Thirteen years old. I've got to tell you, mate, I'm worried sick."

"Ah, jeeze," said Donny. "Thirteen, eh? Last time I saw the little tacker he couldn't have been more than five or six. Anything I can do?"

"You can tell me where I can call a cab," I said. "I need to get home, change my clothes, pack a bag."

"Forget the cab," he said. "Stick around. The rally won't take long and then I'll run you home. Drive you to the airport, too, if you want. It'll be faster that way, I guarantee. You can't leave before you've had the chance to see us in action." Donny glanced across the cafe and grinned. "Hello, here's Heather."

Heather was Donny's sister-in-law and the partner in his trucking business. Once upon a very short time, I was a frog that she'd kissed. She was, I feared, still on a quest for my inner prince. And she was steaming towards us, weaving through the tables, denim skirt swirling at mid-calf, a chunky little Dolly Parton. Heads turned, tracking her progress.

"Uh-oh," I said.

Heather joined us at the counter and signaled for a coffee. "Well, well," she said, a devious smile dimpling her cheeks. "Look who's here."

"What an unexpected surprise," I said.

"I'm here to talk to clients," she explained. "Try to hustle up some jobs. Times are tough and this union crap isn't going to make life any easier." She nodded at the leaflet in my hand. "You should know better than to encourage him."

Donny climbed off his stool and surrendered it to Heather with a sarcastic bow. "Leave the boy alone," he said. "Can't you see he's been in the wars. Here five minutes and some dickhead tries to rearrange his face."

"You're kidding?" Heather registered the swelling on my forehead and her tone softened. "You're not kidding, are you? You look like shit."

"She's a real charmer, isn't she?" said Donny. "See you in the parking area in half an hour, Murray. Tough customer like you might be handy, push comes to shove."

I nodded. Another thirty minutes weren't going to make much difference, one way or another. Donny took his campaign leaflets and his impregnable confidence and vanished into the vegetal world of the market.

"So," demanded Heather. "What happened to you?"

It was too humiliating to recount. I stared down into my coffee, brown sludge, lukewarm and oversweetened. "Long story," I muttered.

"It always is." She shook her head, no stranger to the infinite foolishness of the male species. "And I thought you were a nice boy."

"You should know better than that," I said, absently probing the tender spot.

She dug in her bag and found a pack of aspirin. I washed down a couple of tablets and rubbed my eyes. "Sorry," I yawned. "I haven't been to bed yet."

"C'mon, then." She took my elbow and stood me up. "If you're going to stay, we might as well do something about your war wound."

She had the burger flipper put some ice in a plastic bag, then she led me back through the market, greeting and being greeted. Across the shed, I saw Donny's mate Roscoe in animated conversation with a forklift driver, pressing a handbill on him. A man in a football beanie and leather apron came out of a vendor's stall and rousted him away. Above the stall was a sign with the proprietor's name. It was one I recognized from newspaper stories about pre-dawn slayings in suburban driveways. Incidents attributed to a well-known Italian self-help association.

"It's a world of its own," said Heather. "They'll have Donny for breakfast."

"I'm sure he can look after himself."

"Yeah?" she said.

A fine drizzle alighted on our shoulders as we stepped out into the parking area. Trucks and vans of every size, age and make crowded the asphalt. Motorized trolleys darted between them, ferrying all the roots and leaves it takes to feed three million hungry mouths. An ethereal light leaked down upon the scene from the distant pinnacles of towering stanchions, casting murky shadows between the parked rigs.

The Maitland truck was slotted between a big refrigerator rig and an old Bedford with the word "Foodbank" stenciled on the tailgate. "Strange name," I said.

"A charity," explained Heather. "They collect perishable foodstuffs, then distribute them to worthy causes."

I'd be the one perishing if I didn't get out of the cold.

Heather opened the cabin door. "Up you get," she instructed, indicating the narrow sleeping ledge behind the bench seat. "Make yourself comfortable."

Compliant to orders, I shucked off my shoes and clambered up.

Heather, kneeling on the passenger seat, covered me with a blanket and pressed a cube of ice gently to my brow. "Poor baby," she cooed. "Does that feel better?"

Much better. I closed my eyes and sighed.

"You know what you need, Murray?" murmured Heather. "A bit of tender loving care, that's what."

She spoke a simple truth. "Hmmm," I agreed.

A kind of blank exhaustion settled over me, a state of suspended animation. Time must have passed, but I had no sense of its progress. Then the truck swayed slightly and the door swung shut. I heard the click of the lock and opened my eyes. Heather's face filled my field of vision, her eyes brimming with compassion.

Nope. It was something else. She leaned closer and touched her lips to mine.

It was so long since I'd felt a woman's kiss that I couldn't summon the power to resist. The kiss lengthened, widened, deepened. Heather's mouth was infinitely inviting, wordlessly eloquent, irresistibly persuasive. I felt myself succumbing.

"Yummy," she breathed.

Her hand slid under the blanket and tugged at my sweater. Shivers ran down my spine and a low moan escaped from somewhere deep within my chest. Goosebumps rose as her cool fingers found my skin.

"No," I protested, perhaps less than insistent.

"Sssh." Heather's tongue traced a wet path across my cheek and explored my ear. "Don't say anything."

Then she was up on the ledge beside me, backing me deeper into the narrow space. She pinned me against the curtained rear window, her thigh flung across mine. Her hands were busy between us, probing, unbuttoning, delving.

Pop, pop, pop went the stud-buttons of her quilted vest. Pop, pop went her shirt front. She pushed my jersey up around my neck and the lace of her bra scraped across my exposed chest. Another furtive groan escaped my lips.

"You like that," she whispered. "Don't you?"

The evidence was in hand, the *corpus* was in *delicti*. More kisses devoured my face, fed by every feeble move I made to elude them. My willpower was melting in the heat of our mingled breaths. To prevent Heather tumbling, half-undressed, backwards into the driver's seat, I put an arm around her. Jesus, I thought, I'm in big trouble here.

"Just like old times," she said, hiking up her skirt.

We writhed together on the narrow ledge. It was like trying to have it off in a horizontal phone booth. And there was nothing long-distance about the call that Heather was placing.

"Heather." I used my most forceful tone. "This is not a good idea."

Heather was not of the same opinion. She unfastened her bra and smothered my objections. I tried to turn away, honest I did. It was useless. My resistance was wilting. It was the only thing that was.

"Relax," she purred, her hair falling around my ears, her abundance stoppering my mouth. "I'm not going to do a *Fatal Attraction* on you."

I didn't want to give her the wrong impression about my true feelings. But those breasts, Christ Almighty. A man would have to be made of stone. Part of me felt like it already was.

A veil of condensation had formed on the truck's windows, hiding us from the world outside. I pressed my palm against the glass and smeared the cool moisture across my face. Heather's face was elsewhere and not at all cold.

"Please," I moaned. Through the hole in the condensation, I glimpsed the corporate slogan on the rear bumper of a Stuhl Holdings truck: BOB STUHL IS BIG. Mine was too.

Further across the parking area, Donny was climbing onto a stack of pallets, his pea-jacket buttoned to the neck. He raised a bullhorn and the muffled sound of his voice swept across the bitumen, echoing off the sides of the sheds. I could just make out Roscoe, standing beside the pallets as if on sentry duty. A small, tentative cluster of onlookers began to form.

"The rally," I said. "Donny'll notice if I'm not there. Heather, please stop."

She did, raising her eyes and fixing me with a wicked smile. Then, suddenly, she tried to pull my sweater off. "Skin," she demanded. "I want more skin."

Her recklessness was exhilarating. Her knees were planted on either side of my chest, blanketing my nether regions in the tented folds of her skirt. She reached down and began to tinker with my front-end alignment.

"Um," I said, not meaning a word of it. According to Saint Augustine, a standing prick has no conscience. Neither, for that matter, does a reclining one.

Donny's voice rose and fell and his arm pumped the air. More figures materialized in the pre-dawn gloom, converging on the pallets. Among them I recognized Frank Farrell, the Haulers' enforcer, his fist raised. Heather, meanwhile, was engaged in a complex docking maneuver. "Murray," she said sternly. "It takes two, you know."

An overcoated figure broke from the fringe of the crowd and vaulted up beside Donny. "Something's happening," I reported.

It certainly was. Heather bore down, mission accomplished. A rare pleasure suffused my loins. I closed my eyes and surrendered. At that moment, Donny's oration ceased.

With Heather's clutch fully engaged, I strained to see through the smeared glass. The man who'd jumped up beside Donny was reaching into his coat. He pulled something out and pressed it to Donny's temple. The crowd began to scatter. A confused tangle of bodies contested the rostrum. A sharp crack rang in my ears.

And again. And again.

In her amorous enthusiasm, Heather was pounding the top of my head against the wall of the cabin. Interesting cure for a headache. Unless she stopped, I'd have a cerebral hemorrhage. I squirmed out from underneath her and tumbled down onto the seat.

"What's wrong?" she pleaded. "I thought you liked me."

I fumbled on the floor for my shoes, levering my camshaft back into my pants. "I do," I said. "I'm just not ready for a relationship."

"A relationship?" She started tucking her upholstery back into place.

My shoes were under the seat, along with a hefty shifting spanner. "It's a bit sudden, that's all," I said. Laces dangling, spanner in hand, I hit the bitumen.

"A relationship?" Heather repeated plaintively. "I'd settle for a bit of slap and tickle."

The air was thick with exhaust fumes, the smell of burnt rubber and decaying vegetable matter. Everywhere, trucks were in motion, great wheeled walls of steel and chrome, pumping a grimy haze into the air, their towering bullbars advancing before them.

I picked my way through the obstacle course of vehicles, some moving, some stationary. By the time I reached the stack of pallets, the crowd had vanished. It was like it had never been there, as if I'd imagined everything. The only evidence that anything had happened was a broken megaphone. It lay in a shallow puddle, its handle shattered, batteries strewn across the ground.

I climbed the pallets and scanned the scene. The drizzle was thickening into a solid rain. The parking area was rapidly emptying. Here and there, hunched pedestrians flitted through the semi-darkness. I headed for the floodlit shelter of the main shed and loped into the market. Stalls were closing up. Loads of produce were being shunted into coolrooms. Nothing for me there. Breathless, wondering what was going on, I sprinted back towards the truck.

Head down against the rain, dashing past the Foodbank truck, I slammed head-on into Frank Farrell.

He dropped his mobile phone and it skittered across the wet asphalt. As he bobbed down to snatch it up, the hard man ran his hard eyes over the spanner in my hand. "Been tightening somebody's nuts?"

I ignored him, kept going and found Donny with one foot on his driver-side step, beginning to climb aboard. He was wild-eyed, hyperenergized, rain streaming down his face. "Did you see the crowd? Twenty-five, thirty, that's good for here," he babbled. "When Farrell and his hoons realized we were prepared to stick up for ourselves, they put their tails between their legs and took off."

"Was that Darren Stuhl?" I interrupted. "Was that a gun he was waving around?"

"Fucking idiot. Trying to prove what a big man he was. I knew he didn't have the guts to use it. Not in front of witnesses, anyway. Don't say anything to Heather, eh? She gives me a hard enough time already."

He dragged the door open and swung himself up into the driver's seat. I headed for the passenger side, skirting the front of the truck. Checking for oncoming vehicles, I glanced back in the direction of the market. Frank Farrell had reached the canopy and slowed to a casual amble, heading inside with his hands rammed into the slit pockets of his jacket.

I climbed aboard, tossing the spanner back where it belonged. Heather scooted to the center of the seat, bone-dry between two dripping men. She gave me a withering look, then folded her arms across her ample chest and stared straight ahead. "You two had your fun?" she sniffed.

Donny tapped the top of the steering wheel impatiently as he pumped the accelerator, revving the engine. "We can do it," he muttered, half talking to himself. "I had my doubts before, but I'm certain now. We can win this thing."

Noise filled the cabin. The roar of air from the demisters, blasting the fog from the windshield. The slap and sluice of the wipers, the percussive pounding of rain on the metal roof. I checked the time and felt a surge of panic.

Heather saw me look at my watch, registered my anxiety. "Murray's a man in a hurry," she told Donny. "Isn't that right?"

Absolutely. Thanks to Heather's ministrations, time had got away from me. It was past 5:30. We were cutting it fine. If I missed the plane, it would definitely prove my failure as a father.

Donny slammed the stick into first and the gears screamed like a Jimi Hendrix solo. We inched forward, a wall of heavy-caliber traffic blocking our way, bottlenecked at the exit gate. A gap opened, Donny swung the wheel and we lurched forward. Heather put her hand on my knee.

"Shift it," I muttered. I was talking to the truck in front. Any slower and it would've been going backwards. An air horn sounded behind us, one long continuous blast, on and on.

Then came a pounding on Donny's door, the bang-banging of a balled fist. His arm pumped and his head went out the window. Somebody shouted up at him, staccato sentences, inaudible against all the background noise. Donny cursed, slammed the truck into neutral, hauled on the hand-brake and climbed down.

"With Donny there's always something," muttered Heather.

I swung open my door and craned back. A curtain-wall truck was pulled up behind us at an angle. The name on the side ended in a vowel. A dwarf-like Sicilian in a leather apron was remonstrating with Donny. Even by the usual standards, he was agitated, jabbering and gesturing into the space we'd just left.

A dark shape lay there on the ground. Whatever it was, we'd made a mess of it. Rolled over it with the rear trailer wheels, burst it open and smeared its contents across the asphalt.

"We've run over something," I told Heather. "Sack of tomatoes, by the look of it. Donny's getting an earful from some Italian bloke."

"Damn," she said. "It'll be pay up, or spend all day arguing the toss."

Not what I wanted to hear. And now more of them were arriving. The United Nations General Assembly, plenary session. Donny was down on one knee, assessing the damage. Slap, slap, slap went the windshield wipers, escalating my impatience, now at the jiggling, buttock-clenching stage.

"I'm going to leg it, try to get a taxi," I told Heather. "I've got a plane to catch. Donny will explain."

She eyed me skeptically. "Is it just me, or are you like this with all women?"

I hoisted my jacket over my head, took a parting glance at the damaged-goods conference and trotted towards the gate, shoes slipping on the rain-greasy asphalt. I felt bad about running out on Donny, but not bad enough to stay behind and risk missing my flight.

If I'd looked back, even for a moment, I might have seen what was looming. I might have seen the great tidal wave of shit that was about to break over me. Just one backward glance and Donny might still be alive. And I wouldn't be languishing in the place where I am now.

2

IT WAS ALL ANGELO AGNELLI'S FAULT, of course.

If it wasn't for Angelo, I would never have been at the market in the first place. I wouldn't have been trying to play funny buggers with the most powerful and dangerous union in the state. I most certainly wouldn't have found myself trying to second-guess a man like Frank Farrell.

The Honorable Angelo Agnelli, member of the Legislative Council, was the Minister for Transport in the sovereign state of Victoria. And it all began in his office on the previous Friday evening. His Parliament House office, to be precise, in the majestic old legislature atop the gentle rise at the eastern edge of Melbourne's central business district.

As government leader in the Upper House, Ange was entitled to one of the building's more imposing bureaux. Its antique desk, French-polished bookcases, overstuffed chairs, velvet curtains, flock wallpaper and molded cornices dated from the time when our city was a shining colonial jewel in Queen Victoria's crown. His office, in short, looked a cross between Lord Palmerston's study and a Wild West bordello.

It was August 1991 and even Blind Freddy could see that his enjoyment of these facilities was nearing its conclusion. After a decade in office, Labor had lost the plot. It was common wisdom that our defeat at the next state election was inevitable. But the election was still a year away. In the meantime, the sorry business of government went on.

There were three of us, men in suits. Agnelli was standing behind his desk, his waistcoat unbuttoned. Pushing fifty, he was no longer the boy wonder and his once-beaming dial had turned into a doughy ball in which his wary eyes were set like raisins in a slab of stale fruitcake.

Out on the floor of the chamber, Angelo did his best to project an image of senatorial gravitas, gray of temple, thick of waist, measured of speech and glad of hand. In the privacy of his office, during the parliamentary dinner recess, he dispensed with any such pretense. He held a tightly rolled newspaper in his fist and was smacking it against his thigh as he spoke.

"As if I don't have enough on my plate, *thwap*, what with Treasury screwing me to the floor over the budget estimates," he said. "Now I've got a *thwap* bushfire to fight. What am I paying you for, Nev, *thwap*? If it isn't to keep this sort of crap, *thwap*, out of the papers?"

Neville Lowry was Agnelli's press secretary. He was a tall, sad-faced ex-journalist with a permanent stoop, a reedy voice and about as much hair as it would take to stuff a pincushion. He was perched like a heron on the arm of the office chesterfield, his shoulders slumped forward in the melancholic posture appropriate to his vocation. "It's the *Herald*, Ange," he pleaded. "You know what they're like."

Lowry did not need to elaborate. Melbourne's afternoon broadsheet had never been sympathetic to the Australian Labor Party, in or out of office. And its current editor, a Murdoch hack with the physique of Jabba the Hut and the morals of a conger eel, had made it his mission in life to torment us at every opportunity.

"But the *Herald* wouldn't have it, *thwap*, if somebody hadn't, *thwap*, leaked it." Agnelli turned his ire on me. "And that's your *thwap* department, Murray."

Neville Lowry was a comparatively recent addition to Angelo's staff and he still tended to pay the boss some degree of deference. Not a mistake I was likely to make. I leaned forward in my chair and displayed the palms of my hands. "What am I now?" I said. "The resident plumber?"

For almost seven years I'd worked for Angelo. Stoking the boilers of policy analysis. Tending the vineyards of administrative superintendence. Fixing his fuck-ups and burying his boo-boos. Almost seven years. It was beginning to feel like eternity. First I was Angelo's electorate officer, inherited with the fittings and fixtures when a factional deal handed him a safe seat in the northern suburbs. Back then I managed his constituent affairs, fending off cranky voters and stroking the local party apparatus. And when, in our second term, he was appointed Minister for Ethnic Affairs, he took me along for the ride. This was designed to fend off any suspicion of wog favoritism. As he pointed out at the time, with his characteristic mastery of the bleeding obvious, Murray Whelan is not an Italian name.

Other portfolios followed, rungs in Angelo's ascent up the ladder of political preferment. We'd climbed them together. Local Government. The Arts. Water Supply. Agriculture and Fisheries. And now the big one, the jackpot. In a Cabinet reshuffle the previous month, Angelo had been catapulted into the job of head honcho of the state's rail, tram and road networks.

In better times such a promotion would've been cause for celebration. Unfortunately, Transport had become a poisoned chalice, claiming the careers of two of Angelo's predecessors in less than a year. The problem was money. The government had run out of it. The boom days of the eighties were over and the chickens of fiscal profligacy had come home to roost. With the state deficit running at Brazilian levels, the minister's task was reduced to screwing as much revenue out of the system as possible while presiding over a one-hundred-million-dollar budget cut.

A man of conviction and inner resource might have been able to cope. But those terms had never been applicable to Angelo. In the previous three weeks he'd veered from steely resolve to catatonic retreat to blustering bravado. Now he was tearing strips off his advisors. "A leak," he repeated, *thwap*. "Somebody's got it in for me."

"That's a pretty wide field, Ange," I said.

"You know what the *Herald*'s like," moaned Nev Lowry again. "And the Buzz doesn't even pretend to be factual."

The Buzz was the *Herald*'s gossip column, a vehicle for all manner of kite-flying and bait-laying. It was a gadfly in that day's Buzz which had flown up Angelo's trouser leg, a snippet headed TRUCK CASH GRAB.

"The Buzz has it that incoming transportation supremo Angelo Agnelli has been cooking up plans to slap a hefty new tax on trucks. Makes you wonder how the government's union cronies will react to attempts to slug their members. Not to mention the big wheels of the Transport Industry Association. Somebody should warn the minister that you tangle with the truckies at your peril."

This was a complete beat-up.

Okay, it was true that a Treasury proposal had recently crossed Angelo's desk, arguing for a tonnage levy on heavy trucks to help defray the damage these multi-wheeled behemoths inflicted on the public highway. It was also true that the last time the government tried to make the private transport industry pay its way, irate truck-owners had blockaded the state's milk supplies, forcing a humiliating backdown. Angelo's response to the Treasury proposal had been to bin it. Our administration might have been terminal but it wasn't suicidal.

"Nev here has issued a press release denying any planned increase in motor registration charges," I said, throwing a bridge over Angelo's troubled waters. "And, if you want, I'll interrogate the girls in the Treasury typing pool."

Angelo nodded, tossed the newspaper aside and sat down, as though content that his clumsy minions were now showing some evidence of competence. But we both knew that the real cause of his agitation wasn't the piece in the paper. Nor the possibility of a leak. The entire government administration, after all, leaked like a prostate patient with a prolapsed bladder. No, the gossip column item had merely triggered an inevitable event, one that Angelo had been dreading.

"Howard Sharpe's got a damned nerve, turning up on my doorstep like this," he said. "If the state secretary of the United Haulage Workers has something to talk about, he can make an appointment like anyone else."

Nev Lowry unfolded his legs and began edging towards the door. Not that he wasn't interested in relations between the government and the unions. As a young journalist Nev had often dreamed of covering first-hand the horrors of war and pestilence. He just didn't want to be around when the Haulers arrived. Who could blame him? Angelo flapped his wrist, dismissing his press secretary.

"Just tell Sharpe it's a typical piece of *Herald* mischief," I said. "A minor variation on their usual union-bashing theme. Or a bureaucratic cock-up. Disavow all knowledge. Better still, I'll go out and tell him you're not available. Like you said, he should've made an appointment."

"Might as well front him now, get it over with," said Angelo. "If it isn't this, it'll be something else. Soon as I got this job, I knew that Sharpe'd be looking for a pretext to ambush me, to let me know what a tough customer he is. This job's difficult enough already. It'll be impossible if Sharpe thinks he can just waltz in here and throw his weight around any time the mood takes him."

Howard Sharpe's weight was considerable. The United Haulage Workers was bigger than some of the government departments that Angelo had headed. Its twenty-five thousand truck and tanker drivers, aircraft refuelers, baggage handlers and forklift operators moved everything from beer to bricks. Or not, if Howard said so. As well as buildings and cash assets totaling at least twenty million dollars, the Haulers controlled a pension fund in the region of five hundred million. And, not least, a sizable block of votes on the Labor Party's central administrative panel.

But the Haulers were more than an association of honest toilers, more than just a power base for the right wing of the party, more than just Howard Sharpe's personal fiefdom. They were a law unto themselves. Judge, jury and, it was whispered, executioner.

"Perhaps this is an opportunity to mend some fences, get a bit of dialogue happening," I suggested, not altogether facetiously.

"Too late for that," said Angelo. "Sharpe's got a long memory and he's a man who knows how to nurse a grudge."

Agnelli was referring to an encounter during his pre-parliamentary incarnation as an industrial relations lawyer. Acting on behalf of the Construction Laborers' Union, Ange had successfully sued the Haulers after several of their members, cement-truck drivers, crossed a CLU picket line at the urging of Haulers' officials. In the ensuing scuffle, a CLU member was drowned in wet concrete. No criminal charges were ever laid but Ange won the CLU handsome civil-action damages, which it used to foil attempts by the Haulers to poach its members.

"Howard Sharpe came here for a test of strength," said Angelo, standing up and buttoning his voluminous midriff into his waistcoat. "And that's exactly what he's going to get." He inflated his shoulders, tugged downwards to firm the fit of his suit, adjusted the knot of his tie and stiffened his upper lip. "Time to grasp the nettle."

"The United Haulage Workers isn't a nettle," I muttered, falling into step. "It's the spinning blade of an electric blender."

The entrance hall of Victoria's Parliament House is paved with mosaic tiles in the pattern of the state bird, a forest-dwelling litter-fossicker. The ceiling of this grand vestibule is so high that you can get a crick in your neck just trying to find it. It is a space designed to impress. The three representatives of the United Haulage Workers did not look impressed. They rose as one from a padded bench and advanced to meet us.

"Gentlemen," declared Agnelli. "What a surprise. Just happened to be in the neighborhood, I suppose. Thought you'd drop in and say hello. Very considerate of you."

Howard Sharpe was a florid-faced, obese man in his early sixties. His belly preceded him in a bullish, self-satisfied way and his bibulous nose seemed to be glowing even more ominously than usual. He returned Agnelli's greeting with a cursory nod. "You know Mike McGrath, don't you?" he grunted.

McGrath was his deputy secretary, a thin-lipped individual with round, horn-rimmed glasses and the tapering face of a high-minded ferret. Despite his title, Mike would've had trouble distinguishing a tip-truck from a tenor trombone. His true function was that of Howard's bag man, number cruncher, head-kicker and general gofer. He was being groomed, it was widely believed, for a safe spot on the Senate ticket. To Mike McGrath's way of thinking, anybody entering politics with motives other than ulterior was a *prima facie* idiot.

"And this is Frank Farrell." Sharpe indicated the third man. "Our membership welfare officer."

Sharpe and McGrath were wearing suits, strictly off-the-rack. Farrell wore a gray leather blouson-type jacket over a black turtleneck sweater and neatly pressed jeans. He was somewhere between forty and fifty with thick, brushed-back hair and pumice-stone skin. He shook Angelo's hand, then mine. He had a breezy, masculine manner and a grip that left no doubt about his physical capabilities. Despite his job title, there was no hint of the caring professions about Frank Farrell. Nor was there any hint of the extent to which our destinies would intertwine. If there had been, I probably would have turned tail and fled.

Muscle, I thought. When it came to finesse, nobody beat the Haulers.

"Better come into the parlor," said Agnelli, leading us down the corridor and back into his office. "Sit, sit," he urged, assuming the power position behind his desk.

Sharpe and McGrath glanced around as if trying to decide what to smash first. Or, in McGrath's case, steal. Eventually, they figured out the purpose of the chairs. Farrell remained standing, leaning against the door frame, well behind the action. I took up a position beside Agnelli's desk, put my hands in my pockets and did my best to impersonate an innocent bystander.

The boss leaned back in his chair and spread his arms. "Fire away," he said. I hoped that our visitors would not take his words literally.

Sharpe was out of breath from his waddle down the corridor and the exertion of sitting down. "So, Agnelli," he wheezed. "Tell us about this plan of yours."

"Plan? What plan?" Agnelli raised his shoulders theatrically, a gesture bred into his Latin genes. "Do we have any plans, Murray?"

"Plenty of plans," I said. "No shortage of plans around here."

"You want to talk plans, Howard," said Agnelli, "you should drop in on the Minister for Planning. He's got plans coming out his arsehole. Isn't that right, Murray?"

"Arsehole," I agreed.

Sharpe leaned forward, his shirt buttons straining, and rested an elbow on his broad knee. He wanted it clearly understood that he was not to be mocked. "Cut the crap," he barked. "You know very well what plan I mean. This truck tax increase. We're not going to wear it, you know."

"Ah, yes." Angelo pressed his fingertips together and contemplated the ceiling for a moment. "The item in this afternoon's paper. Had somebody read it to you, did you? And then you thought you'd drop around, demand to know where I got the temerity to think I might have the right to read my own departmental correspondence without first asking your permission."

"So it's true," said McGrath.

"Maybe," said Angelo. "Maybe not. Either way I certainly don't intend to be made to account for myself on the basis of an item of gossip in a rag like the *Herald*. Nor do I appreciate being bushwhacked like this, Howard."

To Sharpe this was no more than preliminary small-talk. He'd come to flex his muscles and nothing Agnelli said was going to stop him. "Because a tonnage levy is the most stupid fucking idea in the entire fucking history of stupid fucking ideas," he fulminated. "And if you think we're going to sit still for it, you need your head examined.

The big outfits might be able to afford it. My blokes, the owner-operators, out there busting their guts every day just to survive, you might as well put them out of business, be done with it."

Agnelli nodded sagely, as if ruminating upon some ancient, imponderable mystery. "Your loyalty to your members is commendable, Howard. More of whom, by the way, work behind the counter in the airport cafeteria than own semitrailers. And while I'm always perfectly willing to consult with their duly elected leaders, that doesn't mean I'm prepared to have an ugly fuck of a bull-elephant wander into my office any time he likes and shit on the carpet."

Perhaps he was being a little provocative but I had to admire Angelo's moxie. This was Sharpe's ambush, after all, and he could hardly expect Ange to cop it sweet. He was in Agnelli's backyard now and if a dog can't bark in its own kennel, where can it? Not that a bit of barking ever deterred the Haulers. One time, story was, Sharpe wanted to make a point to an adversary. Bloke came home from work and found the Fido nailed to his front door.

If Agnelli's attitude was designed to aggravate, it was doing the trick. Sharpe flexed his jaw and I thought his nose was going to explode.

During all of this, I was studying Frank Farrell as he leaned against the deep frame of the closed door, his manner both relaxed and attentive, his hands clasped in front of him. He was a confident one, that was for sure. His face was expressionless but from time to time his black Irish eyes lit with a kind of sardonic glint, as though bemused that grown men could behave in such a manner. He was no mere meathead, that much was evident.

McGrath now spoke, the voice of moderation. "You know that you're going to have to deal with us, Angelo," he cooed. "So why make a stick to beat yourself with? Time like this, the Labor Party on the nose with the punters, we should all be pulling together. And you wouldn't want to jeopardize your preselection, would you?"

Melbourne Upper was one of the safest seats in the state. Safe for Labor, safe for Angelo. In all the time he'd held it, Ange had easily retained the endorsement of both the local branches and the party central office. Challengers had come and gone, of course, for ours is a democratic party and any clown is welcome to a tilt. But as the incumbent member, and a minister, Angelo had a secure grip on his seat. Despite the premier's attempts to convince the factional bosses to nominate more women as parliamentary candidates, the outcome of the preselection ballot in a little over a month's time was a mere formality.

"You must think I came down in the last shower, Mikey-boy," said Ange, leaning forward and putting his elbows on the desk. "But since you've raised the subject, aren't the Haulers due for an election in a few months? Your members must be getting pretty jack of officials who treat their union as no more than a launching pad for private political ambitions. It wouldn't surprise me if you boys find yourselves facing a bit of competition for once. There's a contender lurking in the wings, I hear."

"Bullshit," growled Howard Sharpe, his eyes narrowing. "What would you know about it?"

Angelo tapped the side of his nose. "All in good time, my friend. All in good time."

Mike McGrath, meanwhile, was peering through his spectacles at the bookcases, first at the calfskin-bound volumes of Hansard, most of which had not been opened since before the Boer, and then at Angelo's personal collection of political philosophy, which had not been opened at all.

McGrath started reading the titles aloud. *"A Critique of Political Economy,"* he sneered. *"Retreat from Class: The New Socialism."* He stood up, removed a volume, flipped through it and returned it to the shelf. "This is pretty dry stuff, Angelo. Where's your copy of the *Kama Sutra?*"

"That your idea of a witticism, is it?" said Agnelli. "A subtle hint that I should change my position."

Howard Sharpe gave a wheezy chuckle. "A word to the wise, that's all," he said, his belligerent tone now transformed into one of infinite concern. "We all have our weak spots. Especially those of us in the public eye." He formed a circle with his thumb and forefinger and made an illustrative gesture. If there'd been an Eskimo or a Hottentot in the room, even a member of the Liberal Party, Sharpe's meaning would have been obvious.

Angelo wasn't taking the bait. He shook his head with an air of disappointment. "Stop pulling yourself, Howard," he said. "You'll go blind."

An insistent ringing erupted in the background. The bells announcing the end of the dinner break and summoning members back to their places on the parliamentary benches. Angelo put his palms on the desk, applied his full weight and stood up. "It's been lovely chatting," he said. "But some of us have work to do. Don't hesitate to drop in again. No need for the bodyguard next time, Howard. Murray here isn't half as dangerous as he looks. Now fuck off."

That was my cue to open the door. As Farrell stepped aside, he gave me a collegial nod. Nothing personal, it seemed to say. All in a day's work for the likes of us, the common foot soldiery.

Sharpe continued to sit in poisonous silence, a lump of surly malevolence. He grunted at last, made a Darth Vader noise in the back of his throat, got up and lumbered out the door, his associates in his wake. "Round one," said McGrath as he filed past. "Nil all."

The moment I closed the door, Agnelli flopped back into his chair and heaved a small hurricane of relief. "Is that the best they can do?" he said.

I doubted it. This was no more than a courtesy visit, a presentation of the Haulers' calling card. A reminder, just in case he needed it, that if Angelo ever contemplated making a decision that might impinge on the Haulers' interests he should expect the worst for his political career and personal reputation.

"So who's this mystery contender?" I said, leaning back against the closed door as if to bar any attempt at re-entry by Sharpe and his associates.

"You," said Agnelli.

3

"ME?" I TILTED MY HEAD to one side and tapped my ear, like maybe my invisible hearing aid was on the fritz. "What do you mean, me?"

"I mean that Howard Sharpe and his cronies have been re-elected unopposed for as long as anyone can remember. It just occurred to me that rather than sitting around waiting for them to come to us, we should be taking the battle to them."

Angelo had come up with some crackpot schemes in his time, but this one took the tortellini. If I was hearing him right, he was instructing me to run against Howard Sharpe in the upcoming United Haulage Workers election. What button had been pushed in my employer's febrile temperament to generate such a deranged plan, I wondered?

Surely not the suggestion that he was involved in some kind of sexual impropriety. As well as being a tired and feeble scare tactic, the implication that Angelo was putting it about a bit would only have served to boost his middle-aged ego. He'd been married to the same woman for twenty years and there was nothing in his history to suggest Casanova tendencies. You only had to look at Ange to realize the idea was preposterous.

Could it have been the threat to his preselection? The Haulers had clout in the central party processes by dint of their delegate entitlements at the state conference and the funds they contributed to the organization's coffers. But Angelo's allies in the left-wing unions more than matched the Haulers' baleful influence. And the Sharpe gang cut little mustard among the rank-and-file party members in the electorate, the other component in the preselection equation.

"There is just one small obstacle to your plan, O Wise One," I said. "How can I run in the United Haulage Workers election? I'm not a member of the union."

Agnelli heaved an impatient sigh and began gathering papers off his desk, budget briefs to review while he was sitting in the chamber, making up the quorum. "Don't be so literal-minded," he said. "Of course you can't do it yourself. But a man of your broad acquaintance shouldn't have too much difficulty finding somebody to give it a shot. We throw a few dollars into the pot, stir gently, and then maybe Howard Sharpe's got something better to do with his time than think up ways to bust my balls."

"There's a very good reason why nobody challenges Howard Sharpe and Co," I reminded him. "It's a health hazard. Last time anybody so much as nominated, the poor bastard spend the next six months in traction." Or so the story went.

Agnelli tucked his papers under his arm, strode across the office and put his hand on the doorknob. "I have every confidence in your abilities, Murray," he said. "And turn off the lights when you leave. We're on an economy drive, don't forget."

I stood for a long time at the window, staring down into Spring Street. Rush hour was over, the working week at an end. The city was slipping into evening clothes. Across the road, a crowd was milling in front of the Princess Theatre. Its shingled roof was the shade of ashes and the highlights in its stained-glass windows glowed the color of clotted blood. A golden angel stood poised upon its roof, trumpet in hand, as if sounding the summons to Judgment Day. The words *Les Misérables* were blazoned across its marquee. I knew what they meant.

Out on the parliamentary terrace, the broad sweep of steps leading down to the street, stood a horse-drawn carriage, an open-topped landau. A top-hatted coachman sat stiffly at the reins, brass buttons gleaming, tall whip in hand. A bride and groom cavorted in the passenger seat, striking romantic poses while a photographer snapped away, framing his shots against the facade of Parliament House. It was a common enough Melbourne sight, a wedding album cliché.

In the stroboscopic stutter of the photographer's flash, the horse raised its tail and deposited a stream of steaming turds. The driver immediately reached under his seat and produced a whisk and a shovel.

That was me, I reflected. And I didn't even have shiny buttons or a broom. I headed for the door.

A trickle of honorable members was emerging from the dining room, braced with lamb cutlets and cabernet shiraz for a long and drowsy night of law-making. Howard Sharpe and Mike McGrath had waylaid one of them at the entrance to the main lobby, the Queen's Hall. A Labor backbencher from a marginal seat, he looked like a startled rabbit caught in the headlights of a runaway road train.

As I padded through the foyer, a woman bustled past, the press secretary of the deputy leader of the opposition. She looked the part, a snooty brunette in her late twenties with serious legs and a fiercely businesslike bearing. And a penchant for older men if the salacious scuttlebutt was to be believed. Obviously, I didn't qualify. She gave me a brusque nod and continued on her way. Considering that all the Liberals needed to do to win government was wait until it fell into their laps, I found her self-important manner mildly amusing. Her pins, on the other hand, warranted serious consideration and I sneaked a second appreciative look before heaving open one of Parliament House's massive bronze-inlaid entrance portals and slipping out into the night.

The sky was inky black, the air colder than a conservative's heart. The honk of a saxophone was faintly audible above the rhythmic clatter of a passing tram. At the foot of the terrace, overcoated couples strolled arm-in-arm beneath the fairy-lit trees of Bourke Street. Bound for dinner, I supposed. At Pelligrini's or Il Mondo, perhaps. Mietta's or the Florentino, if they could afford it. Maybe somewhere in Chinatown, a scant block away. Or one of the Greek joints on Lonsdale Street. To any of the cafes, brasseries, bistros, curry houses, pancake parlors and sushi salons that made Melbourne the epicurean epicenter of the nation. If it was edible, we'd eat it. If it wasn't, we'd suck it and see.

I paused for a moment, considering my options. A flame flickered a few paces away. Frank Farrell was standing in the colonnade, having a cigarette while he waited for his employers to emerge. We exchanged nods.

"Off home to the missus, then?" he said.

These were the first words Farrell had spoken since we were introduced. His tone was amiable, his voice a melodious baritone with residual traces of the bush. "No missus," I said. "No pets, either. Sorry to disappoint."

He chuckled and extended his pack of Marlboro. My daily limit was four and I'd already smoked three. I usually saved the last for after dinner but I found myself accepting his offer, bending to light it from a flame he conjured from a gold lighter in the cup of his blunt fingers.

"Bit rich, don't you think?" I said. "Sharpe and McGrath toting you along to put the frights on a government minister. No personal offense intended."

"None taken," said Farrell. "I was there to make up the numbers, that's all. Any meeting he ever goes to, Howard likes to know he's got the majority."

"He's quite a character, your Howard," I admitted.

"How about Agnelli? What are you doing working for a dipstick like that? No personal offense intended."

"It's a living," I shrugged.

"Not for much longer, it won't be. Plan to stick around until the election, sink with the ship?"

"You're not offering me a job, are you?"

"Something can always be found for a friend," he said.

"Ah, there's the rub."

Farrell nodded at the Windsor Hotel, catty-corner across the intersection. "Got time for a beer?"

I consulted my watch. "Thanks, but I've got a previous." And drinking with toughs was not high on my must-do list.

Farrell tossed his cigarette butt aside. "If you change your mind, give me a call."

"About having a beer?"

"About going down with the sinking ship." Abruptly he extended his hand.

I shook it. No union of any size, whatever its ideological disposition, can operate without a bit of brawn. Farrell at least had the virtue of not pretending he was anything else. Doubtless we would have dealings, and neither of us wanted to poison the wells yet. Like we both said, nothing personal.

I continued down the steps. The previous appointment was a fib. I had no plans. If I turned right and walked briskly, I'd be home in Fitzroy in less than fifteen minutes. But home exerted no irresistible attraction. I headed down Bourke Street, shoulders hunched against the cold, hands thrust deep into my pockets, my breath advancing before me in a white mist that vanished even as it appeared, ephemeral as an election promise, enduring as a good intention.

Three minutes later I was shouldering open the door of the Rumah Malaysia, breathing deep the aroma of ginger and chilli. The small restaurant was crowded, rackety with the clatter of cutlery and good cheer. The waiter held a single finger aloft, just in case I didn't speak Malay. "One," I agreed, and was led to a tragic, tiny table beside the kitchen door.

That was the way it had been for longer than I cared to contemplate. There had been the odd woman in my life since my divorce from Wendy. Odd as in infrequent, not peculiar. But none of them lasted. Not Helen the librarian or Claire the art restorer or Phillipa the doctor.

Phillipa was the most recent. I consulted her about my cigarette habit. She prescribed nicotine patches. Therapy proceeded to dirty weekends at charming little country hotels. But general practice was a tad dull for Dr. Phillipa Verstak. And so, apparently, was I. Six months earlier, at the end of summer, she'd gone back to her old job, fitting artificial limbs to land-mine victims at an Austcare hospital in Phnom Penh. How could I compete with legless Cambodian kiddies?

I would've felt a whole lot better about it if she'd managed to cure my cigarette habit. The very thought was enough to make me fire one up. I smoked it while I drank a bottle of Crown lager and waited for my meal to arrive. Four, five, what was the difference? I could die of lung cancer and nobody would shed a tear. Except my son, Red. He'd care. But Wendy probably wouldn't even bother telling him.

The laksa came rich and spicy, helped down with another bottle of beer. By the time I paid the bill, my blood was warm and my head was light. I sauntered back to Bourke Street, half thinking of catching a tram home, half drawn by the tinkle of feminine laughter coming from a line of people extending along the footpath to the front door of the Metro.

Time was, the Metro was a movie house, one of the town's grandest picture palaces. In the seventies, Callithumpian evangelists used it to stage spiritually uplifting productions of *Puff the Magic Dragon and His Technicolor Dreamcoat*. Recently, fashionable architects had transformed it into what the entertainment pages described as a cutting-edge dance club.

I wasn't entirely sure what that meant. Back when I was a barman at the Reservoir Hotel, we used to get some bloke with a panel van to bring in a mobile sound system and one of those modular disco dance floors with the flashing lights underneath. But that was hardly a dance club, was it?

Only one way to find out, I thought. The night was not yet middle-aged. Nor was I, if you counted forty as the starting point. And those bottles of beer had taken off at least a couple of years apiece. I checked out the line.

I put the median age at twenty-eight, give or take five years. Take, mainly. I was ten years older, but not offensively so. The boys tended to designer jeans and white T-shirts, the girls to scoop-neck dresses and balcony bras. Despite the nip in the air, there was plenty of skin on display. And some of the women were definite lookers. But I was hardly an impartial judge. After six months of celibacy, I was starting to get an erotic frisson from the dummies in shop windows. Nobody screamed when I joined the line.

The screaming would come later. And I'd be the one doing it.

4

A MATCHING PAIR OF BLONDES in micro-minis and stiletto heels stood sentinel at the Metro's entrance. They cast an appraising eye over my navy-blue Hugo Boss suit, concluded that I was pathologically unhip but otherwise both harmless and solvent, and raised the red rope. Doof, doof, doof, came the beat from the interior. Wang, wang, wang.

Twenty-five years earlier, I'd sat in the Metro and watched Gregory Peck and David Niven destroy the guns of Navarone. There was still plenty of smoke and noise and flashing light, but no sign of David Niven. Not his scene at all.

The seats had been ripped out, replaced by a dance floor. The movie screen was now a wall of video monitors, an animated matrix of MTV images, winking and blinking. DJs in white overalls tended a console of turntables, the bridge of the Starship Enterprise, warp-factor nine imminent. A central bar dispensed backlit liquors and bottles of Mexican beer with wedges of lime shoved in their necks. Beams of colored light zapped from gimbaled prisms set in huge robotic arms that swung out above the dance floor, flexing and pumping to the relentless beat. Doof, doof, doof.

It was still early, not quite eleven, and the place was only half-full. Hardly a thousand people were milling about, crowding the bars or bopping on the dance floor. There were so many blond tips that I wondered if they were spiking the drinks with peroxide. I shed my tie, left my jacket at the coat-check counter, rolled my sleeves to the forearm and elbowed my way to the booze. The happy-hour special was bourbon. To my surprise, it wasn't watered.

Glass in hand, I surveyed the dancers. Criss-crossed by searchlights and enveloped in clouds of artificial fog, they moved with jerky, pixilated movements to a persistent, all-encompassing, unvarying bass thump. Doof, doof, doof.

A suspended gangway led to the balcony where I'd once sat between my parents and watched *The Parent Trap*. It was now a lounge, booth seats with waitress service and a view of the video wall. There was no sign of Hayley Mills. Instead, clusters of frighteningly glamorous women sat around elaborate cocktails, checking the prospects. Even if I'd had the courage to approach one of them, I couldn't imagine bellowing pick-up lines over the top of Tina Turner. If the music got any louder, I'd start bleeding from the ears.

What I had in mind was a statuesque redhead with a come-hither look, the ability to read lips and a lapel badge that said "Take Me, Murray, I'm Yours." It looked like she hadn't arrived yet.

Some sort of VIP area occupied the topmost level, admission by membership key-tag only. Doubtless this was where the real fun was being had, the stuff involving rolled-up hundred-dollar bills and celebrity cleavage. Techno-beat clanging in my cranium, I retreated to a glassed-in area with a bar along one wall and a half-dozen pool tables covered in blue baize. It was less crowded and marginally quieter.

I took a stool at the bar, ordered another Wild Turkey and pondered my instructions from Agnelli. Any attempt to find a proxy challenger to the Hauler incumbents was bound to be noticed, further aggravating existing antagonisms. And if I persuaded some sucker to stick his head in the lion's mouth and he got hurt, I wouldn't feel very comfortable, ethics-wise.

In this sort of situation, the best way of handling Agnelli was the go-slow. His attention would soon turn elsewhere. First thing

Monday morning, I would begin to drag my feet. Meanwhile, I'd clock off, loosen up and try to make the most of the weekend. The hooch was a good start. A bit of female companionship would be even better.

At the nearest pool table, three guys were putting their moves on a trio of girls. All six were in their mid-twenties, well oiled and kicking on. One of the girls was bent over a cue, poised on the toes of one foot. She was slender, fine-boned and wide-eyed, her dark hair cut short. An Audrey Hepburn lookalike, I decided.

The notion amused me. I began to think of screen equivalents for the other players. Nobody too recent, that was the rule. It had to be someone I might conceivably have seen in this very theater.

The tallest of the girls had long, straight hair and a wide mouth full of perfectly even teeth. Seen from a distance of several miles by a man with glaucoma, she might have passed for Ali McGraw. The fleshy one with the sultry lips was definitely Maria Schneider. *Last Tango in Paris.* Butter on that popcorn, please.

The short dark guy was playing to type, doing a Jean-Paul Belmondo. Cigarette at the corner of his mouth, up-from-under smoulder as he bent over his cue. Maria Schneider was buying it. Give them a couple of hours and they'd be propped on post-coital pillows, swapping subtitles. The tall thin bloke was a limp-limbed Montgomery Clift. He was doing a line for Ali McGraw.

Male number three was a stocky, cocky, corn-fed Steve McQueen. Whenever Audrey Hepburn potted a ball, he grabbed her hand and hoisted it aloft, referee-style. If she bent to take a shot, he draped himself across her, the better to deliver a coaching tip. Any excuse to touch her. She didn't like it and kept skipping free. Bullitt persisted, convinced of his irresistibility.

The others were too busy pairing off to notice. Lover boy caught me watching and tried to stare me out. I let my eyes drift elsewhere. The last thing I needed was amateur aggravation. One more drink, I decided, then bye-byes for Murray boy.

The crowd was thickening by the minute. I found myself doing the arithmetic. Fifteen hundred people, say. Five bars, all working flat out. Three drinks per person per hour, absolute minimum. Spirits at six bucks a pop, champagne at five a glass, imported beers at top dollar.

For three generations, Whelans had owned and operated licensed premises. Nothing in this league, of course. Country and suburban pubs, no smoke machines or six-foot door-blondes. Fifteen years since my father sold up, retired to Stradbroke Island, the last of the publican line. Hard to guess the margins, joint like this. Any way you figured it, somebody was doing nicely.

Unlike Steve McQueen. The more Audrey eluded him, the more he drank. And the more he drank, the more pissed off he got. You could read his growing frustration in the curl of his lips and the way he held his bottle by the neck when he drank. His mates were well on the way to scoring. He was starting to look like a loser. What was wrong with this bitch?

An ugly drunk is an arid source of amusement, even if he's playing pool with a goddess. When he caught me looking again, I held his hostile stare. Same to you, I thought. Not my problem if you flunked out of charm school.

Madonna vogued across the video wall, dividing and multiplying like some collagenic amoeba. Seamlessly the music segued into a track by the artist then still known as Prince. Doof, doof. Wang, wang. Time to hit the frog.

As I skirted the dance floor, I felt my tail-feathers begin to twitch. Weakened by alcohol, my body was succumbing to the all-pervasive beat. Some of these women are here to find a man, my libido wheedled. Perhaps one of them will show a little pity. "You should be so lucky," warbled Kylie Minogue.

What the hell. I shuffled into the fray. The dance floor was sardine-tight with bodies, a roiling cauldron of half-glimpsed faces and lurching torsos. As I sashayed deeper into the throng, Audrey bopped into frame, dancing by herself, flushed and radiant, a picture of pulchritude.

Sweet dreams were of this, and who was I to disagree? I hove off at a respectable distance, took in the view and gave myself over to a little gentle grooving.

Then Stevie-boy appeared, hot on Audrey's delectable tail. He sidled up close and proceeded to get as grabby as ever. But the bits he was trying to grab were strictly off limits, at least in a public place and without prior permission.

Audrey's expression made her annoyance apparent. Girls just wanna have fun, not be mauled by monomaniacal morons. She removed his hand and mouthed something succinct and unmistakable.

Clearly, Audrey was a girl who knew how to take care of herself. Gallantry, on the other hand, did not permit me to stand there, swaying on the spot, waggling my buttocks. When McQueen lunged again, I shoulder-shimmied into the breach and wang-dang-doodled him aside. He tried a flanking maneuver but I headed him off with a series of rapid-fire John Travolta arm-thrusts. Then I blocked all further attempts at advance with a space-invading frug-jerk combo enhanced with Elvis-inspired pelvic thrusts and I-Dream-of-Jeannie neck wobbles.

Hep, I hoped, to my chivalrous intent, Audrey took the opportunity to vanish backwards into the crowd. Her foiled suitor scowled and gave me the finger. I flexed my groin in his general direction. Steam appeared to come out of his ears, but it was just artificial fog. Then he, too, melded into the crowd and disappeared.

My innovative terpsichorean technique had attracted a certain amount of attention. Beautiful people of every sex, gender and lifestyle orientation began backing away at a rapid pace. My career as a babe magnet was in tatters.

Hip-hop melded into rap. I collected my jacket and headed for the exit, pausing only to visit the men's room. The original urinals were still intact and fully operational. I gave one of them the traditional greeting, then turned to the hand basins.

Despite the heavy bar traffic, there was only one other customer. It was Steve McQueen. He must have followed me in. I could see at once that he wasn't there to relieve the pressure on his bladder. "Reckon you're clever, don't you?" he slurred.

For a drunk, he was very fast. He swung wide and his fist connected with the side of my head before I saw it coming. I stumbled backwards, skidded on something slippery and landed flat on my backside on the floor.

Vicious Steve said something in Anglo-Saxon and cocked his foot for a kick. I rolled sideways and started scrambling to my feet. He grabbed the back of my collar and propelled me into a toilet stall. My fingers grabbed for the frame but found no purchase. A white ellipse rose to meet me. Pressure bore down on the back of my head, shoving my face into the toilet bowl. A flushing sound thundered in my ears. Niagara Falls descended.

I fought it hard, gripping the rim of the bowl and arching my back, legs flailing and kicking, my mouth and eyes screwed shut against the torrent of water. The grip on my neck was relentless.

I'm drowning, I thought. What a way to go. Ducked to death in a dunny. I thrashed and heaved and jerked, gasping for air, spluttering and retching. My head banged against the bowl like the clapper in a bell. My mouth collided with the hard enamel and I tasted salty blood.

"Jesus," declared a distant voice. "Not again."

Feet scuffled in the cubicle. Abruptly, the downward pressure ceased. The cavalry had arrived. My head flew backwards and I sucked at the air, triggering a coughing jag. Stars exploded in my eyes. Wrenching myself upright, I spun around. The men's room was empty. I rushed towards the door. Angry. Dizzy. Intent on revenge. Justice. Something. Anything. A towel would've been good.

The doors swung inwards and my path was blocked by a pair of pretty boys in knit tops and bell bottoms. They stopped dead in their tracks and exchanged scandalized looks. Beyond them, the Metro was a seething mass of bodies, an inferno of swirling lights and deafening noise. My assailant was nowhere in sight. My hair was dripping, my shirt soaked. "Are you all right?" inquired one of the tweenies.

Not according to the mirror above the wash basins. My lips were a pulpy red mass. My fingers went into my mouth and confirmed what my tongue had just discovered. My two front teeth were gone, sheared off just below the gum line. The canines jutted down on either side of the yawning gap, giving me the countenance of a drenched vampire. Dracula meets the Creature from the Black Lagoon.

A ponytailed punter brushed past me, entered the stall and commenced to decant. I jerked him aside, narrowly avoiding a hosing. Down beyond the lip of red-smeared white porcelain, way down in the yellowy murk, lay something that might have been a pair of shirt buttons.

As I stared down in disbelief, it suddenly occurred to me that maybe they could be reattached, restored by the miracle of modern dentistry. Averting my eyes, I thrust my hand into the liquid.

"You pervert," gasped the evicted pisser.

Just as my fingers touched their target, he slammed down the lever and a torrent of water flushed my fangs from my grasp.

"Security!" yelled a voice.

5

SECURITY WAS A BRACE OF GORILLAS in black polyester James Brown tour jackets.

"Walk into a door, didja?" insinuated the one trained to speak.

The other one thrust a wad of cocktail napkins into my hand, something to stop me from bleeding all over the floor. My white linen-blend shirt was a write-off. Only worn twice. Sixty bucks at Henry Buck's winter sale.

"I've been athaulted," I complained, spraying pink saliva. "He'th about twenty-thicth, medium height, brown thuede jacket."

Grudgingly, they escorted me around the premises in search of my assailant. He appeared to have absconded. Nor was there any sign of the rest of the cast, Montgomery and Ali, Jean-Paul and Maria. Audrey, too, had made the great escape.

"Call the copth," I demanded.

This got me nowhere but the front door. One of the blondes indicated a payphone across the street, slammed the velvet rope behind me and turned her pretty face to stone. The phone had been trashed, the handpiece torn off. I toyed with finding another, but not for long. The result was all too easy to predict. An extended wait on a freezing-cold street corner. The eventual arrival of a couple of teenage coppers. Unsubstantiatable allegations against an absent and unknown perpetrator. The pointless taking of details. Polite inquiries as to whether sir had been drinking at all this evening. The inevitable suggestion regarding a taxi and a good night's sleep.

Might as well cut out the middle-man, I figured. Save myself the forty cents. Flag down a cab and get myself home, take a proper look at the damage in the privacy of my own bathroom. At every breath, frigid air whistled thorough the gap in my pearly whites. After a couple of failed attempts to hail a taxi, I turned my face north.

Damp and shivering, I trudged past the now-dark Princess Theatre. *Les Misérables,* I reflected, had nothing on me. Compared with the nightclubs of Melbourne, the sewers of Paris were the fields of Elysium. This was going to cost me a small fortune. Already I could feel the pressure on my hip-pocket nerve.

This sort of thing doesn't happen in Melbourne, I told myself. Ours is not a violent city. We have our share of bank robberies, to be sure. The odd terrorist outrage, for ours is an international city, even if it happens to be located at the far end of nowhere. From time to time, a psychopath goes berserk, opens up on the passing public with an automatic weapon. The police training manual was written by Dirty Harry. But things like this, a vicious attack in a public place, don't happen to people like us. Men in suits. Respectable citizens.

Almost respectable, anyway. No member of the Australian Labor Party is entirely respectable. Not to himself, at least.

The late-night streets had a ghostly air, misty at the edges as though viewed through a vaseline-smeared lens. Traffic was minimal and the office buildings had the abandoned, monochromatic feel of some 1950s science-fiction movie. *The Day the Secretariat Stood Still* or *Attack of the Killer Memorandum.* Here and there, cleaners could be seen silhouetted in windows, vacuums strapped to their backs like the life-support systems of a visiting race of anally retentive aliens.

Other windows showed TO RENT signs, a reminder that we were in the midst of a recession. The recession we had to have, according to the federal treasurer. We deserved it. It would cut the national flab, make men of us. Lean and mean and competitive men. Men like that arsehole known to me only as Steve McQueen.

God, I hated him. A gutless wonder, groper of women and cold-cocker of innocent ministerial advisors. My tongue kept worrying the stumps of my departed dentition, probing the sharp edges of the fractured enamel, reminding me of my victimhood. Perhaps I should vandalize a public telephone, I thought. That'd show him.

But I passed no phone. Even if I did, I wouldn't have had the energy to attack it. Exhaustion was replacing outrage. I soldiered onwards, past St. Vincent's Hospital and the Academy of Mary Immaculate, its walls topped with broken glass. Perhaps the nuns knew something, after all. Perhaps there was more to be feared in this world than the chastening hand of Sister Mary Ursula.

"Why did God make me?" she'd demand.

"To know Him, to love Him and to be with Him forever in heaven," I'd recite.

Fat lot of good the catechism had done me. God's protecting hand obviously didn't extend to the men's toilets of cutting-edge dance clubs.

Abandoned by the Almighty, a mouth like steak tartare, I entered the narrow residential streets of Fitzroy. The tight-packed terrace houses of my neighbors were dark, shut up against the night. Their occupants were already abed, dreaming of childhood in some Calabrian village. Or bonged into oblivion. Or out the back in the new renovations, sipping a Sambuca at the conclusion of another successful inner-city dinner party.

No light burned in the window of my humble single-story abode, no fire in the hearth. The framed Spooner caricatures on my hallway wall and the kilim runner on the floor had a reassuring familiarity but they emitted no welcoming warmth. Shit, I didn't even have a cat.

Nor did I bother to look inside as I passed the open doorway of my bedroom. Nobody, I knew for a certain fact, was waiting for me in the bed. The same nobody who'd failed to straighten the covers and clear last weekend's newspapers from the floor. I continued down the hall past Red's room. No point in looking there, either. I knew what I would see. His skateboard, his Spiderman posters, his boxes of dog-eared comics. All untouched in the five months since he last slept there.

Sometimes, occasionally, I'd come home at night, flick on the light, and stand there in the doorway, trying to visualize the outline of his body beneath the covers. Trying to frame the shape of his face in my mind. Imagining that my son was living here with me, not an hour's flying time away, sleeping beneath another man's roof, carried thence by his witch of a mother, Wendy.

Wendy wore the big banana's trousers in the public affairs department at Telecom, a busy career woman with a busy career husband and a house with a view of Sydney Harbor. According to the terms of our no-fault divorce, I was entitled to regular access visits from Red. For practical reasons, this usually meant he came down for the school holidays. But a sporting obligation had nixed the May stay and the upcoming September break had become a victim of Wendy's new maternal status.

Pushing forty, my ex-wife was a mother again. Twins. A matched pair of infant girls were barfing Gerber all over her Chanel suits. And giving her yet another excuse to monopolize Red.

"I think Redmond should come to Noosa with me and Richard instead," she informed me, when I called to confer on the September visit arrangements. Richard was the new husband, a hot-shot blue-blood lawyer. "Melbourne's too cold, you'll be busy with work and we've rented a house on the beach. It'll give Red a chance to bond with his new sisters."

"Can't they bond at home?" I protested. "Surely he doesn't need a beach to bond." What were they, babies or fucking mermaids?

Wendy sucked in her breath and, through a thousand kilometers of fiber-optic cable, I heard the skin around her mouth tighten. "That's the trouble with you, Murray," she said. "You're so selfish."

"Selfish?" Twenty seconds into the conversation and I was already on the ropes. "I'm lucky if I get to see Red four times a year."

"And have you ever considered how emotionally disruptive he finds those visits?"

You can't argue with a line like that, and I knew better than to try. I had her put the kid on the phone and we traded a few masculine monosyllables about getting together later in the year. "See you, son," I said. But I didn't know when. Christmas, I supposed, unless the bonding didn't take or Wendy found another novel excuse.

It seemed such a long, long time since Red and I were bachelor boys together, hunkered down in congenial suburban squalor while Wendy gadded about the countryside, pursuing her brilliant career. He was seven, then, and we were a collective of two, socialism in one kitchen. He was a teenager now and our time together was gathering dust in an empty bedroom.

I continued down the hall. My living room was as I'd left it. Untidy and smelling slightly of those liberties a man who lives alone permits himself. The good elves, I was not surprised to discover, had yet again failed to visit the kitchen in my absence. But three fingers of whiskey remained in my medicinal bottle of Jameson's. The first mouthful stung, the second burned, the third numbed.

Examining my reflection in the tarnished chrome of my toaster, I could just make out the stumps of my frontal tusks peeking from outraged gums. A fortune, I mumbled. An absolute fucking fortune.

On the other hand, I told myself, things are worse in Cambodia. And self-pity is a mug's game. Count your blessings. I counted them out in the back courtyard, pissing on the lemon tree.

For a start, I had a job. This was more than many of my countrymen could say for themselves. Nearly a million at the last count. But Frank Farrell was right. A little over twelve months remained until the election it was universally understood we would lose. After which, my prospects were anyone's guess. First Monday after the vote, I'd be down the dole office.

Previous experience? the form would ask.

No form in the world had enough space to answer that one, not if I told what I could. Which I wouldn't. Secrets were safe with me. Good old Murray Whelan. Party member from the age of sixteen. Assistant secretary of Young Labor, Northern Metropolitan Region. Research officer for the Municipal Employees Union, retired injured. Associate director of the Labor Resource Centre, now defunct. Electorate officer for the Member for Melbourne Upper, Charlene Wills, since deceased. Ministerial advisor to the Honorable Angelo Agnelli, loose cannon.

My lemon tree and I, upon reflection, had a lot in common. Much pissed upon, but still bearing fruit. "Buck up," I told myself. "Or bugger off." The Whelan family motto.

The telephone began to ring. Past midnight and somebody was calling. I was not alone, after all. I foreshortened my micturition and rushed through the back door just as my answering machine kicked in with the message that I was not available.

"Yeth," I gasped, snatching up the handpiece. "Hello, hello."

The caller had hung up. I noticed then that the counter on my machine had registered a half-dozen other calls in my absence. I pushed the playback button and listened to the messages.

The first was an invitation from a cold-canvassing tele-marketer, an exciting offer on time-share resort accommodation in New Zealand. As if things weren't bad enough, I thought. The second was a jackal of the gutter press, trawling for the inside running on the tonnage levy. Then came a series of hang-ups, three in a row. Maybe I should change my message, I thought. Make it more alluring.

I wondered who my most recent caller had been. But I didn't wonder long. I was battered, bruised, miserable and alone. My head was thumping and I sprayed when I spoke. Bed was looking like a very attractive proposition. Dumping my damp, blood-spattered shirt into the laundry tub, I gingerly brushed what was left of my teeth and crawled between my cold and loveless sheets. Nobody had remembered to turn on the electric blanket. Again.

As I lay there in the dark, shivering slightly, knees drawn up to my chest, the pillow cool against my cheek, I fixed my despicable assailant's features in my memory. That well-fed smirk, that air of entitlement, that flop of rufous hair. I'd remember him always, I vowed. And if I ever saw him again, I'd punch his fucking head in.

"Come on," I sighed, losing the battle against sleep. "Have a go, you mug."

6

WHILE I SLEPT, a front of low pressure advanced across the conti-
nent, sucking moisture-laden air out of the icy wastes of the Southern Ocean and depositing it on the lower edge of the land mass. By
the time I awoke, a steady drizzle was drenching the city, rendering
the roads slippery and the outlook gloomy.

Mine in particular. I steamed my lips open under a hot shower,
rinsed my mouth with orange juice and worked my way through the
telephone book until I found a dentist who was open for business on
Saturday mornings. Dr. Freycinet had a cancellation, his receptionist
informed me, in half an hour. His emergency ministrations, she did
not need to add, were going to cost me plenty.

With that thought in mind, I pulled on a sweater, donned a
waterproof jacket, sprinted to the end of the street and climbed
aboard a city-bound tram. Sitting among other glum-faced, wet-
shouldered passengers, I scanned the morning tissues. To my considerable relief, it appeared that the tonnage levy beat-up had
withered on the vine. Then, as I flipped through the business section
of the *Age*, I noticed a half-page spread headlined STUHL SLAMS
GOVT COSTS.

Bob Stuhl was the founder and CEO of Stuhl Holdings and
nobody had more clout or more trucks than Bob. Over seven hun-

dred of them at latest count, readily identifiable by their distinctive orange livery and the punning brag that each bore on its rear bumper bar: "Bob Stuhl Is Big."

Big Bob was a legend. A rough-nut among the silvertails. The man they couldn't root, shoot or electrocute. Not just trucks but shopping centers, hotels and a major stake in an airline. You name it, Bob had a piece of it. Net worth, according to the *Business Weekly* annual rich-list, in excess of eight hundred million dollars. But doing it tough, he wanted us to believe. The story quoted him as warning that transport industry margins were tight and the rumored state government tonnage levy would send freight costs soaring and bring the economy to its knees.

Wondering if an economy could really be said to have knees, I studied the photograph which accompanied the piece. The *Age* had chosen Stuhl's corporate portrait, head-and-shoulders, full-face. It showed a besuited bulldog with heavy jowls and a thick neck, his luxuriant head of silver hair teased into a grizzled quiff with matching sideburns.

Although he looked like some kind of superannuated old rocker, Bob Stuhl managed to project a potent aura, an amalgam of physical bluster, raw willpower and grasping ambition. Nothing, it was clear to see, had ever been handed to Bob on a silver platter. What he had, he'd wrung from the world with his bare hands. Wrung it until its arteries burst. His eyes, staring out from their sacks of flesh, had an unflinching hardness that made the Ayatollah Khomeini look like Bambi.

In the manner of all great tycoons, Stuhl's ruthlessness was matched by his philanthropy. His largesse included an entire intensive-care wing, donated to the Mercy Hospital after his eldest son was brain-damaged in a swimming pool accident.

The story was a put-up job if ever I'd seen one. First the Haulers, now Bob Stuhl. Head throbbing, I could sense Angelo's irritation turning into a full-blown persecution complex.

I got off the tram at the top end of Collins Street, a block from Parliament House and the Metro. Flecked with drizzle, I hurried along the footpath, counting off the street numbers. At the entrance of almost every building were the brass plates of specialist quackery. Fellows of the Australasian College of Radiology. Dermatologists, hematologists, ophthalmologists and gastroenterologists. Every one of them with a string of hungry polo ponies or a daughter at a Swiss finishing school. Even their poor cousins had shingles on display. Podiatrists, osteopaths, physiotherapists, contact lens practitioners and dentists.

Dr. Freycinet's surgery was in one of the street's few remaining art deco buildings. He had a mottled pink scalp and well-scrubbed fingers like hairy little weisworst sausages. Prodding me with chromium implements, he stared down at the poignantly truncated stumps of my tusks. "Bet that hurt," he tut-tutted, with all the cheerful certainty of a man well on his way to his second million.

I scarcely had time to agree before he snapped on a pair of rubber gloves, jammed a dental dam in my mouth, plunged a syringe into my upper gum and proceeded to drive a pair of self-threading stainless steel posts into the front of my face.

"Relax," he urged. "A couple of temporary crowns and we'll have you out of here in a jiffy."

Ninety minutes later, I was teetering in front of his receptionist's desk, numb from the navel up, wearing a pair of interim plastic incisors. "Have a nice day," she chirped, handing me a bill. Four hundred dollars, plus an estimate for the installation of permanent porcelain crowns. Grand total, two thousand three hundred dollars.

The sum reverberated like a gong in my befuddled brain. Twenty-three hundred dollars could've bought me a business-class return trip to Los Angeles, including eight nights' accommodation, car rental and a family pass to Disneyland. Two mobile phones with carry cases and battery recharger units. A second-hand car, if I wanted one. Five months of child support payments.

Not that I'd made any recently. Not since Wendy decided to be bloody-minded about Red's access visits. Anyway, Wendy and Richard were probably pulling a cool quarter million a year between them. My maintenance checks, intended to keep the boy in tennis shoes and subscriptions to *Marsupial Monthly*, were probably going on pool-care products or subsidizing Richard's marina fees.

To compound the issue of cost, I felt like I'd just escaped from a cement mixer. All that drilling and grinding, compacting and scraping had taken its psychic toll. Waves of peevish misery sloshed around inside me, searching for an object upon which to break. Had my cowardly assailant been there, I would gladly have throttled him on the spot. Taken my revenge in full view of the passing traffic, confident that no jury in the country would have convicted me. But the prick wasn't there, was he? I didn't even know his name.

Back home, I devoured a handful of industrial-strength aspirin, crawled back into bed, pulled the cover over my head and once again sought catatonia's embrace.

Occasionally, the jangling of the telephone hauled me up from the depths. But I let the machine answer in the other room, slipping back into a dazy doze as soon as the ringing stopped. Probably Angelo, I thought, aerated about the story in the *Age*. Let him share his hair-trigger insecurities and hare-brained schemes with somebody else. His departmental bureaucrats, for instance. There were plenty of those. His other advisors. His factional cronies. His press secretary. His wife.

Even Angelo had somebody to share his bed, I grumbled to myself. Could he really be getting a bit on the side as well? It was just too ludicrous to contemplate. Not to say unfair. I was single and the closest I ever got to romance was the occasional fling with Mrs. Palmer and her five daughters. And I wasn't even in a fit state for that sort of consolation.

A bang woke me, an insistent rapping on the back door. A six-year-old child stood on the step, her face beaming up at me, a tiny moon in the murky twilight. "Mum thed to come and have dinner at our plathe," she lisped, the gap in her milk-teeth mirroring my recent condition. "If you want."

Her name was Chloe and she lived on the other side of the cobbled lane that ran behind my house. Her parents, Faye and Leo Curnow, were my closest friends. Family almost. The sort of people who take an active interest in a man's misfortunes. Faye was a journalist at the *Finance Weekly* and Leo lectured in something mathematical at Melbourne University. Their other child, Tarquin, was the same age as Red and the two boys had been pals since kindergarten.

Now passably fit for human intercourse, I accepted the invitation. While Chloe rushed home to lay me a place at the table, I dressed and checked the phone messages. Four calls, all hang-ups. Crossing the lane, I stepped into the fug of domesticity, the heady aroma of drying laundry and vegetable soup, the reassuring cacophony of the television: "Hey, Hey, It's Saturday."

Reading glasses perched on the tip of her nose, Faye was simultaneously whisking the contents of a saucepan and consulting a cookbook. Leo was wrestling the cork from a bottle of red wine. The kids were arrayed on beanbags, glued to the box. Tarquin glanced up, then did a double take and squinted at my lips. "Have you got cold sores or something?" he demanded. "You look really gross."

"Somebody smacked me in the mouth," I said. "If you're not careful, it could happen to you."

Faye hitched up her glasses and took a closer look. "You're kidding?"

"I wish I was."

As I reprised the Metro massacre, Faye rolled her eyes and shook her head reproachfully. Trouble, she firmly believed, didn't just happen.

Leo, however, was impressed. "Brawling in a nightclub," he grinned through his beard. "There's life in the old dog yet."

When I got to the bit about the dentist bill, Faye leaned close and scrutinized my temporary prosthetics. "They're very white," she said. "But apart from the fact that they glow in the dark, they almost look better than the originals."

I tried them out on her gourmet experiment, a *tagine d'agneau à la Morocco*. It melted in the mouth, for which I was grateful. Apart from the thrashing it had copped in the Metro toilet, my cavity had taken a fair buffeting from Dr. Freycinet's tubby fingers and shiny appliances.

"How come this stew's got apricots in it, Mum?" said Tarquin.

After dinner, the children watched television while the adults sat around the kitchen table, chewing the cabernet sauvignon. Faye, cat on her lap, took up a recurrent theme. "You know what you need, Murray?" she said. "A woman."

The next morning I got a call from one.

7

HER NAME WAS LYNDAL LUSCOMBE and she was my successor as Angelo's electorate officer. She had a husky voice, a throaty laugh and she gave great telephone.

I was lingering over breakfast in the pale sunshine that was filtering through my kitchen window when she rang. I'd slept late and woken to a succession of minor miracles. My head was clear. My mouth felt almost normal. There was nothing in the papers about the tonnage levy. The sun was shining and I was considering how I might fritter away the rest of the day, make the most of the unseasonably fine weather.

"Hello Murray," she said. "It's Lyndal."

"Murray's not here," I said. "He died of a broken heart. The woman he loves left him for another."

"Really?" she said. "The way I understand it, he dithered around, never declared his intentions, left his play too late. She had no idea about his true feelings."

"He didn't think it was right to make a pass at a professional colleague," I said. "He's a very proper person."

"As well as being dead?"

"Only from the waist down," I said. "And the sound of your voice has fixed that. To what do I owe the pleasure, Lyndal?"

"The usual," she said. "Our lord and master."

Lyndal had been running Agnelli's constituency office in Melbourne Upper for the previous three years, the reward for some highly effective voter-profiling work for the state secretariat. She was a psychology graduate, a one-time crisis counselor whose experience with the depressed and suicidal amply qualified her to run a local Labor Party office. And, usually, to deal with our boss.

"He's cutting the ribbon at the opening of our new community cultural center today," she said. "When I called this morning to brief him, he interrogated me about threats to his preselection. Went right off the deep end, reckoned somebody was plotting against him, wanted me to draw up a list of potential traitors. I think he's flipping out, Murray, and I'd really like your advice. Any chance you can come out to this wingding today?"

It seemed I'd found a place to do my frittering. And I couldn't think of anybody I'd rather fritter with. "Can you hold on a moment?" I said.

I put the phone down and went to the bathroom mirror. My lips were still a little crusty and my frontal fangs glowed several shades brighter than their next-door neighbors, but I was not unsuitable for general exhibition. I picked up the phone again. "Will Nick be there?" I said.

Nick Simons was Lyndal's designated other, the man who'd snaffled her, struck first while I had hesitated.

"That's for you to find out," she said.

Half an hour later, I was dolled up in my best Country Road casuals, boarding the Number 11 tram to Preston.

Out I rode, out beyond the cafes and terraces of Fitzroy. Out across the Merri Creek, dredged now of its industrial effluent, home again to the migrating eel, green with young eucalypts and threaded with bike paths. Out past the Greek Orthodox monastery, its bell tolling noonday prayers across the heathen roofs of weatherboard bungalows and brick-veneer dream homes. Out past discount clothing stores and fried chicken franchises and the temples of gimcrack Protestantism with their couch-grass lawns and peeling facades.

Out past second-hand office furniture showrooms and the wire-meshed windows of licensed grocers. Out into the heartland of the party of the proletariat, to the electorate of Melbourne Upper.

Lulled by the swaying of the tram, I thought about Lyndal. About how I should've made my move when I had the chance. How we met during the '88 election campaign and more than once exchanged the kind of signals that give rise to a man's hopes. How I'd held back, justifying my timidity with spurious reservations about getting involved with a workmate. How I'd let her be snatched away by Nick Simons, an organizer with the Amusement, Entertainment and Theatrical Employees Federation. A ticket seller to the ticket sellers. How Nick was a nice enough bloke, but that didn't mean I wasn't entitled to try to rectify my mistake. Lyndal didn't have children and, by definition, a childless woman is always fair game. She has not yet mated for life.

When the tram reached the terminus depot, I got out and walked. At the Doug Nichols reserve, a little-league football game was in progress, half-pint bruisers contesting the slippery pigskin across a trampled patch of mud, parents howling encouragement from the sidelines. The kids were younger than Red, eight or nine, but I could imagine my son, socks around his ankles, dashing for the goal posts, a look of fixed determination on his face, trying to hide his disappointment when the kick went wide. I turned away and hurried on.

A hundred meters up the road I reached the Northern Region Performing Arts Center, a post-modern assemblage of corrugated steel and tinted cement that rose from a car park between a railway line and an arterial road. "Official Opening Today," proclaimed a banner suspended above the entrance, "Join the Fun."

The fun was already well advanced. Lambs were being spit-roasted and sausages sizzled in a row of open-faced rent-a-tent pavilions. Boys in bum-fluff mustaches, embroidered waistcoats and Nike sneakers tuned fretted instruments beside the stage door. Girls with coin-fringed headscarves rehearsed dance steps between parked minibuses. Community groups had set up stands in the foyer.

The Nursing Mothers' Association and the Movement against Uranium Mining. The Local History Society and the Committee for a Free East Timor. Beside the face-painting stall, an environmental Leninist tried to sell me a copy of *Green Left Weekly.*

Slipping into the auditorium, I found a vantage point against the side wall. Formalities were in full progress, the mayor presiding, a former butcher with a face like a slice of corned beef. On the stage behind him sat a row of dignitaries, including the federal and state members of parliament. Agnelli's wife, Stephanie, was seated beside him, the very figure of wifely rectitude in a russet-toned, knee-length suit and sensible shoes.

The crowd was doing its best to keep the chatter down to a roar. "We are here to salivate the pre-forming arts," the mayor proclaimed, testing the new acoustics to the limit.

I scanned the audience. Nick Simons was nowhere in sight. I found Lyndal in the second row. She was wearing a cable-knit sweater and stretch slacks, leaning forward in her seat, compact and muscular, her chin pointed forward like the figurehead of a sailing ship. Her face was a mask of dutiful attention but the edges of her lips were curling slightly in wry amusement at His Worship's malapropisms.

A country girl, six years younger than me, Lyndal had been drawn to the Labor side of politics by a temperamental disposition towards social justice and an intellectual disdain for the self-serving nostrums of the Liberals. She modestly concealed these attributes behind a flip manner and a technocratic fascination with the intricacies of bureaucratic procedure. She had full, luscious lips and tight curly hair.

How I longed to federate with her, to capture her preferences, to scrutinize her affiliations. To man her booth, to poll her quorum, to table her amendments, to join her in congress, to have her sit on my administrative committee.

She swiveled in her seat to survey the room. Her green, cat-like eyes caught mine and she tipped me a conspiratorial wink. I replied with a little salute and we turned our faces back to the microphone. To Angelo, our boss and our cross.

He wore a sports coat and striped tie, neither too formal nor too casual. Just one of the folks, if a slightly more important one. His speech was mercifully brief. He praised the creativity of the local community, referred modestly to his own role in getting the center funded, thanked all the right people. He read from cue cards, doubtless prepared by Lyndal.

Ange's address concluded the formalities. Lyndal swooped, escorting the distinguished couple to the door, whispering names in his ear as Angelo pressed the flesh. People stood, stretched, hailed friends. A choir filed onto the stage. I nodded to some familiar faces and drifted outside.

Lyndal was standing on the auditorium steps, observing Agnelli as he mingled with the punters, handing out the howdy-doodies. I propped beside her, shoulder-to-shoulder. Our heights were almost equal and it was all I could do not to step behind her, wrap my arms around her waist and scratch my itch on the small of her back.

Angelo had stopped to chat at one of the food stalls. Somebody handed him a sausage in a bread roll. Mustard squirted onto his tie when he bit into it, and he jumped backwards like the victim of an unwelcome practical joke.

"He's never been very comfortable with his constituents," said Lyndal. "But I've never seen him this edgy. Any idea what's spooking him?"

"He's had a recent visit from the Haulers," I said. "They threatened to jeopardize his preselection."

"The Haulers are a very spooky outfit," she said, "but they don't have any influence out here. Angelo should know that."

Choral keening erupted inside the auditorium in an unfamiliar language. English, probably.

"I'm sure he does," I said. "But I'm beginning to suspect that our employer has finally been promoted beyond the level of his incompetence. He could barely handle the burden of his minor portfolios. Transport's a major nightmare and he may not be able to cope."

Lyndal considered this information for a while. It seemed to reassure her. "So it's just general anxiety, then? He doesn't have some specific suspicion?"

"All I know is that he needs a lot of hand-holding at the moment," I said. "Although I'd prefer if it was my hand being held. By you. Where's Nick, by the way?"

"On the road as usual," she said. "Warracknabeal, Ararat, Horsham. Doing a membership sweep of the country racetracks."

If this woman was mine, I'd be superglued to her, not chasing turnstile attendants in the boondocks. "Great," I said. "Then there's nothing to stop you flirting outrageously with me."

"Nothing but that man down there," she said, nodding towards Angelo.

A cluster of constituents had captured their representative and were getting into his ear. A problem with domiciliary nursing-care benefits, possibly, or a wrangle with the office of Consumer Affairs, the Liquor Licensing Commission or the land valuation board of review. A matter, in any case, either beneath Angelo's dignity or beyond his capacity. He put his hand up and started waving in our direction like a drowning man signaling a lifeguard.

We started down the steps. "You've got it cushy out here in the electorate," I said. "The worst Angelo can do is alienate a few pensioners. Back at the ministry, he's at war with the entire trucking industry."

"What do you mean, cushy?" she huffed. "Some of these pensioners can be savage. The worst that can happen to you is an overdose of country and western." As she dived into the scrum surrounding Angelo, the lambent twang of a steel guitar wafted from the far end of the car park.

The music was neither country nor western. It was rockabilly, and its source was a band on an outdoor stage beyond the blow-up jumping castle, the flat-bed of a truck trailer. Figuring I'd continue to pitch my woo at Lyndal when she finished bailing out Angelo, I bought myself a can of beer and joined the meager gaggle of toe-tapping onlookers in the watery winter sunshine.

They called themselves "Over the Limit." Two guitars, a slap bass, a vocalist and drums. Middle-aged amateurs, paunches over their belt buckles, they laid with cheerful abandon into a repertoire of Hank Williams and Carl Perkins standards. Jambalaya Joe and his Blue Suede Shoes.

The drummer's name was Donny Maitland. I never knew he played the drums, but it didn't surprise me. Nothing Donny did could ever surprise me.

8

I WAS SIXTEEN when I met Donny Maitland. One hot summer afternoon, he sprung me reading a novel in the cellar of my father's hotel, the Carters Arms, shirking my chores in the cool of the stainless steel beer barrels. He threw back the pavement doors and stared down at me, nimbus-headed in the furnace of the afternoon, barelegged in his work shorts, the sleeves of his brewery-issue shirt rolled to the shoulders.

"What have we here?" he declared, eyeing my Penguin paperback. "An intellectual?" He must have been in his late twenties then. A man to my boy. A man unlike any other I'd met, and you meet a lot when your father owns a hotel.

I slipped *The Plague* into my back pocket and helped him unload his consignment, taking the strain as he rolled the eighteen-gallon kegs down the ramp. Not that he needed much help. Donny was solid muscle, strong as an ox.

Afterwards, he went into the public bar to get the delivery docket signed and have a beer. They always had a drink, the brewery drivers. I tagged along, drawn as if by gravitational force. Raising a silent toast to our comradeship of labor, he lowered the entire contents of his glass down his throat in one smooth swallow. "You ought to be careful," he warned, wiping his mouth with the back of his hand. "That existentialism shit, it'll rot your brain. Start reading Camus, you'll end up on Kafka."

I wasn't sure who Kafka was. But I'd heard the name, so I asked about him.

Donny and I talked books for the next half-hour, during which he consumed several more glasses of beer. His views were trenchant, visceral, political. Drawn from the certainty of his class, sharpened by his intellect and confirmed by his experience. And he talked to me like an equal. No grown man had ever done that before.

From then on, through school and university and beyond, Donny was a comet that blazed intermittently on the periphery of my vision. A promiscuous reader and tireless talker, he was equally conversant with the thoughts of Mao Tse-tung and the licks of Lightning Hopkins. A hard drinker at bohemian parties, he some-how managed to combine unmoderated radicalism with steady employment. Women loved him. Loved his energy, his humor, his unruly mop of sandy hair and his big, expressive hands.

Hands that were now wrapped around drumsticks, pounding out a steady four-four beat on an el-cheapo beginner-level drum kit. The passage of time had thinned his hair a little and softened the flesh on his frame. He was whiskey-raw at the cheekbones, too. You can get that in your fifties.

Over the Limit weren't bad for a scratch band, though their title was not entirely inaccurate. My attention moved from the impromptu stage to the prime mover. It was a flash rig, a snub-nosed Kenworth with chrome bullbars and vertical exhausts. White with navy-blue trim. Hefty horsepower in high-gloss livery. A name was painted on the door, wrought in the ornate copperplate beloved of the trucking trade. *Maitland Transport.*

Last I'd seen of Donny, a couple of years back, he was still at the brewery, twenty years on the job. By the look of it, he'd cashed in his chips and struck out on his own. I struck out, too. Tossed my empty can and scouted the crowd for Lyndal.

It was slow going. At every turn I ran into familiar faces. Old mates from the neighborhood whose children were in need of my admiration. Minor ethnic luminaries. Chronic conspirers from the local party branches. By the time I arrived back at the auditorium, Angelo's official car was gone from the curb. And his electorate officer, sadly, was nowhere to be found.

I drifted back to the twang just as Over the Limit were finishing their set with a thumping rendition of Lonnie Mack's "Down in the Dumps" that set the friends-and-family crowd whooping and hollering. Donny spotted me as he cleared his kit from the stage and vaulted down off the trailer, surprisingly light on his feet. He greeted me with a slap on the shoulder and a wide smile. "Well?" he demanded. "Whatta you reckon?"

"Tragic old farts," I said. "Should be called Over the Hill."

"Call us what you like, it's thirsty work," he said. "And since you're looking so prosperous, Murray, how about you buy me a beer."

We went into the bar tent, popped the tops off a couple of cans and stepped back into the open air. A Latin combo was setting up on the stage, lots of percussion.

"You can't be exactly poverty-stricken yourself," I said, waving my drink at the big Kenworth. "Looks like you've become a capitalist."

"Nah." Donny chugged on his can and shook his bearish head. "I'm just the wage slave of a petty proprietor."

The owner's name on the door, he explained, was that of Heather, his sister-in-law. "Ex, rather. My little brother Rodney did the dirty on her, shot through with a new cookie. Sold the business, panel beating, twelve on the payroll. Took the money and ran. Heather's got her lawyers on the case, but everything takes forever. Only thing left was the truck. Rodney had it in the wife's name for tax reasons, leasing it out. Lease expired and she tried to sell it, couldn't get a decent price. After I copped the flick from the brewery, she made me an offer. I drive and she handles the business side. No regular contracts, unfortunately. Just bits and pieces. Fruit and vegetables, mainly."

I clearly needed some updating on Donny's recent history. Turfed by the brewery? Before I could ask what this was about, he grabbed me by the elbow and glanced around, acting scared. "You're not still working for that Angelo Agnelli, are you?" he said. "If Heather finds out, she'll be into you about this tonnage levy scheme. She'll make mincemeat of you, mate."

I heaved a weary sigh. "The tonnage levy's bullshit," I said. "Nothing but media mischief. The trucking industry'll be free to pothole the public highway for the life of this administration, I guarantee it."

"Well your boss'd better get the message out pronto," advised Donny, releasing his grip. "The tom-toms are beating in every roadhouse in the state and the CBs are crackling with rumors."

"Being spread by the Haulers, no doubt," I said. "They're keen to keep the government on its back foot. With friends like Howard Sharpe, who needs enemies?"

"Amen to that," nodded Donny. "The bastard stitched me up good and proper."

"Yeah?" I said. "What's the story?"

"The usual one. But I'm planning to rewrite the ending. Let's get something to eat and I'll tell you all about it. Come and meet Jacinta."

"Who's Jacinta?"

"*Mi corazon,*" he said, as the Sandinistas of Samba kicked in.

He led me into the sit-down eating area, a cluster of green plastic garden tables, and introduced me to two men and a woman sitting at a spread of chicken pilaf and pork rolls. "Roscoe, Len and this is Jacinta."

The men gave me curt but friendly nods. They had the same all-weather, hard-living complexions as Donny although they were a little younger and firmer in the body. Roscoe was lank and rangy. Len was the nuggety pug-eared type.

Jacinta was fortyish, tawny skinned with cow eyes, masses of raven hair and a generous gap-toothed smile. "Sit down," she urged. "Help yourself. There's plenty to go around." She had an accent, a glottal sort of American-Asian cross. A Filipina, if I guessed right. Donny beamed at her proudly. Last time I looked, he was flying solo. She seemed nice and I was glad for him.

We sat down and tucked into the food. The band was loud and I butted my seat against Donny's, raising my voice to be heard above the music. "You were saying about Howard Sharpe," I prompted. He put his plate down, as if the subject had ruined his appetite, parked his elbows on the table and gave me the oil.

Twelve months back the brewery fell into the hands of corporate raiders. The new owners immediately set about carving it up, stripping the assets, flogging off everything that wasn't nailed down. Including the fleet of trucks. The delivery contract went to Bob Stuhl, a known associate, who proposed to lay off the drivers on the brewery payroll. The union stepped in and brokered a deal. In exchange for improvements in productivity, the men would keep their permanency and conditions.

"Before long, the squeeze was on," said Donny. "Longer hours, double shifts. Anybody quit, they didn't get replaced. Country runs, blokes were falling asleep at the wheel. Three fatals in three months."

Donny was the shop steward. The men sent him to talk to Howard Sharpe. The union had done all it could, he was told. The men could like it or lump it. Instead, at Donny's instigation, they pulled a wildcat strike.

"Just before Christmas, it was. The period of maximum demand."

Under pressure from his corporate cowboy cronies, Stuhl folded, agreed to new schedules and overtime allowances. Three weeks later, Donny was offered a beer after making a delivery. "Used to be part of the culture. Some blokes'd drink ten, twelve pots a day. Reckoned the trucks knew their own way home. But that era's long gone. Drinking on the job's a sacking offense these days."

The publican insisted. Just the one, he said. No harm in that. Made an issue of it. Wouldn't sign the docket until Donny had a drink with him. "Soon as the glass touched my lips, one of Stuhl's managers tapped me on the shoulder, fired me on the spot. It was a set-up, but Sharpe washed his hands of me. Said I'd dug my own grave, undermined the union leadership's credibility with employers.

Twenty-five years a member and the self-satisfied sack of shit sold me down the river."

I nodded sympathetically. "He came to visit Agnelli a couple of days ago. Paraded his credentials as the champion of the working truckie. Problem is, he's had uncontested control of the union for so long that he thinks he can get away with anything. And that'll never change until somebody steps on his tail."

"Well, that might just be on the cards," said Donny. "I'm not the only one who's had a gutful."

"That right?" I said. "I don't suppose you'd know anybody who might be interested in taking a crack at our fat friend?"

Donny gave me a sly, sideways look. "Our new transport minister wouldn't be looking for a chance to ruffle Howard Sharpe's feathers, would he?"

"Put it this way," I said. "Anybody prepared to tackle the current Haulers' leadership might well find himself the beneficiary of an anonymous donor."

Roscoe and Len were angled back in their chairs, legs extended, beer cans on their laps, soaking up rays and watching the band. Donny reached across the table with his fork and prodded Roscoe in the arm. "Murray here's got a line on some prospective campaign finance," he said. "Show him your T-shirt."

Roscoe looked me up and down with new interest, then unbuttoned his denim jacket and displayed the slogan emblazoned across his chest. *Vote Reform Group,* it read, *Stop the Sharpe Sellout.*

"Reform Group?" I said. "Who's that?"

"Us," said Donny. "Me, Roscoe and Len. We're putting a rank-and-file ticket together to run for the state executive."

"You'll need more than a T-shirt to knock Howard Sharpe off his perch," I said. "And you'd better have good medical insurance. Those boys play rough, by all accounts."

"We're not exactly cream puffs ourselves," said Donny. "Right, comrades?"

Roscoe and Len made clenched-fist gestures and grimaced militantly. "If you don't fight, you lose," declared Roscoe.

And sometimes you just lose. But these blokes didn't look like babes in the woods and, since they already had a campaign up and running, perhaps it'd be possible to meet my brief from Angelo after all. And do my old mate Donny a favor at the same time.

"You got any other backing?" I asked. "Running a state-wide campaign costs money."

"Early days," said Donny. "The vote's still four months away and we've only just lodged our nominations. But I reckon I'll be able to round up some resources from Sharpe's enemies in other unions. He's got plenty."

"And you wouldn't mind getting into bed with Agnelli?"

Roscoe leaned forward and breathed beery fumes into my face. "Listen, mate," he told me. "We'll lie down and spread 'em for anybody who helps us stick it up Howard Sharpe."

"Roscoe's another of the brewery casualties," said Donny, waving his associate back into his seat.

I eyed Donny's running mates skeptically. "Angelo'd want some bang for his buck. He's not a soft touch."

"Naturally you'll want to run the tape over us, see if we're dead-set," said Donny. "Come down to the wholesale fruit and vegetable market tomorrow morning. We'll be in campaign mode. If you like what you see, you can square us with your boss." He rubbed his thumb and forefinger together. "Let's say about three-thirty, four o'clock."

"In the morning?" I said. "Forget it. Agnelli doesn't pay me enough to get up that early. I only assess campaigns conducted in daylight."

The bongo beaters finished their bracket and some sort of ethno-pop ensemble moved onto the stage. Clarinet, accordion, bazouki and tabla. A woman in a down-filled vest arrived and tapped Donny on the shoulder. She was short and busty, her plentiful cheese-blonde hair pinned up with a pair of tortoiseshell combs. Moon-faced, well-preserved, mid-thirties.

"How long before this finishes?" she demanded impatiently, indicating the stage. "Don't forget you've got to be in Nar Nar Goon in time to load those potatoes."

"How could I forget with you around to remind me?" said Donny resignedly. "Murray, meet my slave driver, Heather."

She checked me out, head cocked to one side, scrunching her eyes against the low-slung sun. "Murray?" she said. "Not Murray Whelan?"

I looked at her more closely. It was not painful but it made me none the wiser as to how she knew my name.

"Coburg Town Hall, 1970," she said, smirking a little. "The debutante ball. I was Heather Dunstable then."

The deb ball was the highlight of the municipal social calendar. A chance for the favored maidens of the suburb to don elbow-length white gloves, chisel-toed satin shoes and A-line evening gowns and play at being princesses, escorted beneath a flower-decked trellis archway by young men in hired dinner suits, dragooned for the occasion from the ranks of local likelihood.

A university student, I was well beyond such things. Or so I thought until I got the call. The mayor's daughter, it seemed, had a best friend, a lovely young lass whose intended partner had broken his collarbone when an engine block dropped on him during a clutch-plate replacement. As a prominent member of Young Labor, I was considered an ideal stand-in escort. And since the council provided the venue for our annual conference for nix, the mayor was sure I'd be only too happy to oblige. All I had to do was pick the girl up, lend her my elbow during the presentation ceremony and waltz her around the parquetry a couple of times. His Worship would even swing for the tux rental and the corsage.

And thus it came about that I rang Heather Dunstable's doorbell, boxed orchid in hand, wearing a ruffled apricot shirt and clip-on velvet bowtie. I found myself facing a vivacious little butterball, her hair in coiled ringlets, the front of her dress dropping away to a view that all but sucked my eyeballs out of their sockets. "Pick your jaw off the floor," she said. "We don't want to be late."

By the time I'd met her parents, posed for photos in front of the mantelpiece, bundled her into my Zephyr and driven to the town hall, I'd learned that Heather preferred the Kinks to the Rolling Stones and could hardly wait to start secretarial college.

She could hardly wait for other things, too, but I didn't find that out until later, after we'd ascended the red-carpeted steps of the town hall stage and she'd curtsied before the mayor and the lady mayoress. After she'd got giggly on Brandivino and lemonade and suggested we stop off on the way home and take in the view of Coburg Lake in the moonlight.

"That's not moonlight," I told her as we parked under the trees. "It's the glow from the searchlights at Pentridge prison."

"I'm not stupid, you know," she said, slipping off her shoulder straps. "Let's get in the back seat."

Compared with the pimply adolescents who'd squired her peers, I was probably a bit of a catch. Or so I fancied. "Don't worry," she breathed. "I'm not in love with you or anything." Then she said something that no other girl had ever said to me, certainly none of those stand-offish snobs at uni. A phrase which every red-blooded male of my generation longed to hear. "It's okay," she assured me. "I'm on the pill."

All this flashed through my mind in a nanosecond, sending a rush of heat to my face. "Heather Dunstable," I blurted. "Of course I remember. You haven't changed at all."

"And you're still a smooth talker." She smirked, enjoying my discomfort. "I was only sixteen, you know."

"Yeah," I said. "But advanced for your age." More than I was, still a virgin at nineteen.

She pulled up a chair, moved closer, got chatty. "You were doing law, weren't you?"

"Politics," I said.

Donny was observing Heather's moves with ill-concealed amusement. "Murray works for the transport minister," he said. "He's been telling me how he managed to get this tonnage levy quashed. And I've been telling him about our campaign."

"Your crackpot crusade, you mean," she said. "If you spent as much time behind the wheel as you do plotting to take over the union, we could almost afford to go broke."

Jacinta paused in the middle of packing up the remains of the food. "Choo have to stand up for what choo believe," she flared.

This was clearly a well-gnawed bone of family contention.

"Murray's coming to the market in the morning," Donny told Heather, as though the matter was settled. "He's thinking of getting behind the campaign."

The reedy wail of snake-charming music came from the stage. Heather put her bosom against my shoulder and leaned into my ear. "So tell me," she purred. "Is there a Mrs. Murray?"

According to the calendar, spring was only a few weeks away. But spring in Melbourne is an elusive phenomenon, a largely theoretical construct. It finds expression less in the behavior of the elements than in the expectations of the population. It arrives because, having endured winter, we deserve it.

But we didn't deserve it yet. Not by a long chalk. Battalions of black clouds were rapidly advancing from the southwest horizon. By the time the Falafel Quartet went into their big finish, blasts of wind were sending litter flying and up-ending the plastic tables. In the sudden rush of activity to pack up before the rain arrived, I slipped away.

By the time I got home it was pushing 7:30, and rain was drumming on the iron roof. Running into Donny had been a stroke of luck. What with one thing and another, I was due for a win. And what could be better than a win-win deal with an old friend? As I thawed myself in front of the wall furnace and scanned the television guide, the phone rang. I let the machine answer and cocked an ear.

"For God's sake, Murray," a woman's voice pleaded. "If you're there, pick up the phone. Please, please, please."

It sounded a lot like my ex-wife, although pleading had never been part of Wendy's repertoire. The snarl was Wendy's customary mode of address where I was concerned.

Curious, I answered. "Hello, Wendy? Is that you?"

"At last," she said. "At last." A more familiar, hectoring tone came down the line. "Why didn't you answer my calls? I've been trying to reach you all day."

"What is it, Wendy?" I sighed, resigned to a lecture on my evasion of financial duty, cursing my better nature for suckering me into taking her call.

"It's Red," she blurted, her voice quivering at the name. "Our little boy. He's gone."

9

"GONE?" I said. "Gone where?"

She didn't know. And that was only part of it. She didn't know when, either. "It must have been some time on Friday night. The school didn't realize he was missing at first."

"What do you mean, the school? Was he at a camp or something?" I imagined some character-building three-day adventure in hutments on the edge of a national park. Obstacle courses and nature walks, possum-spotting by torchlight and dishwashing duty in the communal kitchen. Then a wrong turn taken on a hike. Search parties thrashing through impenetrable bush, police helicopters, rescue crews abseiling down cliff-faces, an injured child shivering all night in some wombat hole.

"Oh, yes," said Wendy, like she'd just remembered. "I've been meaning to tell you. We enrolled him as a boarder at Richard's old school. It's very hard to get into."

But not, apparently, out of.

"You put Red in a private boarding school?" I could hardly believe what I was hearing.

"He wasn't being challenged in a government school." For once, Wendy was on the defensive.

"Or thrashed or sodomized."

"That's terribly unfair," she snapped, back in familiar form. "Brookside isn't like that at all. We were just doing what we thought was best. I've got my hands pretty full, you know, with the new babies and work. And Richard's job is very demanding. We both have to travel a lot. We felt that Red would benefit from the experience. Anyway, he comes home most weekends."

"But not this one? A fact that somehow managed to escape your attention, what with your busy lifestyle and all."

That really got the acrimony going. When it abated a little, I managed to learn the little that Wendy knew. It seemed that Red had vanished some time after lights-out on Friday night. His absence was noted on Saturday morning yet, due to some crossing of the procedural wires, it was assumed that he'd simply gone home for the weekend. Wendy spent Saturday and most of Sunday oblivious to this misunderstanding. "He left a message at my office on Friday, said he'd be staying at school for the weekend," she sniffed.

"Bonding with the chaps?" I said.

Lashing out at Wendy gave cold comfort. There would be time for recriminations later. In the meantime, our thirteen-year-old boy had been missing for forty-eight hours and nobody had the slightest idea where he was. The police had been notified, inquiries made, bulletins posted, potential accomplices interrogated. It looked like he'd done a bunk. Emptied his bank account, packed a bag, gone over the wall.

"We're looking everywhere, all the usual places runaways go."

Wendy didn't need to specify what that meant. My bushland visions were replaced by urban images: street kids, gutter crawlers, used syringes. It was a nightmare so precise, an apprehension so specific, that it even had a name. Kings Cross, sleaze capital of a nation.

This wouldn't have happened if I'd been more concerned about Red, I told myself, and less preoccupied with exchanging long-distance artillery salvos with Wendy. "How could you let this happen?" I demanded. "I'll be on the next plane up there."

"What earthly good will that do?"

I had no idea. But I knew for sure that I couldn't just sit on my backside in Melbourne and await further bulletins. If necessary, I'd turn Sydney upside down. First I had to get there. I hung up and called the airlines, couldn't get a seat for at least twelve hours. The next available flight was eight the next morning. I booked the ticket and stood beside the phone, flexing and unflexing, my guts churning. What now?

An accident would have been easier to cope with. An illness. At least Red would be there, visible, tangible. With a jolt of dismay, I remembered the mysterious hang-ups on my answering machine, those pregnant silences. It was him, no doubt about it. He'd reached out, time and time again, and found me wanting.

I checked the machine in case he'd called again. There was only the rebuking hiss of erased tape. Clutching at straws, I called Telecom, hoping my phone records might identify the source of incoming calls and provide some clues about Red's movements. Call back during office hours, I was told. I called Wendy instead, urged her to use her insider clout, pull whatever strings she could wrap her senior executive hands around. "I'll be up there by eleven tomorrow morning," I told her.

"I really don't see the point."

"I'm coming anyway," I insisted, teeth clenched. "In the meantime, call me the moment you hear anything. Anything at all."

I felt powerless. There was so much I couldn't even guess at. I'd never met Red's Sydney friends, didn't even know their names. Not to mention this shit with the boarding school. My derelictions reared before me, full of reproach. I went into Red's room, paced among his boxes of comics, chastised myself, fingered his clothing as though I might conjure him up out of sheer willpower. His clothes seemed so small. He was still just a baby. Now he was somewhere out there in the jungle, fresh meat for the wolves.

There was nothing I could do until the morning. A headache ticked at my temples. Alert for the jangle of the phone, I went across the back lane, tapped on the Curnows' kitchen door and beckoned

Faye into the yard. Tarquin stared goggle-eyed through the glass as his mother wrapped her arms around me and rocked me side-to-side. "Wow," he said, when he heard the news. "Unreal."

Faye and Leo sat with me into the night, watching me smoke far too many cigarettes. Faye called Wendy, made clucking noises, learned there were no new developments. Around midnight I convinced the Curnows that there was nothing else they could do, chased them off home.

A mantra echoed in my head. *A child is always better off with its mother.* For years, my whole relationship with Red had been predicated on that single assumption, the reason I had not contested custody. Now it sounded like a hollow rationalization for abdicating my responsibilities. A child needs its mother, certainly. But a boy needs his father, too. Whether either of them fully realize it.

Occupying myself with mindless and repetitive tasks, I cleaned and tidied, willing the phone to ring, the news to be good. Eventually, I put myself to bed. I'd be no use to anybody if I arrived in Sydney ragged as a rat's arse.

At 3:15 I was still wide awake, lying on my back, staring at the pattern on the ceiling where the streetlight seeped through a chink in the curtains. I was out of cigarettes, out of ideas, out of things to tell myself.

I pulled on a waterproof and walked the empty streets. Past the silent tower blocks of the Housing Commission high rise, down Gertrude Street, on and on, washed by squally little showers that ended almost as soon as they started. At the all-night 7-11 on Victoria Parade, I bought cigarettes, put one between my lips and walked another three blocks before I realized I didn't have a light. Went back for matches, wet hair plastered to my forehead. "You all right, mate?" said the Lebanese kid behind the counter.

A taxi came up the hill, the only car on the road. I put my arm out. Where do you go at four in the morning, killing time? "Wholesale fruit and vegetable market," I told the driver.

I hunched in the back seat, staring out the window, fending off the cabbie's attempts at conversation. I was all talked out, exhausted from futile speculation, from picking at the balled knot in the pit of my stomach. Silence was better. To contain was to control. To forestall, somehow, the worst possibilities. That Red had been lured away, enticed, entrapped.

In fifteen minutes we were on Footscray Road, an industrial artery running between the docks and the railway yards, a hard-edged world bathed in a space-port glow. The road's margins were a pulverized wasteland of busted-up concrete, broken glass and shredded tires. Trucks appeared out of the night, throwing slush onto the taxi windshield. We joined their flow, converging on a boom gate in a chain-link fence. I paid the cabby, sucked damp air into my lungs and tramped up the access road.

The market was somewhere up ahead, beyond a parking apron crowded with maneuvering trucks, big refrigerator rigs, bug-splattered eighteen-wheelers, minivans, the runabouts of suburban fruit shops. A motorized cart stacked with boxes darted from between two semi-trailers, missing me by inches. "You wanna die?" yelled the driver.

I headed for safer ground, scanning the scene for Donny's truck, half grateful for the distraction, half wondering what the hell I was doing there. Open-fronted buildings bordered the parking apron, the depots of major freight companies. A small cluster of men loitered in front of the Stuhl Holdings shed, hands in the pockets of their work jackets. One of them detached himself from the group and advanced to meet me, a mobile phone in his hand. It was Frank Farrell, the Haulers' welfare officer. Up to some skulduggery, no doubt.

"Morning, Murray," he declared cheerfully. "Or is it still last night?"

"Bit of both," I said, nodding towards the group of men. "Attending to your members' welfare, are you?"

A figure emerged from the building. He was wearing a stylish woolen overcoat and the splash of a too-bright tie showed against the white of his shirt. His features were indistinct in the murky half-light but there was something familiar about them.

"Who's that?" I asked.

Farrell followed my gaze. "Him? That's Bob Stuhl's son, Darren."

As I narrowed my eyes, straining for a clearer view, headlights swept the man's face. No doubt about it. It was Steve McQueen, the truculent party-boy who'd rammed my head down the toilet at the Metro.

"Did you say Darrell or Darren?"

"Darren," said Farrell. "Bob Stuhl's got him familiarizing himself with company operations down here."

"Hey, Darren," I called.

He sauntered over, answering to his name. As he closed the twenty paces between us, my pulse soared. Play it cool, Murray, I told myself.

Darren Stuhl's skin was pasty and razor-scraped. By the look of it, he was hungover and not long out of bed. He glanced at me without a glimmer of recognition. "Yes, what is it?" he demanded, his tone peremptory, managerial. He slid back his plush cashmere cuff and looked at his watch. He was an important man with important things to do.

"Forgotten me already?" I said.

He peered at my face for a couple of seconds, then shrugged.

"The Metro," I reminded him. "Friday night." For all my efforts at cool, the words had a squeezed, slightly hysterical tone.

A memory began to take shape somewhere in Darren's recesses. His eyes flicked to Farrell, then back to me. He gave a dismissive shrug. "So what?"

"Two grand's worth of dentistry, that's what," I blurted. "You knocked out my front teeth, you arrogant prick. And now I know who you are, I know where to send the bill."

He gave a contemptuous snort. He had better things to do with his time, it said, than stand in a car park listening to the pathetic bleating of some wild-eyed loser. "Your teeth look okay to me, pal," he said. "It's your head needs fixing."

As he turned away, I felt a flush of humiliation. "Before you go," I said, putting my hand on his sleeve, "I think you owe me an apology."

He stared down at my hand like it was freshly extruded from a dog's rear end. It occurred to me that his overcoat was worth more than all the teeth in my mouth. When he tried to jerk his arm away, I grabbed a handful of the fabric. "Say you're sorry, Darren."

"Get rid of this idiot, Frank," he ordered.

Farrell stood blank-faced, immobile as a statue.

Darren put the palm of his free hand on my chest and shoved. Not a smart move. I saw red. I saw purple. I saw a seething mass of ugly vengeful images that erupted up out of my guts and blew the top right off my fragile self-control. Lashing out, I smacked him across the chops. He reeled back, even more astonished than I was. Then he took a swing.

This time, I was ready. I dodged, grabbed his lapels and sent him sprawling onto the ground. I stared down at him, reckless with rage. If this jerk thought he could assault me with impunity, just because Daddy was worth a couple of hundred million dollars, he had seriously underestimated the mettle of Murray Theodore Whelan.

"C'mon," I urged, beckoning him to his feet. "Have a go, you mug."

10

THE HALF-DOZEN MEN from the depot rushed forward and formed a circle of spectators. The Marquess of Queensberry was not among them.

Darren got to his feet, dragging the back of his hand across his mouth. He peeled off his overcoat and tossed it to one of the onlookers, then squared off and shaped up. A brawler with an audience, relishing it. Not without reason. Hungover or not, he was fifteen years faster and ten kilos fitter. Rolling his shoulders beneath his fashionably baggy olive-green suit, he tilted his chin upwards, urging me on. I was seriously outclassed, over my head in very deep shit.

He led with his bathroom-proven right hook, aiming for my face. I dropped my shoulder and ran at him, feeling the blow land on my ear as I slammed into his chest. If he thought I was going to box him, he'd mistaken me for a man who knew what he was doing. Get in close, I thought desperately. Compensate for my lack of skill by kneeing him in the knackers.

We scrabbled and scuffled across the wet asphalt. I tried to topple him over, wanting nothing so much as to be somewhere else. Anywhere else. His breath was in my face, his eyes wild and savage. The guy was cut-snake mad, completely off his fucking tree. A forearm jolt to the throat sent me reeling backwards. Then I was on the ground.

A pair of shoes filled my field of vision. Black leather brogues, wing-tipped, buffed to a shine, spattered with mud and patterned with little punched holes. A swift kick to the stomach drove the wind out of me and flooded my eyes with spinning red atoms. My left arm shot up to shield my face. The taste of bile filled my mouth, mingling with shame and anger and confusion.

Darren took a backward step, taking his time now, enjoying the moment. He unbuttoned his jacket and cocked his leg for the *coup de grâce*. In the pit of his arm, he was wearing a leather holster, the butt of a gun clearly visible. The kick came towards me. I shut my eyes.

Nothing happened. I took a peek and saw that Frank Farrell was dragging Darren backwards, pinning his arms to his side, wrestling him under control. "Enough," he was saying. "Easy, easy."

As fast as I could, I clambered to my feet. Darren was still trying to get at me, struggling against Farrell's restraint. We glowered at each other, chests heaving. But the fisticuffs were finished and we both knew it.

"Go," Farrell ordered me. "Just go."

Go? It was all I could do not to turn tail and run. But the tattered remnants of my pride could face no further humiliation. "Come near me again, you useless piece of shit," I panted, my legs as firm as instant noodles. "You won't know what fucking-well hit you."

Darren shrugged off Farrell's grip. "Any time," he sneered. "Any time."

"Break it up, you two," growled Farrell. "This isn't the time or the place."

Brushing the mud from my sleeves with as much dignity as I could muster, I turned on my heels and strode away. I had no idea where I was going.

Ahead of me, the wholesale produce market was a cavernous,

floodlit hive of activity. I let it swallow me. It was either that or fall twitching to the ground, a gibbering wreck.

Mountains of oranges reared up before me. Ramparts of onions. Avenues of avocados and corridors of celery. Mesh sacks bulged with butternut pumpkins and waxed cartons glistened with iced broccoli. Red peppers and purple eggplants. Uncountable heads of cauliflower and crate-loads of cabbages. And everywhere the frenetic lurch of forklifts, the squeal of brakes, the flash of banknotes peeled from tight-rolled wads by men in leather aprons.

I went deeper and deeper into the vast, high-roofed building. Above the stalls hung the names of the vendors. A lot were Italian and Greek but there were Asian names, too, Vietnamese and Chinese, above bundles of bok choy and white radishes the size of torpedoes.

Adrenalin was pounding in my ears, my abdomen ached and a lump was rising at my hairline. Fuck, what a psycho. And Frank Farrell, what was that all about? For a lowly union head-kicker, he seemed pretty familiar with the son of one of the biggest plutocrats in the country.

This is insane, I thought. Trying to kill time, I'd nearly got myself killed instead. And now I was wandering aimlessly through a gigantic shed full of tubers and foliage, dodging trolleys and forklifts, wondering what the fuck had possessed me to come here. My hands, I realized, were trembling. Where was Red at this moment, I wondered? How was he passing the night? Was he alone? Safe? What had impelled him to strike out into the big, bad city?

Donny and his mates were nowhere to be seen. The place was so big, so busy, they could easily not notice that I was here. I felt a sense of relief at that fact. I just wanted to call a cab and go home. If I wasn't at the airport by seven o'clock, they'd sell my ticket to somebody else. I calculated the travel times. Half an hour back to Fitzroy, same again to shower, shave and pack. Forty-five minutes to the airport. A total of two hours, say. It had just gone four, giving me nearly an hour up my sleeve.

I arrived at the market cafe, a steaming, glass-walled hubbub of muffled conversations and toasted sandwiches. I went in, looking for a payphone, didn't find one. Sleep was now off the agenda. Caffeine and nicotine were the order of the day. I bought a cup of cardboard coffee, sat down at a battle-scarred formica table and sucked hungrily on a cigarette. My son, I said to myself, your father is a fool.

The coffee was crap, but it was warm and wet. Halfway through it, Frank Farrell came through the door. He sat down and laid his cell phone on the table between us. Big man, I thought, flashing his big, expensive status symbol. "You okay?" he said.

I crushed my stub in the overflowing tinfoil ashtray. "Never better."

"Pompous prick, aren't you?"

I had to agree with him. "Okay, so I didn't exactly cover myself in glory. But a man can forget his manners when he runs into the total stranger who attacked him in a nightclub and rammed his head down a toilet."

"Darren did that?"

"Hilarious, eh?" I peeled back my top lip and tapped my teeth with the crooked knuckle of my forefinger. "Twenty-three hundred bucks."

He gave a low whistle. Whether this was in disgust at Darren's behavior or amazement at the high cost of dentistry was not immediately apparent. "Send me the bill," he said. "I'll make sure Bob pays it. And something in the way of compensation, too, if you'd care to put a figure on it."

"Sounds like you've done this sort of thing before," I said. "I've heard the Haulers are snug with Stuhl Holdings but I didn't realize you also babysit the owner's children."

Farrell gave a resigned shrug. "I prefer to call it managing the management." He lit a Marlboro. I could see him up there on the horse, squinting into the distance, riding herd on the herd. "There's background here," he said.

"And I suppose you want to share it with me?" I drew back my cuff and looked at my watch. 4:15.

Farrell rested his elbows on the table and leaned into his cigarette, considering where to begin. Then he started. "Bob Stuhl has two sons, right. Half-brothers. Adrian's the child of his first marriage. High achiever. MBA, champion rower, the works. The apple of his father's eye, the very nectarine. Being groomed as future chief executive, seat on the board at twenty-seven."

"Until he had an accident," I said. "Read about it. Dived into the shallow end of a swimming pool."

"That's the public version," said Farrell. "Real story's a bit more interesting. Involves your friend Darren."

"Surprise, surprise," I said.

"Darren's ten years younger than Adrian. Never what you might call foreman material. Piss-poor academic record, no good at sports. Generally failed to meet his father's expectations."

"Boo-hoo," I said. "Low self-esteem, so he turns into a delinquent."

Farrell narrowed his eyes. "You want to hear this or not?"

I yawned. "Wake me up when it gets interesting."

Farrell waited until the silence got uncomfortable, then started back in. "The accident was about six years ago. Darren's in his last year of school. He's supposed to be doing his homework, but he's bored. Bob had him at one of those places where they don't mind if you're dumb as dogshit, long as the checks keep coming. Anyway, Darren decides to climb out his bedroom window onto the roof. This is the Stuhl family compound in Toorak, a thirty-room French chateau."

"I see Bob more as the Graceland type."

"You got it," said Farrell. "This is more the wife's speed. The number two, Darren's mother. Social climber. Anyway, it's a hot summer night and Adrian's down below, taking a dip in the French provincial swimming pool. Darren's up on the roof, arsing around. Accidentally dislodges a sheet of slate. Eighth of an inch thick, edge like a blunt machete. It shoots down the incline, frisbees off the guttering and lobotomizes big brother. Cost Bob a hospital wing to bury the truth. Also cost him fifty million when the market expressed its sympathy by shaving ten percent off the Stuhl Holdings share price on account of succession uncertainties."

Good story. As stories went. "Lifestyles of the rich and famous," I said. "Your point being? I should consider myself lucky that Darren only cost me my front teeth?"

Farrell tapped the edge of the ashtray with his cigarette. It didn't have any ash on it.

"My point being that Bob lost his heir apparent," he said impatiently. "Suddenly dipstick Darren was the great white hope, promoted into his brother's shoes. First Bob shipped him off to America so he could get himself some sort of ticket in business administration. Now he's back with a vengeance, learning the family racket from the ground up. Running around making a nuisance of himself at every Stuhl depot and office from here to the Black Stump. Not only isn't he up to it, he's a chip off the old block. Thinks the way to get things done is to be the meanest dog in the yard."

The adrenalin had ebbed away and I was suddenly very, very tired. "Okay, I understand your problem," I said. "Bob employs, what, nearly a thousand of your members. And Darren represents what you might call an occupational hazard. So you keep a close eye on him. You drag him away when he's about to give some poor prick a kicking. You manage the management. I can sympathize. But I'm not going to roll over, help poor benighted Bob with his dynastic succession problems. Now that I know who Darren is, I'm going to lay a complaint of aggravated assault, have him charged, brought before a magistrate."

Farrell's mobile phone chirped. He pushed a button and hoisted the black plastic brick to his ear. "Yeah?" He listened briefly, frowned, then turned it off and laid it back on the table, its stubby antenna quivering. I considered asking him if I could use it to call a cab. But I was already obliged to him for saving me from a kicking and wasn't inclined to go begging petty favors.

"You'd be well within your rights," he told me, straight back onto the topic of Darren Stuhl. "But why take him to court, deal with all that shit, when a private settlement can be reached, put some dollars in your pocket?"

"Because it's not just a private matter," I said. "The guy's a public menace."

"Up to you," he shrugged. "I know what I'd be doing. His lawyers'll make mincemeat of you."

He was probably right. I was in no fit state to think about it. Four-thirty. Time to be making tracks. I nodded at Farrell's phone, wondering again why he was here. "Darren bites again?"

"Not this time. Minor irritation. Nothing we can't handle."

"Especially with Darren on the team," I said. "And all tooled up, too."

"That thing?" said Farrell dismissively. "Rich kid's toy. Darren's got himself a gun club license, not supposed to take it anywhere but the firing range. I've warned him before about toting it around like some sort of fashion accessory. Might go off and blow his tiny dick away." He shook his head with weary exasperation. "The things a man has to deal with."

We both stood to leave. "You didn't say why you're here," said Farrell.

"I came for the color and movement. Got more than I bargained for."

"If you change your mind, send me your bill. Bob can be a very reasonable man. And go home to bed. You look fucked."

Good advice. I should've taken it.

11

I WENT TO THE COUNTER to ask the whereabouts of the nearest public phone. The chief sandwich toaster was flat out filling orders. While I was trying to get his attention, Donny Maitland arrived. He breezed through the door with his handbills in his pocket and greeted me as though there'd never been an iota of doubt in his mind that I'd be there waiting.

So I ordered more coffee and told him about my run-in with Darren Stuhl. Then I warned him about Frank Farrell's lurking presence and accepted his offer of a free ride after the campaign rally. Half an hour later, I was pinned against the back window of the Kenworth with Heather's lipstick on my dipstick.

Through the mist-smeared glass, I witnessed Donny's campaign rally descend into a wild affray when Darren Stuhl decided to start waving around his artillery. Then came the frenzied burst of activity as I quit the truck and went hunting for Donny.

And then I was jogging through the rain, not looking back, thinking only that I'd barely have time to swing past the house and throw some duds into an overnight bag before zooming to the airport. I trotted through the exit gate, past the clog of departing vehicles, and made for the Mobil roadhouse on the other side of Footscray Road. A mustard-colored smudge was beginning to stain the sky beyond the office towers of the city center. Maybe Red had turned up. It occurred to me that I'd forgotten to turn on the answering machine when I went out to buy cigarettes. Shit, shit, shit.

Footscray Road was a death trap, eight lanes of speeding trucks. I sprinted across, nearly getting skittled in the process. Drying my face on a paper towel at the pumps, I went into the roadhouse, found the payphone and called the cab company. Fifteen minutes, I was told. My watch said 5:42. By the time I'd finished waiting in line for a doughnut and bought a copy of the *Sun,* it was saying 5:55.

On the dot of six o'clock, a police car came screaming down the road, lights flashing, and turned into the market. Shortly after, an ambulance did the same.

Had the squished tomato incident gone ballistic, I wondered? I hoped Donny was okay but I figured he could look after himself. Was he not the victorious general who had just swept his foe from the field of battle?

I sipped what Mobil called coffee and thumbed through the paper, looking up every time a car pulled into the forecourt, frantic for the roof-light of an arriving taxi. MOSCOW COUP SHOCK, read the *Sun*'s front-page headline. Hard-liners had seized power in Moscow. Mikhail Gorbachev was missing, location uncertain.

Fuck Gorbachev. It was my son's whereabouts that concerned me. Was it raining in Sydney? Was Red sleeping rough? Five past six came and went. Another cop car turned into the service road leading to the market. What the hell was going on over there? Had some mafioso greengrocer decided to get antsy about a few dollars' worth of hothouse tomatoes? Had hot-blooded Heather decided to take the situation in hand? She'd handled me so well that I was still sticky with her transmission fluid. I wished I could get Lyndal's motor racing like that.

The news from Moscow was late-breaking, too recent for the *Sun*'s cartoonist. He'd found a more parochial topic. Angelo was depicted as an uncomprehending wombat, caught in the headlights of an oncoming semitrailer. Bob Stuhl was behind the wheel and the grille bore the words "Tonnage Levy."

Fucking Stuhl family, I thought. They're out to get me. I'd have to call Angelo as soon as I got to Sydney, explain my absence, try to smooth his feathers. At least I'd found him a stalking horse to back against the Haulers.

At 6:07:14, a taxi pulled up and tooted its horn. For once, the driver was the silent type, a pockmarked Somali with skin like a chocolate-coated cookie. I slumped low in the back seat, my fingers beating a fretful tattoo on the vinyl. Shrouds of cloud were swirling around the city office towers, lights beginning to appear in house windows, traffic building. To what kind of dawn was my baby boy waking, eight hundred kilometers away? Where and how and with whom had he passed this night? This one, and the one before it?

We reached the house and I told the driver to wait while I bolted inside. There was no time for personal hygiene or even a change of clothes. Wendy would have to take me as she found me. I rushed into the bedroom, pulled out an overnight bag and was feverishly ransacking my laundry basket, sniffing for packable jocks, when I heard a voice from the living room.

"You wascally wabbit," it said.

12

A GANGLY PREPUBESCENT BOY was standing in my living room, shoveling cereal into his mouth and watching Elmer Fudd chase Bugs Bunny around a tree with a blunderbuss. "Hi, Dad." He spoke through a mouthful of Wheaties, taking his eyes off the screen just long enough to acknowledge my presence. "Where have you been?"

A wave of relief buckled my knees. "Don't you fucking-well 'Hi, Dad' me," I said. "And never mind where I've been. Where the hell have *you* been? Your mother and I have been worried sick."

"I took da wrong toin at Alba-koiky," said Bugs.

"And switch that fucking TV off," I said, moderating my tone. "You're lucky I don't put you over my knee." I would've had my hands full if I tried. Red had shot up a good three inches in the months since I'd last seen him and his knees and elbows bulged in his baggy clothes like a handful of coat hangers in a sock. If he was a girl, it suddenly struck me, he'd be sprouting tits and getting his period. In Angola, he'd be in the army.

"Sorry, Dad," he said sheepishly. "I didn't know what else to do. You won't make me go back, will you?"

"That depends," I said.

"On what?"

I widened my arms. "On whether you're too big to give your father a hug, for a start."

His expression said he thought he was, but his better judgment prevailed and he submitted to a long paternal embrace. I added a light cuff around the ears for good measure. "Now tell me what's going on. No, wait." I dashed out the front. The meter said fifteen dollars. I gave the cabby twenty and told him to keep the change. He was lucky I didn't hug him as well. "Okay, start talking," I told Red. "And this had better be good."

Red sat on the couch with his knees tucked under his chin and poured out his plaint in a continuous, meandering stream. It boiled down to this. His situation sucked. Big time. The reasons were numerous and well-rehearsed. For a start, there was his new school. Everything about it was stupid. The teachers were stupid, the rules were stupid, the uniform was stupid. "We have to wear a straw hat," he said. "It's called a boater. How stupid is that?"

Pretty stupid, I had to admit.

He'd been enrolled in the middle of the year, filling a vacancy created when the son of a Singapore businessman was required to leave because his father had lost his fortune gambling and could no longer afford the fees. He didn't have any friends and he didn't like all the rules and regulations. Red, that is. Not the lad with the bankrupt dad. When he complained to Wendy and Richard, they insisted he'd soon settle down and learn to like it, that many new boys underwent a similar adjustment period.

"Richard said he cried for months when his parents first sent him there and it hadn't done him any harm. And Mum, all she thinks about is Nicola and Alexandra."

Wendy's choice of names for her twin daughters never failed to bring a smile to my lips.

"They cry all the time. And I mean all the time. Totally. They've been through four nannies already."

"So you decided to run away?" I said, doing my best to sound stern.

"I told Mum I wanted to come down here," he said. "Live with you, go to Fitzroy High with Tarquin. But she said that was out of the question. That you weren't responsible enough."

That was Wendy, all right. "If you were so unhappy, you should've called me," I said. "We could've talked."

"I called and called, but you were never here."

The reproach struck home. "You can't just disappear because things aren't going your way." But that was exactly what he had done. He'd fled to Melbourne to front me in person. Crack of dawn Saturday morning, he walked out of Brookside, used a teller machine to empty his bank account, then went to the Greyhound terminal. He'd done his research. The bus was cheaper than the train. Thirty-nine dollars, student price.

"In case you had to be sixteen or something, I asked this older kid to buy the ticket for me. Except he ripped me off. Took my money and never came back. I only had twenty dollars left and it wasn't enough."

He spent the rest of Saturday trying to hustle small change. "I said I'd lost my bus fare, which was true, so I wasn't lying or anything."

But panhandling is hungry work for a growing boy and food purchases ate into his takings. When night arrived, he was still twelve dollars short. He called me again but got no answer. I thought back and worked out that I must have been at the Curnows' place. He snuck into some bughouse screening a midnight-to-dawn Star Trek marathon and dozed off during *The Search for Spock*. "I'd seen it before," he said. "So I knew where he was."

The next morning, figuring he was in too deep to change his plans, he shook down a couple of Klingons for the balance of the fare. This time, he braved the counter himself, bought a ticket on the next bus to Melbourne, the overnighter.

"That reminds me." I interrupted his saga for long enough to call the airline and cancel my booking. "I was flying to Sydney to look for you," I told him.

"You were?" He swelled with momentary gratification, then realized that remorse was the more appropriate response. "Sorry, Dad."

The story continued. Ticket in hand, he lashed out on an Egg McMuffin, killed Sunday in a succession of video arcades, then spent fourteen hours beside a fat lady who snored all the way from Gundagai to Tallarook. Arriving on my doorstep at six o'clock, he retrieved the spare key from its hiding place, let himself in and proceeded to eat every flake of cereal he could lay his hands on. At which point, I arrived.

"Have you got a girlfriend?" he said.

"Several. That's why I look exhausted."

Jesus, the kid could've got a job writing low-budget travel tips for Lonely Planet. I didn't know whether to laugh or cry. But I did know two things for sure. Never again would my son be forced to wear a straw boater. And never again would he spend an entire night in a darkened room full of Trekkies. Not unless I was there, too. "So what do you think we should do now?" I asked, a leading question.

"Ring Mum?" he ventured. "Tell her not to worry any more."

Correct. I placed the call, told Wendy that I wouldn't be coming to Sydney, after all. She was right, I could do nothing useful up there. "Red's here with me. And he'll be staying here until we get a few things sorted out."

"What things?"

"Stupid things." For once I was holding the trump card in the access game. "Things that suck."

Red took over then, faced the maternal music like a man. "I *do* love you, Mum," he insisted. "It's just that . . ."

Respectful of his privacy, I withdrew into the bathroom and splashed water on my face. All things considered, I didn't feel too bad. In fact, I felt great. Not only was Red safe and well, he'd flown to me for sanctuary, forgiven me my negligence, offered me the opportunity of fatherhood once again.

On top of which, I now knew the identity of the shithead who clobbered me in the kisser at the Metro, marring my haunting good looks. Okay, so I'd embarrassed myself with a pathetic attempt to even the score. But an offer of compensation now lay on the table. I'd taken the high moral ground with Frank Farrell, blathering on about having Darren Stuhl locked up. In the cold light of my bathroom mirror, though, I was more inclined to take the money. Darren's delinquency, I decided, was going to cost Bob Stuhl plenty.

I'd even had my wing-wang wiggled for the first time in living memory, although not in a manner with which I was completely comfortable.

Red, his contrite conversation with mama completed, appeared at the bathroom door. "We're out of cereal," he announced.

I scrambled us some toast and we ate in silence, content with full mouths and each other's company. In the middle of his fourth slice Red nodded at my plate. "You going to finish that?"

"Keep this up," I told him, "and I may not be able to afford you."

Thanks to the snores of his traveling companion, the runaway had got little sleep on the Greyhound red-eye. He readily accepted my proposal of a few hours' kip. Within minutes, he was unconscious. For a long while I stood in the doorway of his room, gazing at the lump beneath the covers.

That's when it came to me, fully formed and with dazzling clarity, as if it had been waiting in the wings for the right instant to step forth and declare itself. For too long I'd been content to drift, to let other people set my agenda. The time had come to take the bullshit by the horns. Red's arrival was a sign that it wasn't too late for a second chance in the lottery of life.

Time was, even a minor political flack could see himself as part of a larger project, something from which he could draw pride sufficient unto the day. But that day was long gone. My life's work was reduced to helping a clapped-out mediocrity retain his fragile grip on an office whose powers he was incapable of exercising. Not a lot of *amour-propre* to be derived from that. The moment had come to tell Angelo that I was popping outside for a little walk in the snow.

My requirements, after all, were modest. Employment that provided a modicum of self-respect, kept the bank at bay and the refrigerator stocked. Time to devote to the long-neglected tasks of fatherhood, to cultivate my own garden. If I couldn't find an employer to replace Angelo, I could always work for myself, set up shop as a consultant. Use my contacts in the public sector to build a client base. Flog my experience as a bureaucratic fixer. The more I thought about it, the more I liked the idea. I could get a card printed. *Murray Whelan & Associates.* It always looked more impressive if you had associates. Maybe I might even get some.

It was past eight now. I called Faye. "Naughty little sod," she said. "Tell him to come visit Tarquin after school."

Doubtless I'd be seeing a lot more of Tarquin from now on. I set the alarm for 1 P.M. and had just hit the hay when the phone rang. It was Agnelli's private secretary, Trish. "Are you coming into the office this morning?"

"Not if I can help it."

"He's very keen to talk to you."

"About what?"

"About eleven-thirty."

I got out of bed and began drafting my resignation.

13

TRANSPORT HOUSE WAS A SPIT-COLORED office tower at the western edge of the downtown grid. Its fifteen floors were dedicated to the administration of the public transport system, the undertaking of feasibility studies into the implementation of multi-modal ticketing systems and the issuing of fifty thousand weekly pay checks. This work was conducted by men in comfortable trousers and women in bum-freezing skirts, who spent their coffee breaks standing on the pavement outside the main entrance, smoking the sort of cigarettes that come in packs of fifty.

The Minister for Transport's office was located on the top floor. When not fulfilling his obligations in the legislature, or conferring with his factional colleagues, its current tenant could usually be found there, in his ministerial suite, surrounded by ambitious schemers, cynical cronies and time-serving paper-shufflers. And me.

By the time I stepped into the elevator, showered and suited, a note for Red on the refrigerator door, I'd done my homework.

According to my calculations, taking into account the full gamut of accrued leave and sick days, unpaid overtime, severance pay and sundry other entitlements, the total sum due to me on resignation would amount to exactly four-fifths of five-eighths of fuck-all. Or approximately three months' wages, whichever was the lesser.

Not much, after all my time with the firm. And now, with my mortgage rate topping 13 percent, plus the additional outlay on Frosty Flakes and other juvenile sundries that would be required, my decision to quit was not ideally timed. So I'd torn up my letter of resignation. I had another strategy. I'd get myself sacked.

Dismissal would trigger various premature termination clauses in my contract, netting me six months' salary in lieu of notice. Double what I would get if I merely quit. Plus, if a new job proved elusive, the fact that I'd been laid off would entitle me to claim forthwith my birthright as an Australian citizen, a fortnightly dole check.

As I entered the ministerial suite, Trish glanced up from her keyboard. "Walk into a door or something?" She fluttered a yellow message slip in the air between us. "Your wife wants you to call her."

"My ex-wife, as well you know." I crushed the slip into a ball and tossed it into the nearest WPB. Wendy was nothing if not predictable. She thought she'd have more luck convincing me to send Red back to Sydney if she got to me at the office, away from the boy's influence. "If she calls again, tell her I don't work here any more."

"You wish," said Trish. "Go straight in. He's waiting for you."

Angelo's Transport House office was bigger than the one at Parliament House but it was strictly utilitarian. Its only feature of note was the view, a panoramic vista that occupied one wall like a gigantic photorealist painting. In the middle distance, the cooling tower of the Newport power station was a gigantic cigarette, wisps of white wafting from its red-painted rim. Cars the size of ants crawled across the twisted parabola of the Westgate Bridge. A seething stratosphere pressed down upon this scene, the writhing clouds as black as Bible-binding.

Angelo was standing in front of the window, hands clasped behind his back, Napoleon crossing the Alps. Neville Lowry sat primly on the edge of a chair, knees crossed. His hairless pate was glowing like an oiled halo.

Angelo waved me inside with an impatient gesture. "You see the cartoon?" he said, rocking on his toes. "Made me look like an idiot. Cabinet meets this afternoon and I want to demonstrate that I'm taking action to nip these leaks in the bud. I've decided to make an example."

Neville moved his attention to a point beyond the clouds. To the hole in the ozone layer, perhaps, or an orbiting satellite. Angelo, too, turned to the window, avoiding eye contact with me. I waited, very alert, my mouth suddenly dry. Did I dare hope, I wondered, that the head to drop into the basket would be mine?

Angelo turned to face me. "Nev here has agreed to accept full responsibility," he said. "I've just terminated him."

Neville smirked and gave me an amiable shrug. For a man whose cue ball head was rolling across the carpet, he was inexplicably buoyant.

"In six weeks," continued Agnelli, "when the dust has settled, he'll be taking up a new position within the department. Deputy director, Corporate Communications. Not a political appointment, you understand. A purely administrative one."

I understood all right. Nev Lowry wasn't responsible for the leak. He'd simply used the opportunity to engineer a move from the political to the civil service payroll, thus ensuring job security beyond the election. "Such self-sacrifice," I said. "It borders on the heroic."

"Ours not to reason why," said Neville, standing up. "Ours but to take a long-overdue holiday. Anything you want me to bring back from Bali?"

"Tropical ulcers," I suggested.

"Just try to look a bit more contrite, Nev," said Agnelli. "At least until you're out of the building. And shut the door on your way out."

I sank into the sofa, wondering if I shouldn't be considering a similar game plan. Angelo resumed his imperial stance before the window. "Any advance on the Haulers front?" he demanded.

"I might have found a taker," I said. "A bloke named Donny Maitland is putting together a rank-and-file ticket. Reckons he can tap into the disaffection with the incumbent regime."

"You think he can knock off Sharpe and McGrath?"

"That's about as likely as the water-fueled jumbo jet," I said. "Still, he's hard to frighten and he might have some impact, given the resources."

"Then see that he gets some. Bury the cost in the policy-development budget, call it industry research or something. How does ten grand sound?"

Like enough to get Donny's little show on the road, pay for some printing and postage. "I'll get onto it," I said, standing up.

Angelo waved me back down. He began pacing, sure sign that he was screwing himself up to some sticking point. What absurdity now, I wondered? Upon what madcap mission was I about to be dispatched? "I saw you speaking with Lyndal yesterday at that community arts crap," he said. This was both a question and an accusation.

"She's an asset to the team," I said.

"Get your hand off it, Murray," said Angelo. "There's backstabbing afoot out there, I'm sure of it. I could feel it in the atmosphere."

"You're being paranoid," I said.

"I'll be as paranoid as I like," he said. "Anyway, it's not paranoia. It's instinct. When you've been in politics as long as I have, you sense these things. Somebody is plotting to knock me off."

Jesus, I thought. Hark to the man. He's dragged me out of bed to pour oil into the storm-tossed teacup of his ego.

"Face it, Angelo," I said. "Nobody in their right mind wants to talk to you. You're a bully and an unprincipled careerist. You take your constituents for granted and treat your employees like shit. Frankly, it's a miracle you're not still chasing ambulances for a living, you slimy arsehole."

Angelo slapped his hands together, rubbed them energetically and beamed at me. I tried again. "You think I'm joking, don't you," I said harshly. "Well that just proves what a dopey cunt you really are."

Insubordination. Personal abuse. Sexist language. He'll have to fire me now, I thought.

Ange looked even more pleased. "You're absolutely right," he enthused. "That's the great thing about you, Murray. You're the only one who's prepared to be up-front with me. None of these toadies" — he flapped his wrist vaguely — "none of them would ever talk to me like that. That's why I know I can trust you implicitly. You're the only one who tells it like it is. Which is why I wanted to talk to you today. I want you to do something for me. It's a big ask, I know. But you're the only one I can turn to. The only one I know I can truly rely on." He paused dramatically.

"I want you to nominate for preselection for Melbourne Upper."

14

THAT DAMNED INVISIBLE HEARING AID was on the blink again.
"You're quitting parliament?" I said.

"Don't be ridiculous," Ange scoffed. "I just don't want to leave anything to chance with my renomination. If you run against me, it'll help split any potential opposition. Then you swing your support behind me in the final ballot and bump me over the line. Simple."

Sure it was simple. It was the oldest trick in the political book.

"Like I said, it's a big ask. But I'm worried, Murray. I wouldn't suggest it otherwise."

I sat there, speechless, staring at him.

"Don't interrupt," he said. "I know what you're going to say. You're going to say that I might be worried, but that you'll be the one at the rough end of the pineapple. End of the day, I'll be back in parliament, you'll be the man who knifed his boss, got the sack. After all, I can hardly keep you on my staff after you declare your intention to run against me. Stands to reason. So there's not much incentive in it for you."

"Not much," I agreed.

"That's why I'm prepared to make it worth your while."

A crack opened in the clouds and a beam of sunshine fell upon the container gantries of Appleton dock. Don't move, I told myself. You'll break the spell.

"You're shocked, I can see," said Angelo. "Please, don't be offended. I know I can't buy your integrity, but I'd be grateful if you give me this opportunity to express my appreciation for your years of loyal service. You know I can't guarantee your job security beyond the election, but at least I can cushion the blow, money-wise."

"Money?" I said, as though the filthy subject never crossed my mind.

"Your current employment contract provides for, what, three months' pay in case of dismissal?"

"Six," I said, a mere point of information.

Angelo was undeterred. "We'll make it nine. Nominations for preselection close in two weeks. Plenty of time for us to amend the relevant clauses. Then wham, bam, ink's barely dry and you decide to run against me — which is your prerogative as a party member. And I give you your marching orders — which is my right as your employer. You pocket the payout and away we go."

"Nine months' severance pay?" I closed my eyes and squeezed thumb and forefinger across them. Any second I was going to wake up, find myself at home in bed, realize this was all a dream.

"Okay then, twelve," said Ange quickly. "A year's pay, lump sum. How's that for a golden parachute?"

Why did I need a parachute? I'd sprouted wings. I tried to look riven.

"I know what you're thinking." Agnelli was a veritable clairvoyant this morning. "You're thinking that you'll have a job until the election anyway. But keep in mind there's a lot of pressure on me to cut costs. Other ministers are shedding staff."

Act now, in other words, to avoid disappointment. "Suppose I agree," I said tentatively. "Hypothetically speaking. For this to work we'll have to put up a pretty good show. I'd need to have a really proper go at you."

"Absolutely," said Angelo, moving in for the kill. "Boots and all."

"In that case, I'll have campaign expenses. Phone bills, entertainment, postage."

"Chicken-feed," said Ange. "I'll pay out of my own pocket. A grand, shall we say?"

The fucking cheapskate had just donated ten times that to Donny out of government funds. "Two," I said, feeling generous, "and it's a deal."

I extended my hand and he nodded in its vicinity.

"Amend your contract and have it on my desk for signature by the close of business," he said. "And mum's the word, okay?"

Trish buzzed to say Angelo's next appointment had arrived, a senior official from the Railways Union. I got out while the going was good and went into my office, a cubicle adjacent to the ministerial document-shredder.

Once I'd located my job contract, it took me all of five minutes to pencil the new details into the margins, ready for retyping. Then I pulled out the phone book, found the listing for Maitland Transport, highlighted the address, copied the details to a check requisition form, added the relevant budget codes and marked it for immediate payment. Not a bad day's work, all up.

I was about to take the paperwork out to Trish when she buzzed me. "There's a gentleman here to see you," she said. "A Noel Webb."

I knew Webb. He was no gentleman.

Surf was up. The waves of shit were about to start breaking.

15

NOEL WEBB was a copper.

We'd had dealings a couple of years back when Angelo was Minister for the Arts, a little matter concerning forged paintings. It was not a happy encounter. I took a couple of deep breaths, asked Trish to send him in, slipped the contract back into my top drawer and stood at my desk, waiting.

Webb filled the door frame. He had the build of an icebox and a personality to go with it. His hair was cut to an assertive two-millimeter burr and his ears stuck out the side of his head like the handles on a cast-iron casserole. He had the sort of face you could strike a match on. It wouldn't light but you'd get a lot of satisfaction doing it.

"Hello, Noel." I didn't offer him a seat. "How's life in bunko?"

"Wouldn't know," he said. "I'm on other duties now."

"Let me guess. Public relations?"

Webb leaned idly against the door frame and surveyed my broom closet as though it confirmed his estimation of my net human worth. "I understand you were at the wholesale fruit and vegetable market earlier today."

It wasn't a question. "So?"

"Why were you there?"

"To buy some asparagus." Until Webb eased back on the attitude, gave me some explanation, I saw no reason to answer his questions. "I'm planning on making a quiche."

"It's not the asparagus season."

He was right. The asparagus season didn't officially begin until they put up a sign at the Melbourne Club requesting that members refrain from urinating in the umbrella stand. "I was misinformed," I said.

Webb sucked in his cheeks. "Still a smartarse, I see, Whelan."

"So this a social call, then?"

Noel Webb liked to be the one asking the questions. "When did you leave the market?"

"Before the asparagus arrived," I said. "But after the last of the stone fruit." Provoking Noel Webb was like shooting fish fingers in a supermarket freezer. I relented. "Five thirty-seven," I said. "Or eight."

He thought I was still winding him up. "Looked at your watch, did you?"

"Matter of fact, I did." I made a show of looking at it again. "It keeps very good time. Which is a valuable commodity. So how about you stop wasting mine with the quiz-show routine and tell me what this is all about."

"Happen to see Darren Stuhl at the market?"

If he was here asking, he already knew the answer. Shit, I thought, Darren's reported me. Got in first, claimed that I was the one who attacked him. Which is what it must've looked like to those blokes who witnessed the fight. Men who, conveniently, were Stuhl employees, unlikely to contradict the boss's son, even if they knew the true story. Which they didn't. Shit. There went my *quid pro quo*. "I saw a lot of people," I said. "It's a very busy place."

Webb ran his tongue around his teeth and pursed his lips. His repertoire of facial expressions was limited but communicative. He wanted me to understand that he could barely restrain his irritation. In that regard, nothing had changed since we were in the same class at Preston East Technical High School.

"And if you blokes were doing your job properly," I said, "you wouldn't be harassing innocent people. You'd have Darren Stuhl behind bars. He's a vicious prick and it's only a matter of time before he does someone a serious injury."

"Not much chance of that," said Webb complacently. "He's on a slab in the morgue."

That gave me pause. "What happened to him?"

"Run over by a truck. Squashed flat as a tack. Raspberry jam from arsehole to breakfast."

Call me uncharitable, but I felt a momentary flash of elation. "Nasty," I said. "Then again, accidents do happen. And they couldn't happen to a bigger jerk than Darren Stuhl."

"Whether it was an accident or not remains to be seen," said Webb. "And your comments about the deceased are not exactly well-chosen, considering."

"Considering what?"

"Considering that you were in the truck that ran him over."

My insides rose, then fell, as if I was in a plummeting elevator. The burst sack, the smear of red on the asphalt. Then another thought jostled forward. Holy moley, I thought, this is about my parting words to young Dazzer. If he came near me again, I'd told him, he wouldn't know what hit him. Now something had.

I sank into my seat. "Do forgive me, Detective Sergeant," I said. Fortunately I had not yet called Webb by his boyhood nickname, Spider, a usage he deeply disliked. "In my understandable excitement at seeing you again, I forgot my manners." I gestured at the visitor's chair. "Please."

Webb sat down. "That's detective *senior* sergeant." He pulled out a small spiral-bound notebook and laid it on his knee. For the moment, he left it closed. "Let's begin again, shall we?" he said. "Why were you at the market this morning?"

"I had insomnia. Couldn't sleep. I was wandering the streets, looking for distraction." I put my hand on my heart. "And that's the living truth."

He looked at me skeptically but let it ride. "And you saw Darren Stuhl there?"

"Like I said, we spoke to each other."

"You knew him from your work here at the transport ministry?"

"We met informally," I said. "He punched me in the face and shoved my head down a toilet."

"An understandable reaction. Must happen to you fairly regularly."

My turn to let it ride. "Happened at the Metro nightclub last Friday. At the time I had no idea who he was. Thought he was just an aggressive drunk. Check with the bouncers if you like. By sheer coincidence, I saw him again at the market this morning, fronted him, suggested he might care to pay my dental bill." I flipped back my top lip and bared my fangs. "Two grand he cost me."

Webb's eyes flicked from my teeth to the graze on my forehead. "And what was his reaction?"

"We agreed to disagree," I said.

"What time was this?" Webb took a pen from his inside pocket and opened his pad.

"About four o'clock."

"What then?"

"Nothing really. We went our separate ways. I ran into Donny Maitland. He was there making a delivery. We had a coffee. He offered me a lift home."

"And what's your relationship with Maitland?"

I shrugged noncommittally. "I've known him since I was a kid. Took his sister-in-law to the Coburg ball in 1970. She was there, too, as you're no doubt aware. Heather. As we were leaving, we got caught in traffic, all those trucks and whatnot. I was running late, had a plane to catch, so I took off, legged it, caught a cab home."

Webb consulted his notes. "This was at 5:37 exactly?"

I nodded. "Just before I took off, we ran over something. I thought it was a sack of fruit or something. But Donny's already told you this, hasn't he?"

"Catch your plane?"

"Obviously not. Circumstances changed and I canceled the trip. A family matter. The reason for my insomnia, if you must know."

He seemed to accept my assurances on that point, or at least he did not pursue the matter. "Know anyone who had a grievance against the deceased? Who might want him dead?"

The deceased. The word had such a blunt finality to it. My acquaintance with Darren Stuhl had been nasty, brutish and short and I'd wished him nothing but ill — but I derived no great satisfaction from his death. Not once my initial surge of *Schadenfreude* dissipated. Apart from anything else, it meant that I could kiss my two grand goodbye. Under the circumstances, presenting a dental bill to his father would have smacked of squalid opportunism. Even in death, Darren Stuhl managed to make a pest of himself.

"Based on my brief contact with him," I said, "Darren was not what might be called congenial. He could've had hundreds of enemies. Thousands, even."

Webb was hoping for something a little more specific. "What about your old mate Donny Maitland? Bit of a stirrer, I understand."

I flashed on Donny, turbo-charged and babbling, grinding his gears. "Donny's got some industrial issues with Stuhl senior's corporation," I said. "And he's got the T-shirt to prove it. But taking things out on the son, that's not his style. Anyway, what makes you think it wasn't an accident? It was pissing down rain, there were vehicles everywhere. Slippery road. Hazardous conditions. And some of those trucks are real monsters, bullbars sticking out a mile. He might've slipped, fallen under. Could happen to anyone." If Farrell's story about the roofing tile was true, Darren had a history of clumsiness.

Webb wasn't there to speculate on possible scenarios. "So the last time you saw Stuhl alive was at approximately four A.M.?"

It was, apart from a quick glance through a misted window across a crowded parking lot in the pre-dawn gloom while having my motor tuned. At which time he was holding a pistol to Donny Maitland's head. If I'd seen him then, so had others, men with a better view. And if they wanted to share their recollections with the police that was their business. For my part, I preferred to wait until I had a clearer idea of what was going on. I had no wish to feed an old friend into the maw of the law.

"Yep," I said.

Webb jotted something down, flipped his notebook closed and stood up. His glance alighted on the phone book, open on the desk between us, where Donny's entry was highlighted. "I sincerely hope you're not trying to play funny buggers with me, Whelan," he said. "Because if you are, rest assured that you'll live to regret it."

"I have no reason to want to play anything with you," I said, also standing up. "And I've answered your questions to the best of my ability. If you have any other queries, you know where to find me."

Webb put his notebook in his pocket and turned for the door. When he reached it, he looked back. "You should be careful how much you bite off, Whelan," he said. "Make sure you can chew it all."

As soon as he was gone, I slumped back into my seat. My mind was racing or at least hobbling as fast as it could. It was more than twenty-four hours since I'd slept. Hectic and draining hours, many of them. Fatigue was beginning to tell. I could scarcely string two beans together.

The note I left for Red on the refrigerator, the one place I was sure he'd find it, said that I'd be back about midday. It was that now. Before I went home, however, I needed to make a call.

I looked down at the phone book and started to dial.

16

A MACHINE ANSWERED the Maitland Transport number. I started to leave a message for Donny to call me when Heather picked up.

"How's Sydney?" she said. "Any news about your son? Donny told me he's gone missing."

"Red turned up here in Melbourne," I told her. "Made a unilateral decision to come and live with me."

"Well, at least you've got something to be pleased about," she said. "That thing we ran over, it was Bob Stuhl's son."

"So I heard," I said. "How's Donny?"

"Shook up, as you can imagine. It was a pretty grisly sight. The police didn't finish with him until ten o'clock. First the uniforms, then the plainclothes lot. They took him up to Citywest station to sign a formal statement. He kept your name out of it, by the way. Thought you had enough on your plate, what with your kid missing. Save you any hassle. I didn't say anything either."

The only other person at the market who knew my identity was Frank Farrell. He must have supplied that information to the cops. "I appreciate the thought," I said. "Any idea how it happened?"

"Beats me," she said. "He was a fair way under when the wheels went over him, that's all I know. Soon as you left, there were people coming from everywhere. You could've sold tickets. Until the cops arrived, that is. Then the cone of silence descended. The only one left to do any talking was Donny."

"Any suggestion of culpability?"

"Why should there be?" said Heather, slightly alarmed. "It was an accident, wasn't it?"

"Let's hope so," I said. "Get Donny to call me when he can, okay? I'll be home in bed."

"Alone?"

"Asleep. Five minutes with you and I'm all shagged out."

I got off the line before she could come back at me, gathered up my paperwork and took the contract to Trish for typing. "That Webb guy was a cop, wasn't he?" she said.

"Road trauma squad," I said. "I'll be out for the rest of the day."

I took the payment requisition down to accounts, kissed some bean-counter backside, extracted a promise that Donny's check would be cut by the next morning, then caught a cab home. Red was on the couch, watching "The Young and the Restless" in pyjamas that were three sizes too small. "Sorry, mate," I said. "I had to go to the office for a while. Work."

He was familiar with the concept, if not the practice. "No worries. A man's gotta do what a man's gotta do."

Clearly what these particular men had to do next was go shopping. Apart from the clothes he was wearing, Red had arrived with a Walkman, some tapes, a pair of Nike cross-trainers and a towel he'd filched from boarding school. Thanks to his hyperactive growth hormones, nothing in his room fitted him. "Just call Mum and tell her to send all my stuff down," he suggested.

That pleasure would have to wait. We lunched at a local pizzeria, then schlepped down the street to the Brotherhood of St. Laurence thrift shop near the Housing Commission flats. The choice was not choice. Eventually we hunted up a couple of pre-loved tracksuits. Perfect condition. Twelve dollars the pair.

"I look like a bogan," Red complained.

"If you want to make a fashion statement, you're welcome to catch the next bus back to Sydney," I told him. "I understand that boaters are all the rage up there."

He didn't push his luck. "Can we go to Tark's place now, before anyone sees me dressed like this?"

Tarquin and Chloe had just arrived home from school. Tarquin was grudgingly babysitting his little sister until Faye finished work. The two boys greeted each other as long-lost soul mates, exchanging high-fives in the time-honored Australian manner. "Hey, man, lookin' like a bogan," declared Tarquin.

"It's the look, man," said Red. "It's the happening look."

They immediately retreated to Tarquin's room to conduct secret boys' business, while Chloe remained, watching television: a "Wonder World" segment about guinea-pig care. I pulled up a bean-bag beside her and rested my eyes for a moment.

"Use plenty of straw," said a voice. "So the little feller is all snuggly-wuggly."

Snuggly-wuggly, I thought. A snoozy-woozy on the couchy-wouchy, that's what I need. Not a kicky-wicky in the heady-weady or a rumpy-pumpy in a trucky-wucky or a squishy-wishy on the roady-woady. Just an eensy-weensy nappy-wappy.

The sound sting for the six o'clock news hauled me back into consciousness. The guinea pigs had been replaced by tanks in the streets of Moscow. Gorbachev was still incommunicado. There was no news from the Crimea. Faye came in from the kitchen to catch the headlines, wiping her hands on a kitchen towel. "You'll stay for dinner?" she asked.

My attention was back on the television screen. A reporter was standing in front of the wholesale vegetable market, an umbrella in one hand and a microphone in the other. It was broad daylight, a light rain was falling and the parking apron was deserted except for a couple of police cars, Donny's truck and fluttering yellow ribbons of crime-scene tape.

"The victim, son of prominent business identity, Mr. Bob

Stuhl, was discovered just before six this morning," the reporter was saying. "The notoriously close-lipped market community is reported to be mystified by his death. At this stage, police have refused to rule out foul play."

Faye noticed my interest. Her journalistic beat lay in the territory of interest-rate fluctuations and the impact of exchange rates on the balance of trade but she was not unacquainted with the nation's premier trucking dynasty. "Apart from the coup in Russia, the Stuhl family was the hot topic at the *Weekly* today," she said as the news went into a commercial and I followed her into the kitchen. "Apparently this Darren was quite a handful. Not that Bob's any angel. The rumors have been around for years that he isn't as legitimate as he'd have us believe. You don't parlay a couple of clapped-out old trucks into a business empire worth millions without cutting a few legal corners."

I decided to wait for a more opportune time to reveal that my interest in the story was based on more than idle curiosity. This was an occasion to celebrate Red's deliverance from perils real and imagined, not for revelations about bare-knuckle brawling and visits from a dick called Spider. Leo burst though the front door, bellowing his hellos and extracting the cork from a bottle of Hunter Valley red.

While pasta percolated and sauce seethed, I sat at the kitchen table, recounted Red's saga and declared my resolve to fight his mother for custody, if necessary.

"Wendy's not just going to roll over and take it," said Leo.

"She never did," I said. "But that's another story."

"This will mean a lot of changes, Murray," warned Faye.

"I've already started to make them," I said. "Can't talk about it yet, but I've had an offer."

"Headhunted?" asked Leo.

"Cannibalized would be a better word. In any case, I'll be able to spend more time with Red."

"And so you should," said Faye, ever the moralist. She dumped a writhing mass of spaghetti into a colander, tilted her head back and bellowed at the ceiling. "Dinner!"

An avalanche of children fell down the stairs and onto the food.

"Can Red stay here tonight?" slurped Tarquin.

"Wait your turn," I told him. "There'll be plenty of time for that sort of thing from now on."

"Look what I can do," giggled Chloe, siphoning a strand of spaghetti through the gap in her smile.

"You must be the grossest little girl I have ever met," I said. She beamed at the compliment, bolognaized from chin to cheekbones.

This was the life. Happy families. Here in Fitzroy at least. Not so joyous in French provincial Toorak, I mused. Poor old Bob Stuhl. Rich as Croesus and tough as nails. But what did it profit him? One son was parsnip puree, the other tomato concasse.

As the kids cleared the dishes, Faye reached into the freezer. "Strawberry crush or tutti-frutti?"

17

THE PHONE JERKED ME from an uneasy sleep soon after eight the next morning. It was a woman. Unfortunately, it wasn't Lyndal Luscombe.

"You can't do this to me, Murray," she started in.

I swung my bare feet onto the floor, wondering if it was too early for a cigarette. "This isn't about you, Wendy," I sighed.

The ability to relinquish control had never been my ex-wife's strongest suit. And when it came to custody of her flesh and blood, she had no compunction in unleashing her inner pit bull. "You clearly haven't given any thought to Red's future," she accused. "Knowing you, you'll send him to a government school. He'll miss out on his chance to sit the International Baccalaureate and end up at some third-rate university. There goes his MBA. God, you are so selfish."

Red's decision to vote with his feet had put Wendy in an untenable position. Short of kidnapping him, she couldn't force the boy to return to Sydney. And it wasn't as if I didn't have previous experience in the prime parenting role, I reminded her, back when it was me who kept the home fires burning, made the playlunch, ran the bath, applied the Band Aids, read the bedtime stories. We finally reached a compromise. Red would remain in my care, subject to review at the end of the year. In the meantime, I was to make sure that he called his mother regularly.

"He'll turn out like you," she warned. "And we don't want that, do we?"

I hung up and stood in the doorway of his room, watching him sleep and contemplating our new life together. My little boy was beyond storybooks now. Beyond bathtime and peanut-butter sandwiches, folded not cut. He'd become a streetwise bus-fare hustler. An illicit crosser of state borders. A fugitive from boarding school. His will was his own. He could be guided but not constrained, enlisted but not compelled. And, whatever Wendy might say to the contrary, I could be a good father to him. I could love him and feed him and watch over him while he slept. And enroll him in a government school.

I proceeded into the kitchen, phoned Fitzroy High and made an appointment with the principal. Then I togged up, put a note on the refrigerator and nipped into Transport House to make sure Angelo had countersigned my revised job contract.

"It's still on his desk," said Trish. "He's been too busy selling his budget cuts to the public transport unions to sign it."

My trip was not entirely wasted, however. The paper-shufflers in accounts had set a new benchmark for efficiency. The check for the Maitland consultancy job was waiting in my in-tray. Since I hadn't yet heard from Donny, I gave him a call.

"Are you awake?" I said, phone in the crook of my shoulder, staring out my twelfth-floor window at a sky that was now the color of dirty bandages.

"I ought to be," he said. "I've just had a visit. A copper, and not nearly as civil as yesterday's lot. Bloke named Webb. Head like a garden tap, personality like a duodenal ulcer. Accused me of obstructing the course of justice. To wit, concealing the fact that you were present when I ran over Darren Stuhl."

"Sorry if I dropped you in the shit," I said. "Webb came to see me yesterday, knew I'd been at the market. I assumed you'd told the cops, didn't realize otherwise until Heather told me."

Donny wasn't fussed, said he'd explained to Webb that he thought I'd gone to Sydney to look for my lost kid, that he didn't think my momentary presence in the truck was relevant to the accident report. "Good thing Jacinta's at work. She'd freak if she knew I'd had a house call from a member of the homicide squad."

"Homicide?" I said. "Webb didn't tell me he was from homicide."

"Very interested in you, he was," said Donny. "Wanted to know if I'd ever seen you with Darren Stuhl. Implied you're involved in some way and I was covering for you."

"He suggested the same to me about you."

"Standard procedure," said Donny. "In my experience, the best thing with coppers is to say as little as possible."

"A man in my position can hardly refuse to talk to the police," I said.

"And what position is that, Murray?"

Good question. "We need to talk," I said. And the telephone, by implication, was not the place to do it.

"Come on over. I'm not going anywhere. They've impounded the truck, pending forensic tests. They've probably got it down the watch-house, belting a confession out of it with a telephone book."

I told him I'd be there in a couple of hours, after I'd attended to some pressing domestic issues. The first of these was a visit to the supermarket for fresh supplies of cereal. The second was to return home, rouse Red and inform him of our imminent appointment at his new school. "If you're serious about wanting to live here, then the sooner we get into a settled routine the better. Deal?"

"Deal."

A box of Nutri-grain later, we set out for the tram stop at the end of the street. "We could save quite a bit on fares if I had a bike," Red remarked casually. "Tarquin rides to school and he hasn't been killed yet."

"We'll see," I said, thinking we'd be needing a car, too. A little second-hand runabout, easy to park, fuel-efficient. In a couple of weeks, the departmental taxi account would be a thing of the past. In the meantime, we trammed the kilometer to the Edinburgh Gardens, then walked between skeletal elm trees to the red-brick high school with its cluster of portable classrooms, its asphalt basketball court and peeling community mural.

The principal, Ms. Henderson, was an ample woman with a Sapphic haircut, her daunting demeanor somewhat moderated by the laugh lines at the corners of her caftan. It may have been my first day at high school, but Red was an old hand, well versed in the jargon. By the time the lunch bell rang, we'd completed the paperwork and taken the tour. "Is it okay if I stay for the rest of the afternoon, Ms. Henderson?" Red pleaded, ear cocked to the burble of voices in the yard.

"If it's all right with your father."

The student prince extended an upturned palm. "I can catch the tram home with Tarquin, Dad."

"Thought you said he rides his bike?" I coughed up five dollars. "Make it last."

"Keen, isn't he?" remarked Ms. Henderson dryly as Red disappeared into the throng.

So was I. To see Donny, to find out what was going on. I trotted back to Brunswick Street and hailed a cab.

Reservoir was two suburbs beyond the Northern Region Performing Arts Center, an undulating expanse of cream-brick working-class suburbia. The sort of place, it was said, where old grayhounds go to die. Donny's place was typical, a low-fenced double-fronted bungalow with a patch of lawn at the front and a driveway leading down the side to a backyard garage. An off-white Commodore with a dinged rear taillight stood in the drive.

A chink creased the venetians as I stepped from the cab and the front door was open by the time I reached it. Donny looked like he'd been through the wringer. He was shoeless and unshaven, his flannelette shirt hanging loose over saggy track pants, the bottoms tucked into a pair of thick socks. "Heather told me about the kid," he said. "Must be a weight off your mind."

"If it wasn't for this shit, I'd be the happiest man in the world," I said.

Donny led me down a short hallway lined with overstuffed plank-and-brick bookcases and we emerged into a combined kitchen–living room warmed by a wood-fired heater. The furniture was mix-n-match. Filipino folk art hung haphazardly on the walls. Donny's drum kit stood in the corner and a geriatric labrador snoozed in front of the fire. Sliding glass doors overlooked a redwood deck with hanging plants and a Webber barbecue. We were in absolutely no danger of being interrupted by a photographer from *Vogue Interiors*.

"What a mess," I said, meaning the general situation.

"You should've seen Darren Stuhl. That's what I call a mess. Nearly lost my lunch, and I hadn't even had breakfast yet. You want a beer?"

"Bit early for me," I said. "Cup of tea'd go down well. If homicide's involved, they must've made their minds up pretty quick that it wasn't an accident."

Donny lit the gas under the kettle and unhooked a couple of mugs. "You'd have to wonder how he got so far under the wheels."

"So what do you think happened?" I said. "Any ideas?"

"I leave the theorizing to you intellectuals."

I sat at the table and stared at my hands. "You tell the cops he pulled a gun on you?"

Donny cocked a worldly-wise eye. "Yeah, sure. And volunteer myself a motive for killing him? Not bloody likely. Besides which, I'm trying to present myself as a credible union leader. If I go bleating to the constabulary every time some twerp tries it on, I might as well toss in the election right now."

"So the campaign's still on?"

"My oath," he said. "I'm not going to let this distract me."

"Don't take this the wrong way," I said. "But what about Roscoe or Len? Maybe one of them decided to engage in a little hand-to-hand class warfare."

"Believe me, if either of them were responsible, they'd be lining up to tell me all about it. Whatever happened back there, it wasn't down to us. You can take my word for it."

"Well it wasn't me," I said. "I swear."

"You don't have to tell me that, Murray," he said. "But you might have a bit of trouble convincing the cops. Like I said, Webb was very interested. Knew about your punch-up with Darren."

"I told him that part myself," I said.

"So how come the cops knew you were at the market?"

"I assume Frank Farrell told them. Apart from you and Heather, Farrell was the only other person there who knew my name. And he'd have no reason not to tell the cops. In a situation like that, a man dead, even a deadshit like Darren Stuhl, I wouldn't expect anyone to withhold information."

Donny plonked a steaming mug in front of me. Garfield the Cat. "There's withholding," he said. "And there's volunteering. And a man like Farrell doesn't talk to the cops out of a sense of civic duty. He's making mischief, Murray."

"I've got nothing to hide, so he's not going to get very far."

"That's not going to stop him trying. Situation like this, a man would be well advised to keep his wits about him."

Through the window I saw a recent model Magna pull into the driveway behind Donny's Commodore.

"Here's trouble," said Donny. "It's Heather. She's been to the bank, telling them we'll have a bit of a cash-flow problem while the truck's impounded. She still doesn't know about the gun, by the way."

Heather stomped through the back door in her bossy boots and shoulder pads, groomed to within an inch of her life. "Oh," she said. "It's you." Her tone was frosty, preoccupied.

"What did they say?" said Donny.

"What do you think they said?" She didn't bother to conceal her exasperation, both with Donny and the bank. She pulled a print-out from her handbag and slapped it flat on the table. "You've been dipping into the truck expense account to pay for your stupid bloody campaign handbills, haven't you?"

Donny made a dismissive gesture. "Relax. I'll pay it back."

"With what? Jacinta's wages?"

Donny flushed. "What Jacinta chooses to do with her money is her business."

"Professional psychiatric help," snorted Heather. "That's what you need."

I tried to make myself as inconspicuous as possible. Total invisibility would've been good. Then Heather turned in disgust from Donny and directed her lasers at me. "If you were as much Donny's friend as you pretend, you wouldn't be encouraging this nonsense."

"Fair go, Heather," said Donny. "This isn't Murray's fault."

She folded her arms and glowered down at us, a woman at the end of her tether. Always a dangerous place for a woman to be.

"Cup of tea?" I said inanely. She tightened her lips and gave a hard little shake of her earrings. I took the check from my pocket and placed it on top of the bank statement. "How about ten thousand dollars then?" I said. "Would that make you feel better?"

Donny snatched up the check. "Jesus, you move fast."

Heather thought I was making some kind of joke. "What's that for?"

"To secure the services of Maitland Transport to undertake an ongoing, open-ended, industry-based research project on behalf of the policy development section of the Ministry of Transport."

"What research project? We don't do research."

"We do now," beamed Donny.

I gave him his riding orders. "Clear any debts you've already incurred," I said. "Then use the balance to pay yourself a salary equal to your income from driving the truck. Enlist support from sympathetic unions. Recruit enough candidates to field a ticket. Beef up your publicity. Start getting up Howard Sharpe's nose."

Heather twigged. "Is this legal?" she said, taking the check from Donny and examining it carefully.

"It's from the government," I said. "How could it be otherwise?"

Her mood began improving. The check disappeared into her handbag and she decided that a cup of tea would be nice, after all.

"Agnelli is to be quarantined from any responsibility for this exercise," I told Donny.

"My lips are sealed."

"You know I don't agree with Donny about this union election thing," said Heather. "But I'm grateful for the help." She put a warm hand over mine and squeezed. "Very grateful."

"Goodness," I said. "Is that the time? I really must be off. Got to pick my boy up from school."

"Here we go again," she said. "The Incredible Vanishing Man."

18

HEATHER WAS NOT THE ONLY PERSON whose attentions I was keen to avoid.

In case Angelo's mental compass suddenly swung about on the backstab payout offer, I thought it wise to keep out of the way until his signature was firmly appended to the contract. As soon as I got home, I called Trish to report that I'd come down with a dose of the Texas flu and wouldn't be fit for the office for the rest of the week.

When Red arrived home from school, I had him call his mother to discuss which of his possessions she should ship south. Then we went into the city and spread some plastic around the retail end of the teenage apparel industry. Despite the intermittent nature of our contact over the previous five years, the old father-son adhesive had stood the test of time. In little more than thirty-six hours, we'd segued into an easy domesticity.

"So when do I meet these girlfriends?" asked Red as he set out on Wednesday morning for the second day of his third-rate education. "This harem of yours."

"Never," I said. "In honor of your arrival, I've taken a vow of celibacy."

"It's not natural, Dad," he advised. "A grown man has certain needs."

"Right now my greatest need is for you to pick your clothes off the bathroom floor," I said. "And for Christsake, turn off the fucking television before you leave the house."

The tonnage levy issue finally bit the dust on Thursday. An item appeared in the *Sun* reporting that the transport minister had issued a firm denial of any intention to implement the tax. This was described as "an embarrassing backflip." I was glad I wasn't at the office.

But that didn't mean I couldn't be found. Just before six, I went to the corner store for a loaf of multigrain and a liter of low-fat. Spider Webb cruised past in a shiny maroon Falcon as I was returning. When I reached the house, he was waiting on the doorstep, legs apart, hands on hips, his center of gravity somewhere around the keyhole. I resisted the temptation to stick my key into it. "You don't look very sick to me," he leered. "Your office said you were bedridden."

"So you dropped around to offer your best wishes for my speedy recovery, did you?"

"You know your problem, Whelan?" he said, like he was the world's leading expert on the subject. "You don't know your own best interests. Let's go inside and talk about it." His tone suggested I didn't have any choice.

"The house is already full of germs," I said. "And you've had nothing from me so far but my full cooperation. So let's talk here, shall we? What do you want this time, Spider?"

His scalp bristles bristled. "To give you a bit of friendly advice, that's what. We've got more officers working on this case than you've had hot dinners, smartarse. Nothing is escaping our attention. And if you think your fancy political contacts can protect you, you're a bigger fool than you look. And that'd take some doing."

"Thanks for the tip," I said. "But I've got no idea what you're talking about."

"Yeah?" he sneered. "Well you might be interested to know that we've now got Darren Stuhl's postmortem results." He delivered this information like a man playing an ace.

"And what do they say?"

"They say you should take this opportunity to come clean, save yourself a lot of trouble."

If there was any logic here, it defeated me. "You'll have to give me a hint," I said. "I don't speak Neanderthal."

Webb rocked back and forth on his heels, giving me the slow burn. "You remember a bloke called Brian Sutch?" he said.

"Vaguely." Sutch was a notorious standover man. He'd given us a few headaches back when I was at the Municipal Employees Union, extorting money from our members.

"Heard what happened to him?"

"Shot, wasn't he?" This was a good fifteen years back. The closest I'd come to the incident was reading about it in the papers.

"That's right," said Webb. "Three rounds to the head in the public bar of the Brickworks Hotel. Twenty-five eyewitnesses. All swore blind they were in the gents at the time. Ever been to the Brickworks? The bog's even smaller than that rathole office of yours."

"And?"

"We knew who did it, but couldn't make the case without a witness. Fortunately, there was quite a bit of old evidence lying around the squad room. Turned out that some of it could be made to fit one of the witnesses. Amazing how fast his memory improved when that fact was pointed out to him."

I reached around Webb and slid my key into the lock. "If you have any other queries, Sergeant Webb," I said, brushing past him. "Don't hesitate to give me a call. I'll be more than happy to consult my schedule. And my lawyer."

I shut the door in Webb's face and leaned my back against it. This is blatant intimidation, I thought. Spider acted like a big swinging dick at school and he clearly believed that membership of the police force was a license to do likewise in adult life. His belief that I was covering for Donny Maitland was now out in the open. His threat to frame me unless I came clean, however, was a waste of breath. I had nothing to come clean about. If Spider Webb thought

I'd perjure myself, he needed his head read. In Spider's case, that was a job for a phrenologist.

The sound of Webb's departing car leached through the woodwork. I took my bag of supplies down to the kitchen where Red was on the phone to his mother, adding further essential requirements to his initial list. "Don't worry about sending the bike," he was saying. "It's too small now and, anyway, Dad's going to buy me a new one."

In accordance with newly instituted practice, the television was running unwatched in the living room. Breaking open a meditative beer, I slumped on the couch, letting the six o'clock news bulletin wash over me. Webb's line about the postmortem, what the hell did that mean?

A man in a police uniform with silver-studded epaulets appeared on the screen. Spider's boss, the Chief Commissioner of Police. He was fronting the microphones at a press conference, an update on the Darren Stuhl case. If Bob expected top-level service, he was certainly getting it.

According to the C.C., Darren Stuhl's autopsy indicated that the cause of death was a blow to the head with a blunt instrument, rather than traffic injuries as initially assumed. The task force undertaking the investigation was confident of an early result. Heavy rain and a high level of vehicular activity in the area at the time of the incident had, however, hampered police in their inquiries. Anyone having relevant information was urged to contact the police.

Red threw himself onto the couch beside me and heaved an exhausted sigh. "Mum said that Richard's upset I can't crew with him in the regatta on Saturday. As if." He reached for the remote control. "Can't we watch something else? This is boring. And what's for dinner?"

"A blow to the head," I said absently.

"I'd prefer a poke in the eye," said Red. "Or how about some of those beef burgers in the freezer."

I was more concerned with what was cooking in the minds of the police. I could appreciate their difficulties. A washout crime scene. The market tighter than a fish's arse. Bob Stuhl breathing down their necks for a result. But the only blunt instrument I could recall at the market was the one Heather had in her hand. And nobody had beaten Darren Stuhl over the head with it. Not as far as I could remember.

"Turn the grill on," I told Red. Then I went into the bedroom and called Donny Maitland, planning to do some grilling of my own. "See the news?" I said.

"I'm too busy cleaning up," he said. "Mr. Plod's been back. Tossed the place. Did a right royal job of it, too. Joint looks like a tornado's been through it."

"What were they looking for?"

"Didn't say. Whatever it was, they didn't find it. They came, they ransacked. Three hours later they left empty-handed. Fishing expedition, that was my impression."

"They have a search warrant?"

"No, I invited them in," he said sarcastically. "Mistook them for interior decorators. What's this about the news?"

I told him about the Chief Commissioner's announcement and Spider Webb's visit.

"Sounds to me like Webb's just shaking your tree, see if anything falls out. As for Darren getting decked, it stands to reason. If they were looking for the murder weapon here, they didn't find it. How could they? I didn't do it."

"I think you should get a lawyer," I said.

Donny scoffed. "What good would a shyster do me? I've got better things to do with your boss's money. You want to help me, get off the line so I can finish cleaning up this mess before Jacinta gets home."

Donny was right, I decided. The cops were beating the bushes. Webb and his task force colleagues were probably putting pressure on every potential informant in town, hoping that something useful would turn up. Well, it wasn't going to turn up from my direction. How could it? I didn't know anything.

Nor, evidently, did the press. Both of Friday's morning dailies carried stories about the Stuhl case. In the absence of hard facts, they fell back on speculation. The market-murder clippings file was dusted off and long-dead, bullet-riddled tomato vendors again got their photos in the paper, although the connection between white-bread Darren and the garlic-munching godfathers remained obscure. To compound the issue, it was reported that some kind of turf war was happening between Vietnamese newcomers and some of the longer-established market interests.

Darren's funeral was held that afternoon at St. John's in Toorak. Bob's elevated status ensured a big turnout. Several former federal Cabinet ministers attended and many a crocodile tear was shed in the memory of a promising young man so untimely squished. Among the shedders, caught briefly in the sweep of the television cameras as the casket was borne down the front steps, was the entire state executive committee of the United Haulage Workers. Watching it that night at home, I glimpsed Frank Farrell's face in the congregation.

Unlike that of his older brother, though, Darren's fate had no appreciable impact on Stuhl Holdings' share price.

Monday saw me back at the office. In my absence, Angelo had signed the contract. It was waiting in my in-tray along with a preselection nomination form and a copy of the party membership rolls for Melbourne Upper. The message was clear. The skulduggery was to commence.

I phoned a real estate agent and made arrangements to rent a one-bedroom flat in Preston. This would allow me to claim to be a resident of Melbourne Upper, always a useful sop to local sensibilities. I spent the rest of the morning poring over the membership list, mapping known factional allegiances, ethnic affiliations and personal networks. When I returned from lunch, I found a telephone message slip on my desk. It stated that Senior Sergeant Webb had called requesting that I call him regarding an appointment.

As a general operational principle, I avoid lawyers. They leave bits of paper everywhere and cost a poultice. But since push was coming to shove, it seemed advisable to share my burden with somebody more acquainted with police procedures. I called a man named Pat O'Shannessy, known to me only by reputation.

Commonly called One-Stop, O'Shannessy was a criminal lawyer who plied his trade in places where more fastidious eagles feared to fly. He listened to the bare bones of my situation, took Spider's direct line and called me back fifteen minutes later.

"Citywest police station, three this afternoon. See you at my chambers at two."

One-Stop's chambers were smack in the middle of the legal precinct, in a Queen Street high rise commonly known as the Golan Heights. The reason for this was apparent when I read the directory in the lobby. Unless I was mistaken, few of O'Shannessy's fellow tenants had been educated by the Jesuits.

One-Stop was a man of Falstaffian proportions, proprietor of the largest collection of chins I'd ever seen. So many that I thought for a moment he was wearing a neck brace. He gazed at me through half-moon glasses from behind his redoubt of a desk, the hem of a red linen napkin wedged into his barely visible collar.

"Lunch on the run," he explained, waving me into a chair with a baseball mitt that might have been a hand. "Care to join me?"

Declining his roast beef sandwiches, I went straight into my spiel. Told him pretty well everything. Apart from Heather going the lunge, of course. And the bit about seeing Darren threaten Donny with a gun. "I don't believe that Donny Maitland killed Darren Stuhl," I concluded. "Apart from anything else, why would he implicate himself by shoving the body under his own truck? It doesn't make sense. And I'm not going to let the cops railroad me into implicating him."

Except for the steady motion of his jaws and the occasional smacking of his lips, One-Stop heard me out in silence. When I finished, he licked his enormous fingers and wiped them delicately on the napery. "It is the task of the police to separate the circumstantial sheep from the evidentiary goats," he pronounced. "The extent to which you are prepared to assist them in that process is up to you.

My advice is this. If you cannot be entirely candid, at least be consistent. If you cannot be consistent, say nothing."

"I've done nothing wrong," I said. "Nothing unlawful, at least."

"Glad to hear it." O'Shannessy ripped the napkin from his neck, stood abruptly and brushed the crumbs from his lapels. "Onward, then," he declared, "into the valley of death."

19

IT WAS AMAZING how fast the man could move. He barreled down the footpath like a galleon under full sail, alarmed pedestrians leaping aside at his approach, while I bobbed in his wake like a dinghy. By the time we'd covered the four blocks to the Citywest cop shop, I fully expected him to barge straight through the front doors without waiting for them to open. One-Stop's legal skills were still an unknown quantity but there was no doubt about his capacities as a morale booster.

"If I think you're getting into hot water," he said, "I'll pull the plug."

Citywest was a low-slung, box-like building across the road from the Flagstaff Gardens. It might have passed for the regional headquarters of a computer software company if not for the pervasive smell of truncheon leather and the Uphold the Right motto above the bulletproof reception desk. Noel Webb appeared promptly, beady-eyed and hot to trot. "One-Stop?" he sneered into my ear as he fed us into the elevator. "You must be desperate."

He took us to an interview room, a windowless cube with washable vinyl walls, and we were joined by a horse-faced man in his mid-fifties with tired, watery eyes and a bad case of the sniffles. His breath smelled of throat lozenges and he carried himself with the resigned air of one kept from his sickbed by the unremitting demands of a thankless job. He introduced himself to me as Chief Inspector Voigt and croaked that he appreciated my cooperation. This pleasantry fooled nobody.

"Consider yourself honored," said One-Stop. "Reg here is *le grand fromage* himself. Head of homicide." He and O'Shannessy were clearly old sparring partners.

We all sat down and One-Stop opened the batting. "I am instructed that my client has already answered a number of your questions. He advises me that he is happy to assist in any way he can. But stick to the straight and narrow, please gents."

Voigt fixed me in his rheumy gaze. "Mr. Whelan," he sniffed. "Can you tell us why you were at the Melbourne Wholesale Fruit and Vegetable Market on the morning of Monday, August 12?"

I explained about Red going missing, that I was unable to sleep and walking the streets in search of distraction.

"But why the market?"

"Impulse," I shrugged. Professional discretion constrained me from disclosing my other reason. It was, after all, irrelevant to the matter at hand. "I was quite upset about my son. And, like I said, I was looking for distraction."

Voigt's inner bullfrog made a skeptical sound. "You didn't go there with the intention of seeing anybody?"

"Darren Stuhl, you mean? Not only didn't I go there to see him, I was unaware of both his identity and the fact that he'd be there."

"But you did know him."

"We'd met," I said. "But I didn't know who he was."

For what felt like the hundredth time, I described our encounter at the Metro. As he listened, Voigt nodded and dabbed his nose with a crumpled tissue. "You were assaulted, yet you made no official complaint at the time."

"I complained to the nightclub bouncers," I said. "There seemed little point in raising it with the police as there were no witnesses and I didn't know my assailant's identity. I only discovered that when I spotted him at the market. A man called Frank Farrell identified him for me."

"And how do you know this Farrell?" said Voigt.

"Professionally," I said. "He works for the United Haulage Workers. I've had contact with him in my capacity as an advisor to the Minister for Transport."

Noel Webb, who was doodling idly on a writing pad, smirked at this, as though I'd exposed myself as a fatuous big-noter.

"So you approached Stuhl," continued Voigt. "What happened then?"

"I suggested he apologize and pay my dentist bill."

"What was his reaction?"

"He was dismissive."

"But you persisted."

One-Stop cleared his throat. Not, I assumed, because he'd caught Inspector Voigt's influenza.

"He pushed me away. I pushed back. There was a minor scuffle. It was all over in a few seconds."

"But you did threaten him."

"I warned him that I'd take legal action if he came near me again," I said firmly.

One-Stop, observing this over the top of his half-moon glasses, gave me an encouraging nod. So far, so good.

"Then what?" said Voigt.

"I walked away. I wandered around the market, took in the sights, had a cup of coffee in the cafe. Donny Maitland turned up, offered me a lift home, so I went and waited in his truck with his sister-in-law Heather. I've told all this to Sergeant Webb."

Webb continued to toy with his pen, as if waiting for the pussy-footing to finish.

"This is in the parking area, right?" said Voigt.

"Yes."

"At approximately 5:15 A.M.?"

"Yes."

"And you didn't see Darren Stuhl there?"

"Like I said, I was sitting in a truck with Heather Maitland. We were engrossed in conversation. The windows were misted up."

"Were you aware that Maitland was conducting a union election rally in the vicinity at the time?"

"I could hear him making a speech," I said. "But I wasn't really paying attention."

"And you remained in the truck until Maitland returned?" said Voigt.

This was where the ice started to get thin. "No, I stepped out briefly. I was booked on a flight to Sydney to look for my son. I was beginning to get anxious that I'd miss it if we didn't leave soon, so I went looking for Donny."

"Alone?"

"Heather stayed in the truck while I did a quick circuit of the area," I said, kissing my alibi goodbye. "Donny turned up, we pulled out, ran over something. I thought it was a bag of fruit, decided I couldn't wait around while it was sorted out. I went across to the Mobil roadhouse and called a cab. When I got home, my son was there, so I called the airline and canceled my booking. They've probably still got a record of it." Even as I provided it, this corroborative suggestion seemed ludicrously irrelevant.

"And when was the last time you saw Stuhl?"

"I wasn't even aware that Darren Stuhl was dead until your colleague here informed me later that day."

That was it. End of story. I turned to One-Stop and shrugged.

"And you definitely didn't see Stuhl in the parking area?" Voigt persisted. "You're sure?"

"I've told you what happened," I said.

"And you have nothing to add?"

"Like what?"

Spider Webb ended his reverie and gave an incredulous snort.

"DSS Webb believes you haven't been entirely frank with us, Mr. Whelan," snuffled Voigt. "Isn't that right, Sergeant?"

"I do indeed, sir," said Webb.

This exchange was conducted in a slightly flippant manner that was intended to convey that the tenor of the interview was about to undergo a distinct change.

"We are now going to show you something, Mr. Whelan," said Voigt. "I want you to take a close look at it and tell me if you have ever seen it before." He nodded to Webb, who laid down his pencil, got to his feet and strode from the room.

One-Stop tilted his head back, stroked his neck flaps and peered at me quizzically through his spectacles. I shrugged apprehensively, wondering what this mysterious exhibit might be. Voigt took advantage of the pause in the interrogation to draw a series of deep nasal breaths, clearing his sinuses.

Then Webb was back. He dropped something on the table in front of me. It landed with an emphatic clunk and I found myself staring down at a clear plastic bag containing a fourteen-inch, drop-forged Sidchrome shifting spanner.

Shit. How had I managed to let that slip my mind? Frank fucking Farrell, I thought. This was down to him. And it was mischief, pure and simple. Nobody else had seen me with the damned thing. Christ, I'd even forgotten about it myself. And to explain why I was carrying it, I'd need to tell them what I'd seen out the truck window. And if I did that, I'd risk dunking Donny in the doo-doo.

"Well?" said Voigt.

"It's a spanner," I said.

"I think we're agreed on that much, Mr. Whelan," said Voigt. "The question is, have you seen it before?"

My mind was racing, figuring the angles. Some of them were acute. Others weren't so cute. None of them were guaranteed to make me look blameless. I fell back on the truth, hoping I wasn't impaling myself. To be on the safe side, I blunted its edges a little. "Possibly," I said.

"Would you care to elaborate?" invited Voigt.

"A spanner similar to this dropped out of the truck when I opened the door," I said. "I held onto it until I got back in. If you found this under the seat of Donny Maitland's truck, then it's probably the same one. If you're implying that I hit Darren Stuhl over the head with it, I categorically deny it."

Webb was still standing. He put his palms on the table, leaned forward and stuck his pie-crust face into mine. His aftershave smelled like formaldehyde. "How about we cut the crap," he said. "It's as plain as day what really happened here. This arrogant, vicious, spoiled rich kid sticks your head down a toilet, humiliates you, costs you an arm and a leg in dental charges. You run into him again, take a perfectly reasonable tone, he tries for an encore. You tell him you're going to have him prosecuted, walk away. A bit later, he finds you alone. He threatens you. This time, you've got a spanner. You defend yourself. But you hit the prick a little bit too hard. You kill him. You panic, shove him under the nearest truck, try to make it look like an accident."

He leaned back, arms wide, QED. Inspector Voigt was looking contemplative, as though this novel and unexpected interpretation of the events might warrant consideration.

"It would've been pretty stupid of me to attack a man with a spanner, knowing he was carrying a gun," I said.

Voigt shot Webb a sideways glance. This wasn't part of the scenario he'd been sold. "What do you know about the gun?" he demanded.

"Only that I noticed Stuhl was carrying one when we were scuffling."

"So why didn't you mention it earlier?" harrumphed Webb.

"Because you didn't ask me."

"And what else haven't you told us?" said Voigt.

There was a scraping sound as One-Stop pushed his chair back. "My client," he announced, "came here of his own free will and in good faith. He came to answer your questions, which he has done. He is not here to engage in hypothetical speculation or to play guessing games. If you have evidence to substantiate your allegations, I suggest you produce it and give my client the opportunity to refute it. Otherwise, I am advising him to terminate this interview forthwith."

Spider ignored him. "Take this chance, Whelan. Clear the air. Don't dig yourself deeper into the shit."

Voigt had stopped sniffling and the two cops were staring at me very hard. Their gaze was about as relaxing as Dr. Freycinet's high-speed drill.

"If Sergeant Webb wants to talk to my client again, Inspector Voigt," said One-Stop, "have him contact me first."

Voigt sniffed wearily and nodded. Spider backed away and sulked.

"I'd like to go now," I said. "If that's all right."

20

"AMATEUR THEATRICS," concluded One-Stop. "That spanner wasn't even tagged for evidence."

He made these reassuring remarks in the bar of the Golden Age Hotel where he took me for a stiffening belt after we left Citywest.

"I told you Webb was threatening to frame me," I said.

"His *modus operandi* undoubtedly contains a degree of bluster," agreed One-Stop, signaling for another round. "But I don't think you need worry too much. They've got no witness, no admission, no evidence and therefore no case. It's a hollow threat. Sit pat. If they want to talk to you again, they have to call me first."

Heartening advice and a snip at eight hundred dollars. But I wasn't going to do nothing while Frank Farrell took advantage of the situation. As soon as I got back to the office I called the United Haulage Workers.

Mr. Farrell was not currently in the office, I was informed by a singsong female voice. "Is it a pressing matter?"

"It's pressing on me," I said.

"You could try his mobile. The number's changed. I'll give you the new one."

I dialed the string of digits and Farrell came on the line. He sounded like he was speaking from inside an industrial vacuum cleaner.

"It's Murray Whelan," I said. "I'm calling to congratulate you on your good citizenship."

"The cops been asking you questions, have they?" he said. "I just told them what I saw, that's all. Why should I keep my trap shut for you? For all I know, you had a hand in it."

"That's bullshit and you know it," I said. "Why would I kill Darren when you'd just offered to negotiate a generous compensation payment? Get real, Frank. You saw an opportunity to associate a member of Angelo Agnelli's staff with Darren Stuhl's death. Howard Sharpe and Mike McGrath must be very happy with your work. You know I had nothing to do with it."

"All I know is that you were sticking your bib where it didn't belong," he said. "Don't tell me that you weren't at the market to connect with that stirrer Donny Maitland."

I stared down at the floor between my shoes and wished I'd cooled down before I made this call. Spider Webb had stoked me up and I'd gone off half-cocked in Farrell's direction.

"Anyway," said Farrell benignly, "how do you know Maitland didn't do it?"

"Thanks again for nothing, Frank," I said, hanging up.

My gaze moved from the phone to the window. It lingered long on a flotilla of battleship-gray clouds while I considered my position. With a week remaining until preselection nominations closed and our deal went into effect, the last thing I wanted was for Angelo to discover that I'd been implicated in the death of Bob Stuhl's son. Fortunately, Ange was out of town until Wednesday, crawling cap in hand through the corridors of Canberra, hunting up federal finance for a raft of redundancy packages for public transport employees. After that, I could only hope that the cutting and slicing required by the Treasury bureaucrats would keep him busy.

And the best way to avoid further implications of collusion with Donny Maitland was to have no further contact with him, at least for a while. Donny was a big boy. Donny was capable of looking after himself. And I had loyalties closer to home. Red should be my most immediate priority.

Do what the man said, Murray, I told myself. Sit pat. And that's exactly what I did for the next seven days.

Sat behind the wheel of a number of bargain-priced second-hand cars, test driving prospective purchases. Sat through *Dances with Wolves* with Red. Sat in on a parent-teacher information evening with Faye and Leo. Sat in Dr. Freycinet's chair while he fitted my new porcelain crowns. Sat and wondered when Spider Webb would next appear on my doorstep. Wondered, too, who had killed Darren Stuhl. And why.

Sat on the phone and trawled for indications of potential challengers to Angelo's preselection. Only one blip appeared on that particular screen. A seventy-year-old ex-communist named Jack Butler. Old Jack was a seasoned activist, a perennial combatant in the ceaseless struggle for universal justice. He'd set up a group called Save Our Trains to campaign against government plans to close the Northern Line of the metropolitan rail network, a community resource that had been losing money since the day it opened in 1884. According to rumor, Jack planned to run against Angelo in order to focus opposition to the closure of the line.

But Jack Butler was a minor-league player. And as a single-issue candidate he represented no threat to Angelo's tenure. So had Angelo's finely calibrated antennae picked up evidence of a more dangerous contender lurking in the wings? Or was I simply the beneficiary of a bad dose of the heebie-jeebies?

On the afternoon before nominations closed, Angelo summoned me to his Parliament House office. "Perhaps you won't need to run after all," he announced. "Apart from that old commo from Save Our Trains, mine's the only hat in the ring."

"Fine by me, Ange," I said. "But it's play or pay. I'm sick of jumping through hoops."

"On the other hand," he said, "nominations don't close until noon tomorrow. And it never hurts to have an extra iron in the fire."

That settled, we got down to brass ballots.

The process employed by the Australian Labor Party to select its candidates for public office is fully understood by only three people. Two are dead and the other is still awaiting release back into the community. As far as the rest of us can work out, half the votes come from party members in the electorate and the other half from a panel elected at the state conference.

In this instance, the vote was scheduled to take place in three weeks' time when an exhaustive ballot would be conducted over the course of a weekend. Since Angelo's factional allies held a slim but firm majority on the central panel, he needed less than half the branch votes to reconfirm his nomination. Short of Nelson Mandela deciding to stand against him, the result was a foregone conclusion. Or so it looked.

My task was to muster the strays. Disaffected individuals, the shell-back left, up-for-grabs ethnics. Convince them that voting for me was the best way to send a salutary signal to the powers that be, then deliver their preferences to Angelo in the second round of the ballot. Easy money for three weeks' work. Better still, there was no penalty for failure. What could Angelo do, fire me?

"You're an independent candidate with an open mind," he instructed. "I don't want anyone to know what's really going on, including Lyndal Luscombe. By the way, she's waiting for you at the Southern Cross Hotel. I asked her to meet you, discuss the lay of the land."

"The lie, don't you mean?"

"Bit late to get moralistic, Murray," he said. "I'm headed down there myself to say a few words at the annual cocktail party of the Victorian Coach and Bus Operators Association. Let's go."

A group of Labor parliamentarians were coming along the corridor as we stepped out of Angelo's office. When we were almost abreast of them, Ange turned to me, his face swelling with rage.

"After everything I've done for you," he sputtered, waving an upraised finger in my face. "You two-timing turncoat. Clear your desk and get out of my sight!"

As interested faces turned our way, I set my jaw angrily. "You're an incompetent disgrace, Agnelli," I hurled back at him. "And the sooner the party wakes up to you the better."

I stormed off, through the foyer and down the parliamentary declivity into the gathering twilight. Five minutes later, Angelo found me loitering in front of the Society restaurant. "I think they bought it," he said. "But there's no need to get personal."

We walked a block down the Bourke Street hill to the Southern Cross, once the city's only truly modern hotel, now just another airport Hilton, indistinguishable from dozens like it. While Angelo went upstairs to the Epsilon Room to bestow his benediction on the captains of the coach industry, I called Red from the lobby and told him I'd be home a little later than usual. Then I went into the lounge.

The place was beginning to fill. The after-work trade, tourists in pre-dinner mode, business travelers on expenses. A blouse with puffy sleeves was inflicting show tunes on a Steinway in the corner. Felines, nothing but felines.

Lyndal was perched on a stool at the bar, glass in hand. A tad more dressed-up this time. Gunmetal gray suit, hem above the knee. A coastguard clipper. On the next seat, angled towards her, was a fleshy man with a nailbrush haircut, tie loosened, getting mellow.

"Hello, Murray," said Lyndal. "This is George from Hamburg. George has been buying me drinks. He thinks I'm a hooker. Isn't that right, George?"

Hamburger George made a noise like lobster climbing out of a hot wok, grabbed his room key off the bar, muttered something about time zones and beat a hasty retreat. As I took his place, I tried not to look at Lyndal's legs. Tried not to imagine lace and a hint of garter. "You're in fine form," I said.

"Nothing a conversation about Angelo Agnelli can't fix."

"Say what you like about Ange," I said. "He has a rare gift for inspiring loyalty in his staff."

"Loyalty in his staff, rapture in the ranks." She hailed the barman, a silver-haired lifer in a tartan cummerbund and matching bowtie, and ordered a gin and tonic. Her third, at least, judging by the emphatic flourish in her gestures. I booked a double Jameson's to catch up.

"So how's he traveling?" I said. "The branches still solid?"

"Solid?" Lyndal graced me with a wry twist of the lips, an arch of her sharp-edged eyebrows. "The local membership doesn't exactly regard itself as the Angelo Agnelli fan club, you know?"

"Diversity of opinion is the lifeblood of the party. Any specific grievances?"

"All the usual ones. He doesn't spend enough time in the electorate. He's out of touch. He's getting too big for his boots. The left think he's too close to the right. The right think he's a prisoner of the left. The Turks reckon he favors the Greeks, the Greeks the Turks, the Anglos the Italians."

"Business as usual, then," I said. "Point is, can at least half of them be relied on to put their hands in the air for him when required?"

"Will they do as they're told, you mean? Of course they will." Behind her flippancy, the *lingua franca* of our trade, I could hear something else, a brittle contempt.

"All that crap about gender equity," she said. "Fact is, you men think that sex is just one of the perks of the job."

We seemed to have jumped ahead a page. I wondered what she was talking about. Our drinks arrived. I took a snort and jiggled my ice cubes. Lyndal did likewise and stared at me like she'd been reading my mail. The items that come in a plain brown wrapper.

"Christ," I said, the loose threads coming together. Mike McGrath's crack about the *Kama Sutra*, Howard Sharpe's obscene finger gesture in a meeting that seemed to have happened a lifetime ago. "He's having an affair, isn't he?"

"How do you know?" said Lyndal, astonished. "Is there talk going around? God, how embarrassing."

"Embarrassing?" I said. "It's almost unbelievable. Although you never know what some people find attractive. And there's the power thing, I suppose. Henry Kissinger and all that."

"He's not that repulsive," she said, defensively. "I mean, I've slept with him, after all."

Now it was my turn to be astonished. "You've slept with Angelo?"

She nearly choked on her drink. "Agnelli? Ugh, what gave you that idea? God, it'd be like fucking Toad of Toad Hall."

"So who are you talking about?" I said.

"Who are *you* talking about?"

"Angelo."

"Angelo's having an affair?" She looked at me like my marbles had taken a hike. "Who with?"

"I thought you might be able to tell me."

"Margaret Thatcher?" she hazarded. "Indira Gandhi?"

"Indira Gandhi's dead."

"That just proves you can't keep a good man down."

"I have absolutely no idea what you're talking about," I said.

She drained her glass, slid to her feet, tugged her hem down and smoothed her skirt. "This gin's going to my head," she said. "And it's time the tonic went somewhere else." She slung the strap of her bag over her shoulder and wove her affirmative way towards the amenities.

McTavish the Barkeep cleared the debris, wiped the puddles and laid out a bowl of complimentary nibbles. "Nuts, sir?"

I put a ten on the bar to reserve our seats and followed Lyndal's lead. The washrooms opened from a vestibule off the lobby containing a cigarette vending machine and a deep telephone alcove. By the time I lightened my load, I'd figured out that I'd been holding my telescope to the wrong eye.

I dallied in the vestibule, pretending to use the cigarette machine, then collared Lyndal when she emerged. "It's Nick, isn't it?" I said. "Your boyfriend, whatever you call it. Your designated spouse equivalent."

"What about him?"

"He's the one having the affair?"

"How do you know?"

"You just told me."

"Yes, I suppose I did," she admitted. "All these trips to the country. Turns out he's been shagging his way across rural Victoria."

"You don't seem very upset."

"I don't give two hoots. Nick and I decided to separate a while ago. It's just a matter of getting the timing right."

"Right for what?" I said. "Are you involved with somebody else, too?"

"You'll find out soon enough," she said.

I wondered who'd beaten me to the punch this time. "Is it anyone I know?"

"What makes you think there's anybody?"

"I'd just like to know, before I make a complete fool of myself," I said.

"It's a bit late to worry about that, Murray," she said, smiling.

"If you were more upset, I could comfort you," I said. "Or if you were angry, I could offer you the opportunity for revenge. If you'd had more to drink, I could take shameless advantage of you."

"Talk," she said. "That's all I ever hear from you."

"Well, try this for talk." I backed her into the phone alcove, wrapped an arm around the small of her back and drew her hard against my torso. I met no resistance, French or otherwise. I put my mouth on her throat and nuzzled my way upwards until I found her lips. They were pretty much where I expected them to be, just south of her nose, tasting slightly of gin. After I'd tasted them for a moment, they moved.

"Not here," they breathed. "Not in a phone booth."

"I'll get a room," I said. "Don't go away."

I detached myself and bolted for the front desk, dizzy with near-success.

"Do you have a reservation, sir?" asked the clerk. Gus, according to his name tag.

A reservation? Until five minutes ago, I didn't even have a hope. "Not as such," I said.

In that case, Gus would see if there was anything available. Lowering his eyes, he began to peck at a keyboard, invisible below the raised edge of the desk. Tap-tappety-tap-tap, he tapped. Tap and peer, tap and peer. Tap, tap, tap. What was he typing down there, I wondered. Madame fucking Bovary?

I looked back the way I'd come. Lyndal had emerged from the vestibule and was loitering beside the fountain in the center of the lobby. She contemplated its marble nymph. Her expression was worryingly pensive. Tap, tap, went Gus. Lyndal began towards me, then hesitated. Gus reached chapter 47, wherein Emma anxiously awaits the arrival of her lover Rodolphe. Hark, the clatter of hooves on the cobblestones. Tap, tappety, tap.

Lyndal was chewing her bottom lip now, definitely besieged by second thoughts. You've overplayed your hand, I thought, beginning towards her, words of passionate reassurance forming themselves in my mind. At that moment, a bell in the elevator bay pinged and Angelo Agnelli emerged, his duties upstairs with the bus proprietors concluded.

Oblivious to my presence behind him, he hailed Lyndal and began to speak with her, drawing her along as he moved towards the main doors. She must have said something unexpected, because he pulled up with a start of surprise. She cast me a quick glance across his shoulder. Sorry, it said. Can't be helped.

Then they were walking again, deep in conversation. Right across the lobby and out the door. Gus finished his manuscript. "I'm afraid I can't help you, sir."

"That's okay," I sighed. "I know a little place in Fitzroy. A sort of boutique operation. There's always a bed for me there."

An empty one, unfortunately.

21

I WENT OUT THE FRONT and let a man dressed like an admiral whistle me up a cab. Had it drop me at the Khyber Pass, the Indian takeout nearest the house, then walked home with a chicken mukhani, two vegetable samosas and a tub of saffron rice. Desire, according to the Buddha, is the fountainhead of all unhappiness.

I found Red toiling over a hot television. "Hard day, Dad?" he said, clocking my comportment, bless his hundred-dollar Nikes.

"It was only hard for a while," I said. "But not any more."

We ate our curry in front of "Sale of the Century," then tackled Red's homework, ancient Egypt. "You haven't forgotten?" he inquired as we whittled pieces of cardboard into a simulacrum of the Great Pyramid of Cheops. "Term holidays start tomorrow."

"How could I possibly forget?" I said, asking myself the same question. "I'll have a bit of free time, changes at work and whatnot. We can go to the museum together, stuff like that."

Red looked underwhelmed. "It's just that Geordie's invited me to go to Mount Buffalo. He's asked Tarquin, too. Can I, please?"

Geordie, if I remembered right, was one of the new peers, a freckly kid, very polite. Considering that Red's move south had cost him two weeks in subtropical Noosa, I could hardly stand in the way of a tobogganing expedition. "What's it going to cost me?" I said.

"Nothing. It's free. His parents have got a lodge."

So Red called Geordie and set up a teleconference. Geordie's mother remembered me from the school information night, and I pretended likewise. Then we trooped across to the Curnows' to filch a sleeping-bag. Faye was working late and Leo was helping Tarquin with the death mask of Tutankhamen.

"That job prospect," I told him. "It's running for Agnelli's seat in parliament."

Leo was a mathematician. He knew how to put seven and nine together. "I'll open a bottle," he said. "Hold this scarab while the glue dries."

When we got back home, there was a brisk message on the machine from Angelo. "Call me," it said. I didn't. I was tired of being Angelo's yo-yo. As far as I was concerned, tomorrow couldn't come fast enough. When it did, I dispatched Red to school with a cut lunch and the Nile Valley in his backpack, zipped my jacket against the breeze and walked up the hill to Carlton, to the Cafe Caruso, a small espresso bar just off the main strip.

The old place had been tarted up since I was last there, the zinc counter replaced by a slab of polished granite, mirror tiles installed in place of the dusty bottles of almond cordial. The card-playing *paesani* had been banished and the ancient aluminum coffee machine superseded by a flash new apparatus of vaguely fascistic design, all bronze eagles and curvaceous chrome. The ancient formica tables had been transposed into Memphis-style structures with surgical appliances for chairs.

"Looking prosperous these days," I told Claudio, the diminutive proprietor.

"Whatta can you do, Murray?" he shrugged. "You gotta keep up."

Apart from a couple of truants playing Space Invaders down the back, I was the only customer. I stood at the bar and ordered a short black, then slid my nomination form across the burnished granite. "I need your signature, Claudio. It's just a formality."

Claudio read the form solemnly, twice. "Angelo, he know about this?"

"Angelo is comfortable." I tapped the side of my nose, then jerked my chin towards the telephone. "Any questions, call him."

That was good enough for Claudio. He shrugged, signed with a flourish. I finished my coffee, thanked him for his assistance, then went down the street to Bernini's bistro and repeated the procedure.

By the time I reached the end of Lygon Street, I had the requisite number of signatures on my nomination form, all Labor Party members in good standing, registered residents of Melbourne Upper. I also had so much caffeine coursing through my system that my heart was fluttering like a distressed damsel's eyelashes. At party head office, a big Victorian terrace in Drummond Street, I lodged the form with the receptionist, watched while she thumped it with a stamp that said "Received."

"Any others for Melbourne Upper?" I asked.

Her nibs was an old warhorse, a stickler for protocol. "Seventy seats, you can hardly expect me to know the candidates in all of them." She indicated the clock. It was eleven, one hour until close of nominations. "You'll find out soon enough."

I walked back to Fitzroy and did a load of laundry. According to the machine — phone, not washing — Angelo had called again. The washing machine didn't say much at all. Probably because it was too busy trying not to gag on the smell of Red's socks.

At midday, the beginning of the rest of my life, I was standing in the backyard, my mouth full of clothes pegs, staring up at the gathering strato-cumulus and wondering if I hadn't made a very big mistake. Wondering if I had blown it with Lyndal. Wondering what Noel Webb and his task force associates were doing, if they were any closer to a result. Wondering if Red had enough warm clothes for five days in the snow.

Agnelli called half an hour later. "I won't tell you to clear your desk," he growled down the line. "There's been nothing on it but dust since last week. But, as of now, you're officially fired."

"After seven years together, Angelo, this is a profoundly emotional moment," I said. "Before I get all choked up, how did the field close?"

"No other takers," he said. "Unless you count Lyndal Luscombe."

"She's nominated?"

"She told me last night. Sprung it on me as I was leaving the Southern Cross."

It all made sense now, sort of. Her vacillation at the birdbath fountain, what I took for second thoughts, could just as easily have been misgivings about the timing. She'd said something about timing, getting it right. Then Angelo's sudden appearance had tipped the balance, probably her last chance for a face-to-face before nominations closed. Even her siren call to the opening of the cultural center fitted the scenario. Her concern about Angelo's state of mind was an oblique way of asking if he'd tumbled to her intentions.

My love life, my political machinations, were all turning into scenes from a French farce.

"I should have guessed," I said.

"You didn't say anything last night, did you?" demanded Angelo anxiously. "You didn't give the game away?"

"My lips were sealed," I said. Most of the time. "I thought she was about to come across with something, then she suddenly left."

"She claims it's a matter of principle. If the factional bosses won't select women candidates, it's up to women to stand anyway, try to force the issue. It's cost her her job, of course, and she realizes she can't win. But it's her business if she wants to make a martyr of herself. My problem is that it's hardly a vote of confidence, two of my closest aides turning traitor. Confirms the wisdom of my decision to have you run."

Forget Aristotle, Angelo's logic was in a category of its own. A thesis which he immediately confirmed. "We can't be seen together from now on," he said. "There's this motel in Carlton, the Gardenview Mews. Whenever I want to meet, I'll book a room in your name, give you a call, let you know the time. Okay?"

"Bit cloak and dagger, isn't it?"

"Don't talk to me about daggers. I've just been stabbed in the back. Twice."

For a year's salary, lump sum, Angelo could be as absurd as he liked. "You're the boss," I said. Force of habit. I'd just hung up when the phone rang again. It was Lyndal.

"About last night," she started.

"I think I've got last night figured out," I said. "I can't help but wonder if you were going to tell me."

"About nominating? Of course I was," she said. "I just felt I owed it to Ange to tell him first. How about you? When were you planning on coming clean?"

"Upstairs in the honeymoon suite," I said. "If Nick's still out of town, I could come around to your place tonight. Since things are out in the open, there's nothing to stop us taking up where we left off."

"Except the fact that we're running against each other."

"That's just politics," I said. "I'm talking lust."

"Goes to credibility."

"Mine or yours?"

"You don't have enough credibility to worry about," she said. "It's pretty obvious that you've cut some kind of deal with Angelo. What's he offered by way of inducement? A permanent public service job?"

"What do you take me for?" I tried to sound offended. "A hooker?"

She laughed at that, a nice teasing sound, rich with possibilities. "See you on the hustings, Murray."

My next call was from Mike McGrath, deputy secretary and chief weasel of the United Haulage Workers. I didn't ask how he got my home number. "I've just heard the news, mate," he said. "Thought I'd call to offer my felicitations. Not that you need them. Agnelli must be making this little charade worth your while."

"Do I detect a note of cynicism?" I said. "Did it never occur to you that I might merely be exercising my rights as a member of our great, democratic party?"

"If that's the case," he said, "I take it you'll be willing to accept our support?"

"You're offering me the opportunity to crawl into your pocket, Mike? Gee, that's generous of you. Thanks, but no thanks."

"I wonder if Ms. Luscombe will take such a high moral tone?" He put a mocking spin on the Ms.

"The enemy of my enemy, is it?" I said. "Anything to keep Agnelli on the back foot. I think you'll find that Lyndal has more sense than to let you poison her wells."

"Maybe," he said. "Or maybe she won't know until it's too late."

"What's that supposed to mean?"

"If you change your mind, give me a call."

"You lot should change your name," I said. "From Haulers to Spoilers."

The phone began to call constantly as word spread through the grapevine. I stuck to the script, reciting the prearranged formula. That I had no personal grievance with Angelo. That I believed the voters of Melbourne Upper should be given a choice. I repeated it so often that I almost convinced myself.

One caller who hadn't yet heard the news was Donny Maitland. He called to update me on the progress of his campaign. "The Haulers' traditional union enemies have been less than forthcoming with their support, I regret to report," he said. "But that hasn't stopped me setting up a base down by the docks to get the word out direct to the rank and file."

I explained that I was now out of the ministerial advisor racket and was challenging Agnelli for preselection. "I'll give you the full story when I can," I said. "There's also something else you should know." I told him about my visit from Webb and the interview at Citywest.

"The cops must be getting desperate for a result," he said. "Any result. I told you Farrell was up to no good. But your lawyer's right. Sit pat. That's what I'm doing. It'll all come out in the wash."

"I wish I had your confidence," I said. "Good luck with the cops and good luck with your campaign. And keep your eye on that dog of yours."

"Don't worry about me," he said. "I've taken your tip. Got myself some medical insurance."

First thing the next morning, Red left on his trip to the snow, piled with the other kids into Geordie's parents' Pajero. "We'll have him back on Thursday night," said Geordie's mother, a reassuringly athletic type. "It's a six-hour drive, so expect him about ten o'clock."

The armed men arrived a little earlier.

22

IT HAPPENED on rubbish night.

In the six days that Red was away, I began the spade work for my preselection campaign. This was not demanding. I called some prospective supporters. I arranged appointments to speak at branch meetings. Mostly, I shopped for a car.

About 9 P.M. on Thursday, I put the bin out and stood for a moment on the curbside, contemplating the silver-gray 1986 Honda Civic I'd purchased that afternoon. One owner, four new tires, eleven months' registration, $11,250. Easy to park, cheap to run, and perfect for my campaign image as the unpretentious, thrifty, environment-conscious offspring of hard-working local parentage.

Just as I was stepping back through the front door, I heard rushing footsteps behind me. Before I could turn a blow struck the back of my head. Down, down I went, the walls sliding past. Then hands gripped my arms and I was being dragged forward. Then came a white radiance. I swam towards it as if from the bottom of a bucket of red jelly. Hello, I thought. Be with you in a minute.

It came to me that I was lying on my living-room floor, looking up at the ceiling light. My arms were twisted behind my back. I told my limbs to move, get out from underneath me, to straighten themselves. They wouldn't. Perhaps they'd gone deaf. Perhaps they couldn't hear because of the thumping inside my head. I tried to speak but my mouth wouldn't open. It was taped shut. Strange, I thought.

About as strange as the two figures looming above me, staring down. They were wearing powder-blue boiler suits and yellow rubber washing-up gloves. They had blobby faces; their noses and lips were all squashed. One of them was holding his penis in his hand. He began to urinate, directing the spray at my face. A hot, stinking stream stung my eyes.

"Wakey, wakey," said the other one, his voice muffled by the stocking over his head.

But I was more than awake. I was thrashing against the tape that bound my ankles and wrists, trying to struggle upright, trying to shout. Something hard jabbed into my chest, pinning me to the floor. When I realized it was the barrel of a shotgun, I got the message.

"Do we have your attention?" said the one holding the gun. He bent over me, a shrink-wrapped pug-dog face.

I nodded. Certainly. Absolutely. Most assuredly. Yes indeed.

"And you know why we're here, Murray?" His voice was calm and relaxed. Very much in control and utterly unfamiliar. I ran the socio-geographical nuances of his accent and drew a blank. He raised the gun barrel a little and tapped me under the chin with it. "Eh?"

I shook my head.

His twin finished buttoning his flies and kicked me in the side. Just hard enough to make the stars tap dance.

"No idea?" said the gun one. "Think about it."

I thought about it, hard. They probably weren't from the Labor Party. Not state, anyway. Nor reporters from the *Herald*. Too articulate. They knew my name, so this wasn't some random home invasion. The Haulers could have nothing against me, now that I was no longer Agnelli's sidekick. Which left only one possibility. This had something to do with Darren Stuhl.

"Ughhgh," I said.

The urinator sat down in my Ikea armchair, sprawled back and let gun-boy do all the talking.

"I'll get straight to the point, Murray, just so there's no misunderstanding," said the voice at the end of the shotgun. "We can blow your head off. We can blow your knees away. We can knock you out and burn your house down around you. We can do anything we like, any time we like. You understand?"

If he was trying to frighten me, he was doing a sterling job.

"Understand?"

I nodded.

"That's the spirit. Now listen very carefully. You listening?"

I nodded.

The muzzle of the shotgun moved up until it was resting on the bridge of my nose. The barrels had been sawn short and the edges filed. I noticed this because they occupied my entire field of vision.

"You haven't been entirely truthful with the police, have you?"

I nodded. Force of habit. Jesus, I thought. It's the cops. Webb has stepped over the line.

"You're covering up for your friend Maitland, aren't you? You forgot to tell them what he did to Darren, didn't you?"

"Urgh," I pleaded. "Grnghf."

"But you're going to tell them now, aren't you?" He tapped my forehead with muzzle of the shotgun. "Because Bob Stuhl is not going to let some pissant like Maitland get away with murdering his son. Understand?"

I was beginning to. These guys weren't overzealous cops looking to cut a few procedural corners. They were representatives of the private sector.

"And Bob's not going to stand back and watch while some vindictive pen-pusher helps his son's killer walk free. Understand?"

By then, my head was nodding faster than the chorus line in a Bombay musical. Bob Stuhl, Christ Almighty. The cops might threaten me, but a threat was all it would remain. But Bob Stuhl? The Prince of Darkness had a better reputation.

Pug-face swung the shotgun aside and leaned closer. "What are you going to do?" Abruptly he ripped the strip of tape off my mouth, taking a layer of lip with it. "Tell me."

"Aya," I said, gulping air.

The shotgun came back up into my face. "Tell me what you're going to do."

"Aya um going to tell them Donny did it."

"Or?"

"Or you'll kill me."

"Good boy."

The tape went back over my mouth. The silent pisser put his heel against my hip and rolled me over onto my front. The shotgun moved to the nape of my neck. Then the light went out. I lay there in the dark, listening to the air surge in and out of my nostrils, the pounding of my heart, feeling the metal against my skull.

"If you haven't done the right thing by this time next week, we'll be back to remind you. We won't be so polite next time."

Then they were gone. Out the back door, across the yard and down the lane.

For a long time I just lay there, trussed up like a Red Cross food parcel, inhaling ammonia-scented wool-blend carpet fibers. I'd been threatened before. I'd been frightened before. But I'd never before been systematically terrorized.

My buttocks gradually managed to unclench themselves. Rolling onto my back, I brought my knees up to my chest and threaded myself through the loop of my arms. I hopped into the kitchen, fumbled in the dark for a steak knife and sawed the plastic tape from my hands and feet. Then I ripped the gag from my mouth, walked calmly into the bathroom and vomited into the toilet.

Red would be home soon. He couldn't find me like this, pissed-on and hyperventilating. I locked every door and window, gathered up the scraps of plastic tape and dumped them in the kitchen tidy. Then I stripped off my clothes, dropped them into the laundry sink and stood under a scalding shower, scarifying my skin, willing myself to wake up from this nightmare.

Sitting pat was no longer an option. Complaining to the police would be pointless. Even if I could persuade them that this had really happened, they could offer me no protection against men like this. Action was being forced upon me. Action I did not wish to take. Still trembling, I wrapped myself in a bathrobe and punched the digits of Donny Maitland's phone number. Jacinta answered from somewhere on the other side of Jupiter.

"He's at the campaign office," she said. "He told me what you did to help him, getting the money and everything. Thank you so much."

I muttered a pleasantry, extracted the number for the campaign office, rang off and punched again.

"Rank-and-file ticket," yawned Donny's voice. "Stop the Sharpe-Stuhl collusion."

"It's Murray," I said. "I've had some unpleasant visitors."

"Cops?"

"Worse than that, I'm afraid. I need to talk to you urgently."

"You want me to come over?"

"Yes, please. No. Wait, let me think."

Red would be through the door at any tick of the clock, full of stories to tell. If Donny then turned up and we went straight into a closed-session conference, the boy would wonder what was going on. Lies would be required. On top of which, I wanted to get out of the house. The place felt like a trap. I didn't want Red there.

"Better if I come to you," I said. "How do I find the place?"

As Donny gave me directions, a horn tooted in the street. I opened the door and found Red heaping his luggage on the step. One arm waving thanks to the departing Pajero, I went down on my knees and embraced the startled boy. "Dad," he protested. "Somebody'll see."

I pointed to the Honda. "Our new wheels," I said. "Let's go for a spin."

He ran an appreciative eye over my purchase. "Only if you get dressed first," he said.

I threw on some clothes, cranked up the batmobile and drove. While Red babbled about chairlifts and nursery runs and snowball fights, I steered a course for the docks, following tram lines that glistened like drawn swords beneath the streetlights. A painful bump was swelling at the back of my skull. I felt like I was wearing a subcutaneous yarmulke.

"Is this to test the shockers?" said Red as we juddered down a potholed service road, barbed-wire alley.

"Since we're out and about, I thought we might visit a friend." I turned into a compound marked by a hand-sprayed sign.

Our headlights swept a quadrangle walled by stacks of shipping containers that rose four-high like gigantic Lego blocks. In the center of the yard stood a white box, a portable site office. Donny opened the door and stood watching our approach. In his black pea-jacket and knitted cap he looked like an extra from *On the Waterfront*.

I parked beside his dinged Commodore and we walked towards the office, gravel crunching. Red nudged me and pointed up. Above one of the container-stack walls, the superstructure of a ship loomed in silhouette against a backdrop of moonlit clouds. "Cool," he said.

Donny read at a glance both the alarm in my eyes and the situation with Red. "Welcome to the liberated territories," he said, spreading his arms. "And this must be the boy." He extended a beefy hand to Red. "Haven't seen you since you were knee-high to a hubcap."

Red shook hands tentatively, somewhat overwhelmed by the sheer masculinity of the situation, and we followed Donny inside. Maps, whiteboards and posters covered the walls. A photocopier was churning out leaflets. Behind a partition was a galley kitchen with a cafe-bar and a refrigerator plastered with stickers. Beer $2, read a note on the door.

Donny steered Red towards a computer with winged toasters fluttering across its screen. "There's supposed to be some games in there, but nobody can find them. How about you take a crack while I talk with your old man?"

Within a few clicks, Red was putting Pac-man through his paces. Donny tilted his chin towards the door and I nodded. As we started back outside, the phone rang. Donny picked it up. "Rank-and-file ticket."

He listened intently for about twenty seconds, then started rubbing the back of his neck. "Of course I'm pissed off," he said at last. "We're trying to present ourselves as a credible alternative, you pull a stunt like this, makes us look like feral crazies."

He listened some more. The fluorescent light made him look old and tired and brought out the boozer in his face. "If that's your attitude," he said wearily, "we're better off without you." He listened a bit longer, then dropped the handpiece back in its cradle with a shake of his head.

"Problem?" I said. It couldn't be as bad as mine.

"Roscoe," he explained. "He was driving past the Haulers' head office in South Melbourne a little while ago and noticed the lights were on. It seems the organizers were all there having a meeting. So Roscoe unilaterally decided to mount a guerrilla raid. The fucking idiot spray-painted our slogans all over their fleet of cars. When I expressed my disapproval, he accused me of lacking militancy and quit the ticket."

"Very mature," I sympathized. "Can you find somebody to fill his spot?"

"It won't be easy. Len's dropped out, too. His wife got the jitters. The bastards were parking in front of the house while he was at work. A couple of them'd just sit there all day. Tell you the truth, things aren't going quite as well as I'd hoped." He glanced at Red, his face lit by the glow of the screen, then chucked his chin towards the door. "Anyway, enough of my troubles. Come for a walk."

We crunched slowly across the yard, hands sunk deep into our pockets. A milky moonlight filtered though the clouds. The air smelled of exhaust fumes, the sea and wet gravel. I fired up a cigarette. "Haven't you heard?" said Donny. "Those things can kill you."

"There's faster ways to go," I said. Then I told him about my visitors, pouring it out in a breathless stream. "They threatened to come back and kill me if I don't do what they want within a week."

Donny's face became redder as he listened. "He *pissed* on you?" he said. "And you reckon these guys are working for Bob Stuhl?"

"They definitely gave that impression. Dropped his name a few times. He must have a direct line to the cops. They share their suspicions, he expedites the process."

"Bob fucking Stuhl," muttered Donny. "What a ruthless bastard. Got his start in business cutting the brake lines of his competitors. I wouldn't put it past him to engage in a bit of vigilante action if he thought it'd nail his son's killer. But maybe it wasn't him who sent them. Could've been the Haulers, trying to set me up. Or even the cops themselves."

I crushed my cigarette into the wet gravel and lit another. The smoke churned my empty stomach. "Whoever they were, they scared the shit out of me," I said. "So what am I going to do, Donny?"

He tilted his head. A growl was coming from the road, the gear-shifting roar of an approaching truck. It was moving fast. Donny grabbed my arm and tugged me towards the parked cars.

Suddenly, a blinding bank of headlights exploded into the compound. A towering prime-mover rocketed towards us, hit its anchors and carved a path through the gravel, fishtailing wildly. As it slowed, the passenger door flew open. Frank Farrell leaned out, one foot on the step. A bottle flew from his hand, tumbled through the air and burst against the site office, spreading a sheet of flame across the wall. The truck revved up again and disappeared behind the portable. Above the roar of its engine I heard the sound of shattering glass.

I ran for the door and wrenched it open. The rear window was shattered and the photocopier was an oily chemical blaze. Flames licked the ceiling and acrid black smoke belched everywhere. Red was stumbling backwards, arm raised to shield his face from the heat, coughing and spluttering. Donny rushed past me and grabbed the boy by the collar. We all fell out the door, retreating crabwise into the yard, crashing to the ground in a cursing tangle of limbs.

The truck was speeding away, heading for the gate, engine shrieking. Donny sprinted after it. As it turned up the road, he pulled a pistol from his waistband and fired after it. Pam, pam.

That was Donny Maitland. Never a dull moment.

23

THE OFFICE WAS GOING UP like a bonfire, crackling and popping as its contents were incinerated. Another few seconds and Red would've been among them.

"Holy shit," the kid declared. His attention was so firmly fixed on the fire that he hadn't noticed Donny's fusillade.

Cinders were raining from the sky and we retreated farther from the heat. Donny began trudging back from the road, eerily lit by the leaping flames. The gun was nowhere in sight. I ran my hands over Red. Satisfied that he was uninjured, I bundled him into the Honda, its sales-lot paintwork already flecked with thumbprints of soot.

"What's going on, Dad?" the boy pleaded, subdued and bewildered.

"Wait here," I ordered. My tone brooked no contradiction. For once, it got none.

Donny and I stood watching his headquarters burn.

"Roscoe wanted to turn up the heat," he said. "Looks like he got his wish. A bit of tit-for-tat, Haulers style."

"First spray cans, then Molotov cocktails," I said. "Now gunfire. What next? Hand grenades?"

Shadows danced across the towering container-stack walls of

the compound and the stench of burning plastic poisoned the air. The yard was a desolate inferno, one of the rings of hell.

Donny said, "You're right. I acted without thinking." He patted his hip. "These things can be a real temptation."

"You should've told me you were planning an armed struggle," I said. "I could've asked Agnelli to fund some guided missiles."

"This isn't usually my speed, Murray," said Donny. "You know that. Call it a lapse of judgment. I realize I can't shoot my way into the union. And, let's face it, I'm never going to get elected either. The wheels were already starting to fall off. Now it's gone way too far. Jesus, Murray, the kid could've been killed. I'm tossing in the towel. It's not worth it. Fuck the union."

Headlights swept across the yard. A security-service patrol car came through the gates. It screeched to a halt beside us and a watchman stuck his horseshoe mustache out the window. "What happened?" he said.

"A cigarette in a wastepaper basket," Donny told him. "Spread to a can of fuel. Nobody hurt. Can you get on your radio, call the fire brigade?"

The driver obliged then got out to watch the show. Donny and I paced around to the far side of the fire. "Where'd you get the gun?" I asked. Across the other side of the yard I could see the pale shape of Red's face peering through the window of the Honda.

"Off a crim who didn't need it," said Donny dismissively. "These guys, your visitors. They gave you a week, right?"

"That's what they said."

"And you trust me, right?"

After what had just happened, I felt entitled to a degree of skepticism. "I'm in a hard place here, Donny," I said. "If it was just me, I might be able to deal with it. But I've got the kid to think about."

The big truckie fixed me in his gaze. "I did not kill Darren Stuhl," he stated firmly. "And I'll get you out of this fix, if it's the last thing I do. Just give me a couple of days, okay? I'll see you right, I swear."

The wail of a siren wafted over the horizon. Donny glanced around, took a small automatic pistol from his pocket and thrust it towards me. The burnished metal of its stainless-steel barrel glowed in the canyon between our bodies. "Do me a favor, will you?" he said. "Chuck this in the river."

The siren grew louder. My hand reached out and the gun disappeared into my jacket pocket, dead weight. Donny jerked his thumb towards the gate. "I'll be in touch. And try to be more careful where you throw your cigarette butts in future."

I left him standing there, watching the guttering slagheap of his ambitions, and drove out the gate. Red's curiosity filled the car's interior, palpable as gas under pressure.

"Those men in the truck don't want Donny running against them in a union election," I explained. "Matter of fact, they don't want anybody running. They're not big fans of democracy." Or having their cars spray-painted.

"Are they after you, too?"

"Nah," I reassured him. "We just happened to be in the wrong place at the wrong time." Other men were after me.

A fire engine sped towards us, crowding the center of the road, lights searing the night. "Exciting, eh?" I grinned, needing to say something, making a joke of it.

"Shit, yeah," Red agreed. "Wait until Tark hears about this."

"You think this could be our secret for a while?" I said.

"How come?"

"Put it this way, how would your mother react if she found out I'd taken you somewhere that got fire-bombed?"

"But Tarquin won't tell Mum," he said.

"Not your mum," I agreed. "But what about his mum? Thing like this, he'd be bound to want to tell her. Could be a bit of a weak link in the chain. He tells Faye, she tells Wendy, one thing leads to another. You with me?"

He was with me, all right. Shit like this didn't happen at exclusive boarding schools. And getting rescued from a burning building outclassed a ride in his stepfather's yacht any day of the week.

We turned into Footscray Road, a stream of thundering trucks even in the midnight hour. Their aggressive bulk dwarfed the two-door Honda, a pitiful trespasser in the kingdom of the whopping leviathan. Contemptuous of both common courtesy and the rules of the road, they cut and wove around us, buffeting our tiny sedan in their slipstreams. The human hands that guided them were invisible, indifferent, somewhere high above. Braking for a red light, I read the slogan on the bumper of the colossus in front of us: BOB STUHL IS BIG.

And his reach is long, I thought.

Despite Donny's alternative scenarios, I remained convinced that Bob Stuhl was behind my unwelcome visitors. Cut the red tape, that would be Bob's attitude.

Red twiddled the radio dial through snatches of music and the somnolent drone of late-night chat shows. Dark water beside us, the floodlit gantries of the container terminal on the edge of my vision, we drove into the empty places where the city washed against the sea. *Dirty deeds,* came the refrain. How cheap, I wondered, did a pair of hired gunmen come? For a man as rich as Bob Stuhl, such men could be bought for the price of a decent lunch.

We crossed a bridge over the Maribyrnong River and I turned to follow its course. Farther upstream, it ran between playgrounds and golf courses, taverns and boathouses. Down here, near the bay, it was an industrial canal, a black ribbon flecked with litter. I pulled into the undercroft of an electroplating works, Customer Parking Only, and told Red that I needed to take a leak.

Cutting through a construction site, I followed the embankment until I was well out of sight of the car. Inky water lapped at the pilings as a dredge motored past. An oily slick glistened in its wake like plankton rising from the deep. When it was gone, I stepped from the shadows, took the gun from my pocket and tilted it into the dull moonlight. Donny was right. Sometimes the temptation is irresistible.

This was the first pistol I had ever held. My knowledge of guns extended no further than the stock phrases of a million movies. Rack it. Lock and load. Safety off.

There should be a catch somewhere, a button or lever to release the magazine. Yes, there it was, where the trigger guard met the butt. I ejected the magazine, slipped it into my pocket. I gripped the slide firmly between thumb and forefinger and drew it back. A shell popped out of the breech, flew over my shoulder, bounced off the concrete and rolled over the edge of the wharf.

The slide remained locked open, displaying the empty breech. I pulled the trigger, felt firm resistance. The thing was empty now, inert. I examined it more carefully, reading the inscription on the barrel. S & W Compact 40.

Okay. Compact was the model. Forty was the caliber.

S & W needed no deciphering. The magazine held six bullets. I slid it back into the grip and released the slide. If I had this figured right, there was now a round up the spout. Drop the safety catch and squeeze the trigger, it would fire. Feet apart, I aimed down at the water. Two-handed grip, the classic stance. Squeeze, don't jerk.

The gun bucked slightly and a sharp bang echoed off the blank face of the cold-storage depot across the water. The sound was swallowed up by the emptiness of the night. The spent shell tinkled at my feet. A faint smell of cordite mingled with the salt tang of the air. I peered down at the water, its surface unmarked. What did I expect? A dead fish to come floating to the surface?

I flicked the safety back on and kicked the spent casing into the water. I tucked the pistol into my waistband, zipped my jacket and walked back the way I had come.

Fuck with me now, Bob, I thought.

24

THAT NIGHT I SLEPT SOUNDLY, the automatic beneath my pillow.

I was a man packing heat. Nothing could unnerve me. Not a damned thing. Not the cat that crossed my roof at one o'clock or the slam of a neighbor's door just after two. Not the rattle of a window-pane at three or even the twitter of birdsong at five-thirty.

At eight, when a garbage truck came down the street dragging an aircraft carrier behind it, I gave up the battle and brewed myself a cup of breakfast. According to the radio, the Soviet Union had ceased to exist as of midnight, Moscow time. The things that happen, I thought, when you're not paying attention.

While Red snoozed on, I showered and shaved and examined my face in the mirror. It looked desperate. Donny had asked for a couple of days. I couldn't wait that long. At 9:15, I called Frank Farrell. He answered with a grunt shrouded in static.

"Hello, Frank," I said. "How's the Citizen of the Year this morning? Or should I say the Haulers' resident terrorist?"

The line fizzed and hissed, an overlay of white noise. For a moment, I thought I'd lost him.

"That you, Whelan?" he crackled. "What are you bitching about this time?"

"I was ringside at your arson attack last night, Frank. Saw the whole thing. Donny Maitland won't go to the cops, but there's nothing to stop me."

"And tell them what? That your mate was party to the malicious damage of a fleet of vehicles belonging to this union? That he's taken to firing pot shots at passing traffic?"

"That I saw you torch a building with a child inside."

"What child?"

"My son, Frank. You nearly incinerated him."

"Jesus," said Farrell. "I had no idea. Is he okay?"

"If he wasn't, you'd be behind bars right now. Not that you should discount that possibility. Assault with intent to do bodily harm. Reckless endangerment of a minor. Can't see Howard Sharpe and Mike McGrath going in to bat for you over charges like that. They'll hang you out to dry, leave you twisting in the wind."

There was another long pause. "I'd never knowingly hurt a child, I swear."

"Convince me in person," I told him. "Midday at the main gate of Luna Park."

"This is a joke, right?"

"Can you hear me laughing?" I said. "Just be there."

Red emerged from hibernation and stuck his head into the refrigerator. If he'd been traumatized by the previous night's events, the emotional scars were not immediately evident. His appetite was certainly unimpaired.

"Let's do something together today," I suggested.

"Not the museum," he begged, his mouth full of oven-popped grain treats. "Anything but the museum."

At 11:30, we were cruising St. Kilda, looking for a parking spot. Spring was putting in a tentative appearance and a good-sized crowd had turned out to express its appreciation. Volvo station wagons choked the streets and the bike-rental operators on the foreshore were doing brisk business. The bay was a sheet of burnished silver, flecked with yachts and wet-suited windsurfers. Lycrathighed roller-bladers whizzed along the pier and seagulls wheeled and dived in the breeze like squadrons of demented Messerschmitts.

I found a parking spot beneath a palm tree on the Upper Esplanade and we walked down the slope to the open-mouthed clown face that formed the entrance to Luna Park. The old funfair was showing its age, though there remained something irresistible about its tawdry attractions. The screams of rollercoaster riders advanced to meet us, echoing the cries of the gulls.

Red had invited Tarquin along and the three of us merged with the masses. Two juveniles in baggy jeans and windbreakers, a fatherly figure in corduroy trousers and a hiking jacket, a .40 caliber semi-automatic in his pocket.

We went to the cashier's window and I bought a wad of ride tickets. "Go pick up some girls," I told the boys, dispensing cash and tickets. "See you in two hours."

At noon, right on schedule, Farrell was waiting at the entrance, leaning against a fortune-telling slot-machine. He was wearing his gray leather blouson, his hands thrust into the front pockets of his tight-fitting jeans, thumbs out, framing his crotch. "Now I see why you chose this place," he said. "The joys of single fatherhood, right?"

"Save the soft soap," I snarled.

"You're pissed off," he said. "I can appreciate that. How was I supposed to know there was a kid there? I'm not the only one to blame here. It cuts both ways."

"You nearly roast my son alive and it's *my* fault?" I said. "Your logic defeats me."

He fell into step as I headed back into the carnival, past the pinball arcade and the hall of mirrors. "Maitland would never have got that office together if somebody wasn't bankrolling him," he said. "It's pretty obvious that Agnelli's behind it and that you made the arrangements. If you start a war then take a kid into the combat zone, you can't blame other people if he gets hurt."

We reached the Ferris wheel. The great machine advanced in fits and starts, one set of riders alighting and another taking their place, swinging seat by swinging seat. A paradigm of the democratic process. When an empty cage dropped into the loading position, I stepped forward and handed the attendant two tickets.

"Let's talk about Darren Stuhl," I said, climbing aboard.

Farrell hesitated, then grudgingly followed me. "What about him?"

A roustabout dropped the safety bar into place and hauled on a lever. Our swaying seat jerked forward and upward. The Big Dipper thundered past, girls screaming, then we began to revolve smoothly, rising high above the swallow-tail pendants on the turrets of Ye Olde Giggle Palace, far above the calliope cadences of the carousel, up into the open air.

The bay extended before us and the crystal towers of the city rose in a cluster that seemed close enough to touch. A gusty wind had begun chopping at the water, raising whitecaps, and the light off the sea was harsh in our faces.

"You've caused me a lot of needless aggravation, Farrell." The wind tore and snatched at my words.

Farrell eased a pair of sunglasses from the narrow slit of his jacket pocket and put them on. "Like I said, I just told the cops what I saw."

"Darren Stuhl was a shit," I said. "But I didn't kill him."

Farrell didn't answer. He just stared out to sea, as if the row of tankers inching their way along the shipping channel was the most compelling sight in the universe.

"I imagine the cops weren't the only ones you talked to," I said. "You offered to talk to Bob Stuhl, or his people, about compensation for what Darren did to my teeth. So I imagine you must have communicated with him on the circumstances surrounding his son's death."

Farrell folded his arms across his chest. "What if I did?"

"Well since you're Mr. High Level Contact," I said, "I want you to tell Bob Stuhl something else."

"You want me to tell him that you didn't kill his son?"

The momentum of the wheel increased. We crested the top and began to descend, gathering pace. The pendants on the turrets of the mock-medieval castle snapped and cracked like whips. I plunged my hands into my jacket pocket and gripped the butt of the automatic.

"Masked men came to my house last night," I said. "They stuck a shotgun in my face and threatened to kill me unless I tell the cops I saw Donny Maitland kill Darren Stuhl."

Behind the lenses of his sunglasses Farrell's face was as unreadable as a Patrick White novel. "And you think Bob Stuhl sent them?"

"I think a grieving father, impatient for justice, might be tempted to take things into his own hands," I said.

Farrell pondered this, then nodded. "Could be," he said. "Are you going to do what they told you?"

"No, I'm not. And since you have access to Bob Stuhl, I want you to see that he gets that message. If those men come near me or my son, I will kill them without hesitation. Then I'll come and kill him."

"Is that right?" Farrell didn't bother to conceal his skepticism at this brave declaration.

We reached the bottom and began to ascend again. I took the automatic out of my pocket and held it casually in my lap, finger curled loosely around the trigger, thumb resting on the hammer. "Tell him that this is not an idle threat," I said.

Farrell's gaze dropped to the gun. He studied it. "Where'd you get that?"

"Won it in a fucking lucky dip," I said. "Never mind where I got it. The point is, I've got it and you're going to tell your pal Bob that I won't hesitate to use it."

Farrell puffed his cheeks and blew out a long, hard breath. "Then I hope you can shoot better than you use your fists."

"Only one way to find out." I thumbed back the hammer and pressed the muzzle into his side. "And if this is part of some job you're doing on Maitland, the same goes for you."

Farrell stiffened, getting it now. "Take it easy," he said. "I get the message. You're quite the hairy-arsed individual, aren't you?"

"When I want to be," I said. We reached the top. There was nowhere else to go. Slowly uncocking the gun, I slipped it back into my pocket. "A little understanding, Frank, that's all I'm asking for."

"I'll see that Stuhl gets your message, if that's what you want," said Farrell. "No skin off my nose. But why don't you just go to the cops, tell them you're being stood over?"

"Let's just say I'm covering my bases." I patted my pocket.

The ride was ending. Our cage dropped to the loading step and lurched to a halt. The bar came up and we stepped back onto terra firma. A little firmer, I felt, than before we boarded. We walked towards the main gate.

"Very cinematic," said Farrell, folding his sunglasses. "The only thing missing was Orson Welles and a zither."

"Make no mistake," I said. "I'm in deadly earnest."

He held his hands up in a mollifying gesture. "I was wondering about that gun," he said. "Compact automatic, chrome slide. Looks a lot like Darren's yuppie toy."

"So what?" I said. "There must be thousands of guns like this."

"But it's an interesting coincidence, isn't it? Did you know that Darren's gun was never found? Word is, the cops think whoever killed him must have taken it."

"Well I didn't kill him," I said. "And I didn't take his gun." I now understood why Voigt and Webb lit up when I mentioned it.

"But you were at Maitland's office last night. And Maitland just happened to have a gun there. This wouldn't be the same one, by any chance?"

We'd reached the pinball arcade just inside the entrance. Red and Tarquin saw us passing and dashed out to block our path. Tarquin brandished an inflatable plastic baseball bat. "This is a hold-up," said Red. "Give us more money."

Farrell sidestepped him and continued towards the exit. "I'm sure Bob'll be very interested in everything you've told me," he said.

25

THE IMPLICATION OF FARRELL'S WORDS hit me like a locomotive. As my head swiveled to watch him go, my mouth dropped wide open. It was a wonder nobody stuck a ping-pong ball in it.

Tarquin, meanwhile, was pummeling me with his inflatable cudgel and Red was thrusting forth an imploring palm. "Donkey Kong ate all our money," he explained. I peeled off fresh cash, recommended the Whip and allowed gravity to draw me down the slope to St. Kilda pier. My mouth was now closed but my brain was spinning faster than a cotton candy machine.

The water beneath the pier deepened from shimmering transparency to impenetrable jade. I walked its length, out past the Victorian pavilion where the concrete pilings ended and the rock groyne threw its protective arm around the yacht marina. Roller-bladers zipped past, mobile phones clutched to their ears. Old Greek men sat on Eskys, jigging for squid with long rods and barbed lures. "PENGUIN VIEWING CRUISES," said a sign on the railing. "JAPANESE SPOKEN."

Clever penguins, I thought. A damned sight more intelligent than me. When I arrived at Luna Park, I was merely terrorized. Now I was catatonic. And this time, it was all my own fault.

Donny said he got the pistol from a crim who didn't need it. I now realized that he'd been finessing the point. By Donny's lights, Darren Stuhl was born into a criminal class. The fact that he was also a thug only confirmed the definition. And Darren didn't need the gun because he was dead. So did getting it mean taking it? If so, when had that happened? And how? And why?

Whatever the answers to those questions, there was one thing I did know for sure. Nothing could have been better calculated to inflame Bob Stuhl's belief that Donny Maitland killed his son than what I had just done. Not only had I blithely brandished a missing item of evidence which linked Donny directly to Darren at the time of his death, I'd found exactly the right messenger to convey that connection to Darren's vengeful father.

I began to pick my way across the rocks of the breakwater, the hollow of my head echoing with the rattle of rigging against the masts of the yachts in the marina. Gulls swooped and bickered. A cluster of English backpackers had stripped off their tops and were sunning themselves in the lee of the wind, their skin ghostly white against the blue-black of the granite boulders.

Bob Stuhl's minions had given me a week. Would Donny last that long? If Big Bob was willing to use terror tactics at the investigation stage, how far would he go as Director of Private Prosecutions? What penalty would he feel entitled to exact?

My hands were in my jacket pockets. One was closed around the butt of the automatic. The other fingered the bullets. I knew better than to walk around with a loaded gun. Test-firing the automatic was one thing, I'd concluded as I tossed and turned through the night, but using it was another. The state I was in, lunging for it nervously every time a shadow crossed my windowpane, I was more likely to shoot Red than to fend off a posse of professional toughs.

My objective in showing the automatic to Farrell was deterrence. After that my plan was to throw it into the sea. Near the end of the breakwater, I found a sheltered spot between two large boulders. Squatting at the water's edge, I marked a suitable place in the deep green of the marina channel and slipped the pistol from my pocket.

Donny had sworn that he hadn't killed Darren Stuhl. But real doubts now hung over that assertion. Could he have been lying? A version of the events at the market that morning swam before me. Darren waving his gun in Donny's face. Donny somehow getting the better of him. Donny taking Darren's gun, then pulverizing his body to escape detection. But why bother? Why not just plead self-defense? Unless, in the heat of the moment, Donny's low opinion of the law's claims to impartiality had got the better of him.

The breeze was cool at the water's edge and I hunched deeper into my hiking jacket, the gun pressed between my palms. The wind pushed a row of triangular sails over the horizon, then pushed them back again. The wake of a passing speedboat slapped the rocks by my feet. Still I squatted there, thinking.

Donny had promised to see me right. But how did he propose to deliver on that assurance? Was it possible that I was putting myself and Red at risk on the basis of a misplaced trust? Donny Maitland was a good man, yet he was unpredictable. I needed to talk to him again. Soon. I put the pistol back in my pocket and walked back along the breakwater to the pavilion. There was a payphone inside.

Heather answered the Maitland Transport number. "Donny's gone to collect the truck," she said. "The police have finished with it at last. And he's decided to give up this union nonsense, so we can finally get back to business."

"Can you let him know that I need to speak with him urgently?"

"It's not about the money, is it? We'll have a problem paying it back. Donny wasted most of it on office equipment and there's been a fire at his campaign headquarters, whatever he calls it. I don't think he'd got around to insuring it yet."

Insurance. Even when you take it out, you're never entirely sure you're covered. There's always some risk you haven't considered, some caveat you've failed to read.

I told her I'd square the money with the ministry but I still needed to see Donny. Then I got off the line before she could ask me if I was alone. The answer this time was yes. Very much alone.

I walked back up the hill to the rictus mouth of Luna Park. The boys had long exhausted their funding and were waiting with bored impatience. "You said two o'clock," whined Tarquin. "It's already ten past three."

"I was thinking," I said. "You should try it."

"I'm hungry," Red remarked.

We went down the road to the Hebrew bakeries on Acland Street and I fed them to bursting with pastries. By the time we'd finished eating, the sun was losing its luster and the pleasures of St. Kilda were exhausted. We drove back to Fitzroy and I checked the messages on the machine.

Donny hadn't called but Angelo Agnelli had. The preselection process was now a week old and it was time for our first clandestine conference at the Gardenview Mews motel. The agreed place, as Angelo's message gnomically described it. Six o'clock.

Angelo's shadow play was the least of my immediate priorities. Until Donny got in touch, though, I decided I might as well go through the motions. I chased the boys off to Tarquin's place, swathed the gun in clingwrap and buried it in a shallow hole at the base of the lemon tree in the backyard. Then, so that I'd have something to report to Ange, I called Jack Butler and mooted a strategic alliance with Save Our Trains.

Old Jack had no illusions that he would survive the first round of the exhaustive ballot. On the second round, his handful of votes would be up for grabs. I offered him an inducement to swing them my way. He agreed to think about it.

I checked the day's papers in case some new crisis had set a cat among Angelo's pigeons. Nothing jumped out at me. But beyond all the end-of-an-era stories about the demise of the Soviet Union, the *Age* ran a piece about women candidates for ALP preselection. Lyndal Luscombe was quoted as urging Labor to honor its commitment to greater gender equity. The party, she warned, was at risk of appearing hypocritical. As if that wasn't a danger with which we had long learned to live.

At 5:45, I trudged through the Exhibition Gardens to my assignation. A damp chill was rising from the lawns and the tail-lights of the Friday rush-hour traffic blazed red to the horizon.

The Gardenview Mews was on Rathdowne Street, across the road from the park, set inconspicuously into a row of terrace houses. The name was spelled out in foot-high brass letters above an entrance archway. Nothing indicated that a place of public accommodation lay within. From Angelo's point of view the place had two great advantages. Not only was it unlikely that he'd be noticed as he came and went, but Parliament House was a scant ten-minute walk away. He could meet me at the Gardenview Mews and be back in his office before anybody noticed he was gone.

I walked through the arch and found myself in a motor court overlooked by a double tier of balconies. These were trimmed with cast-iron lacework, as was the ground-floor walkway that ran around three sides of the quadrangle. Cars were parked nose-in against the walkway, recent model sedans mostly. At the open door of one of the rooms, a young couple with the look of the landed gentry were unpacking a designer-togged toddler from an upscale station wagon. A paunchy man in a business suit, his tie loosened, came down the stairs from the upper levels and began filling an ice-bucket from a machine on the walkway. We all nodded at each other amiably.

The have-a-nice-day clerk in the office at the end of the walk-way confirmed that a phone reservation had been made in my name, took an impress of my credit card and handed me a brass-tagged key to a room on the ground floor. I let myself in, admired the three-and-a-half-star rating and turned on the television. Agnelli's arrival coincided with the sting for the six o'clock news.

"You haven't got much to report yet, I imagine," he announced, shedding his jacket and sprawling on the settee. "But no harm in touching base."

I killed the set and gave him the rundown on my approach to the Save Our Trains candidate, making my phone conversation with Jack Butler sound like a round of shuttle diplomacy.

"What'll he settle for?" asked Angelo, rooting about in the minibar. "Bottom line."

"Public support for the issue while wearing my hat as a former transport advisor, personal solidarity and a five-hundred-dollar contribution to his campaign expenses."

"And what's Lyndal Luscombe offering?"

I shrugged. "Jack's not giving much away."

Ange settled on a pack of peanuts and reclined on the bed, munching. "She's the main game. Get close to her. Offer her a preference swap, then renege in the final round. If she wants to play with the big boys, she'd better learn how the game works. Your payout check's in the mail, by the way."

Angelo then spent twenty minutes giving me the benefit of his opinion on the key ethnic powerbrokers in the electorate. Venal idiots, one and all, he concluded. My mind, however, was elsewhere. "Any further aggravation from the Haulers?" I asked. "Our decoy duck has gone under, I'm afraid."

"Good." Angelo dismissed the issue by lobbing the empty peanut package into the wastebasket. "Save you having to close him down. The Haulers are back on the reservation for now. They've agreed to suspend hostilities in the interest of the party's overall electoral prospects."

"Our man will be glad to know his failure has not been in vain then," I said.

Angelo had moved on. He picked up the phone, dismissing me with an airy wave. "I'll drop the key off on my way out," he said, "after I've made a few calls."

"Long as they're not international," I said. "And leave the minibar alone." He was already dialing, a million miles away.

As I crossed back through the Exhibition Gardens, avoiding the deep shadows, sticking to well-lit paths, it occurred to me that the

Gardenview Mews would make a useful bolthole if I got the heebie-jeebies at home later that night. The room was paid for, after all.

A soot-smudged white Commodore was parked in the street outside my house. Donny climbed out as I approached and eyed me anxiously. "You rang," he said. The statement contained an obvious question.

I shook my head. "They haven't been back. But I need to talk to you."

"Good idea," he agreed. "I've got a proposal for you."

26

I UNLOCKED THE DOOR and waved Donny inside. He lumbered down the hall ahead of me like a bear going into a wardrobe. "How's the boy today?" he said. "That fire must have given him a hell of a scare."

"A mother like Red's got," I said, "he can handle anything."

Donny loitered in the living room flipping through my CDs while I screwed the top off a new bottle of Jameson's. "Chris Isaak," he said approvingly. "Roy Orbison with a creepy edge." He'd already had a drink or two; in the confined space I could smell it.

"I hear the cops are very interested in the whereabouts of Darren's gun," I said, handing him a glass of neat whiskey. "Word is it wasn't found on the body."

He picked up my wavelength. "Probably at the bottom of some river by now."

We sat down in the easy chairs, the bottle on the coffee table between us. "I've been trying to imagine what happened that morning," I said.

Donny avoided my gaze. "Better if you don't know."

"Yeah?" I said. "And why is that?"

Donny took a sip, then stared down at the pale liquor, rotating it meditatively in his glass. A silence hung between us. Donny was measuring his words, finding the right way to distribute the load.

"There's only two people who know what happened," he said at last, raising his eyes. "Me and the man who killed Darren Stuhl."

"And who was that?"

"Farrell." He said it as though stating a self-evident truth.

"Farrell? Why would Farrell kill Darren Stuhl?"

Donny's great shoulders rose and fell. "Dunno," he said, abjectly. "Looked to me like he might've just done his block."

My glass was suddenly empty. I reached for the bottle and refilled it. "And you saw this happen?"

Donny sipped again, heaved a reluctant sigh and proceeded to his confession. "I get up on the pallets, right, start speaking my piece. About fifteen, twenty people gather around, Farrell and his pals included. Farrell starts giving me the raspberry. Nothing to write home about. As soon as I start talking about Bob Stuhl and the way he puts his drivers at risk, Darren appears. He jumps up beside me and sticks his gun in the side of my head." He mimed the action, finger and thumb cocked. "Then Farrell jumps up there, too, and starts dragging Darren away."

"All part of the Haulers' service," I said. "Managing the management."

"Farrell's lot start shoving chests, telling people to piss off, it's all over. Roscoe takes a swing and an all-in brawl erupts. Len's getting clobbered so I jump down to help. Then, fast as it started, it's over. Everybody takes off. I go scouting for Len and Roscoe. Out of the corner of my eye, I register a flash of movement between two parked trucks. Farrell's got something in his hand and he's slamming it down on Darren Stuhl's head."

I stopped him there. This was a matter in which I had a particular interest, thanks to Noel Webb's Theater of the Spanner. "What was it?"

Donny shrugged again. "Dunno. But it must have been solid because when I saw Darren's body later, he had a bloody big gash on his forehead. Anyway, Darren goes down like a ninepin. Just then, Roscoe calls out to me. A bunch of Farrell's mongrels have got him cornered. I dash over and help him sort things out. When I look again, there's no sign of either Farrell or Darren."

"Did Farrell realize you'd seen him?"

He shrugged again. "He had his back to me," he said. "He might have spotted me in the wing-mirror on one of the rigs. I don't know for sure."

"So why didn't you tell all this to the cops?"

Donny shook his head ruefully, sagged back into his seat and showed me his palms. "Perhaps because Farrell had done me a good turn hauling Darren off me like that. But mainly it was because I liked the idea that I had something on him. I thought I'd bide my time, see if I could use it during the union election campaign."

"Use it how?"

"That's a question I've been asking myself ever since," he said. "Let's just say it seemed like a good idea at the time. Even when Darren turned up under the truck and it was obvious that Farrell was trying to set me up, I still didn't say anything. To make things worse, I pinched Darren's gun off his body when nobody was looking, just in case."

"Just in case of what?"

"In case it came in handy," he said. "If things got rough in the campaign." He was a punctured tire, still holding its shape even though the air was gone.

"You've got to go to the cops," I said.

"I've left my run too late. They won't believe me. I was too confident early in the piece. I didn't think they'd believe I was stupid enough to kill Darren Stuhl, then stick his body under my own truck. Well, they were wrong about Darren but they were right about the stupidity. I could win an Olympic medal for idiocy. And now that I'm a suspect, they've got even less reason to believe me. Like you said, why would Farrell kill Darren Stuhl? I've set myself up for a fall here, mate. And it all came to a head last night. First your visitors. Then me, blasting away at Farrell's taillights like a madman."

I struggled to process the implications of Donny's words. And to cross-reference them against my own actions in showing the gun to Farrell.

Donny might have been first ashore on Fuckwit Island, but he wasn't Robinson Crusoe on the atoll. Now I'd have to tell him what I'd just done. That I'd given Frank Farrell the opportunity to finish the frame-up job he'd commenced when he dumped the deceased Darren under Donny's Dunlops. "Darren's gun," I began.

Donny leaned forward, squared his sagging shoulders and interrupted me. "Thanks to my mistakes, Murray, you've got a sword hanging over your head," he said. "I said I'd see you right and that's exactly what I'm going to do. Remember I said I had a proposal to put to you?"

"I'd be lying if I said you had my unalloyed confidence at the moment, mate," I warned. "And like I was about to say—"

"Jacinta's been on my back about taking a trip to the Philippines," he interrupted. "Very nice at this time of the year, I understand. Especially if you've got local contacts who can show you some of the more remote places, the ones off the beaten track."

"Some men are going to kill me and you're talking about taking a holiday?" I said incredulously.

Donny ignored me. "It'll take me a couple of days to get a visa and book a ticket," he said. "But I reckon I can be there well before your deadline expires. Soon as I arrive in Manila, I'll give you a call. Then off you toddle to the cops. Say exactly what you were told to say. That I killed Darren and you've been covering up for me. Tell them whatever you think it'll take to get the bastards off your back. The cops, Bob Stuhl, whoever they are."

I considered what he was saying. Not only would it take the pressure off me, it would place Donny out of range of Bob Stuhl's vigilantes. There was only one problem. "You realize this means spending the rest of your life on the run?" I said.

"That remains to be seen," said Donny. "Once the legal wheels start to turn I can play it by ear. In the meantime, it's not like I've got anything to keep me here. The union campaign's history and I'm sure Heather can find somebody else to boss around. The main thing at the moment is to get you off the hook. And since I hung you there in the first place, I don't want to hear any argument about this, Murray. I've made up my mind."

The back door slid open. "Honey, I'm home," yodeled Red. "What's for dinner?" He erupted into the living room, then pulled up short, sensing the somber atmosphere.

"G'day, young feller," said Donny. "Enjoy our little barbecue last night? Your dad's just been helping me plan my holidays."

Red idled in the doorway, grinning sheepishly. Donny downed the last of his drink and stood up.

"Red," I said. "Isn't it time you called your mother? And before you go, Donny, I've got a travel tip for you. Come out the back way."

When we reached the lemon tree, I scraped at the dirt with the side of my shoe until a plastic-sheathed parcel appeared.

"Darren's gun isn't at the bottom of the river," I started. "You might still need it."

27

DONNY'S DETERMINATION to head for the hills of Mindanao was only strengthened by the news that I'd flashed the pistol at Farrell. "I've got even more reason to go now," he declared.

"Thanks to me," I said.

"This whole fiasco is my fault," he insisted. "Wait for my signal, okay? If you haven't heard from me by Thursday, go to the coppers anyway. Until then, do whatever you'd normally do. And, listen mate, I can't tell you how sorry I am for the trouble I've caused you."

After extracting an oath that I would obey his instructions, he gave me a parting slap on the shoulder and disappeared along the back lane. I stood there watching him go, wondering how long it would be before I saw him again. Wondering, too, if Frank Farrell had whispered into Bob Stuhl's ear yet. Or the ears of those who had Bob's ear.

Donny's decision at least had the virtue of being a plan, or so I told myself. A desperate plan, to be sure, however, one that would allow me to meet the twin terrorists' demands. I slept a bit easier that night. But not before double-checking the locks on all the doors and windows and leaving a light burning in the living room.

By the next morning, Saturday, spring's cautious reconnoiter had become a full-blown advance. The sky was a blanket of baby blue. For the first time in months, the sun shed warmth as well as light. The air refreshed rather than braced. Blossoms emerged from swelling buds with an almost audible pop.

It wouldn't last, of course. It never does. Soon the rain would return, blooms would rot on the branch and Antarctic fingers would again stick themselves up our trouser legs. But, according to the forecast, we could reliably expect at least another five fine days. By then Donny would be out of harm's way and I'd be down the cop shop buying a reprieve with a lying oath. Until that moment arrived, I did as Donny had urged and pretended things were normal. It was either that or take up permanent residence under the bed.

Sunday was Father's Day, a fact which had escaped my attention until Red woke me with a tray. Rock-hard boiled eggs, desiccated toast and a little gift-wrapped something from the Sox'n'Stuff spring sale. "You shouldn't have," I said, pleased as Punch.

"They said you could exchange it if you didn't like it."

"Not like it?" I was scandalized by the very idea. "A tie like this could stop a charging elephant."

We spent the afternoon in the park playing frisbee, intermittently discussing Red's career plans. Acting, he thought, or maybe directing. Possibly special effects, pyrotechnics maybe.

Donny called while we were out, left a message on the machine saying that everything was on track. He'd soon be in that warm place we discussed. As a peace-offering to Heather, he was making a final run, a one-off job up the bush, too good to pass up. On the road, I thought, was probably the best place for him. Out of town was out of sight.

A week remained of the school holidays. A bike was bought for Red. Skateboards cluttered the yard. The television stayed on continuously. We hosted an all-night sleepover for a bunch of the guys. And I went into campaign mode.

I realized, of course, that my imminent confession to conspiracy to pervert the course of justice would do little for my standing in the community. That was a hit I would take to see Donny safe. But until that moment arrived, I buried my fears in the most prosaic pursuit I could imagine. Cold canvassing for votes.

I erected a collapsible card table in my bedroom by way of an interim office, broke open the membership lists and began grubbing among the grassroots.

As I tested the litmus of Angelo's standing, I found the situation much as Lyndal had described. While he was far from universally popular, his status as the sitting member ensured that most of the troops felt obliged to support him. Either that, or they took their cue from ethnic heavyweights who delivered blocks of votes in return for the kind of largesse that could only be dispensed by a government minister. But Ange's footings were not set in quite as much concrete as he might have hoped. With the electoral tide ebbing, there was a growing mood of recrimination within the ranks. And, with patronage reaching its use-by date, some of the clients were sniffing about for fresh sources of pork.

Lyndal was siphoning some of his support, mainly from areas that I, too, was targeting. While many of the comrades agreed in principle that the party should beef up the participation of women, they saw in Lyndal a bit too much of the self-serving apparatchik. Uppity chick, in other words.

On Monday evening, while Red was playing Nintendo at Geordie's place, I toured Melbourne Upper branch meetings, pitching to tiny gaggles of true believers huddled in under-heated supper rooms at Mechanics Institutes and municipal libraries. On Tuesday morning I took coffee and biscotti with Maestro Picone, *éminence grise* of the Italian senior citizen set. In the afternoon, I bought drinks for members of the local schoolteacher intelligentsia at a popular after-work watering hole. I also called Ayisha Celik at the Migrant Resource Center.

Back in my days at the electorate office, Ayisha ran the Turkish Welfare League. Over the years she and I had done the odd favor for each other. Not quite as many as I would've liked, but that's the way the kebab crumbles. Now, according to the word around the traps, she was Lyndal Luscombe's campaign manager.

"Mr. Shifty," she said, in her lilting wog-girl voice. "We wondered when you'd be in touch."

After a bit of banter, I raised the subject of a meeting with Lyndal. Ayisha proposed lunch the next day in the restaurant in the National Gallery where a competing-candidate *tête-à-tête* was unlikely to be observed by some motormouth from Melbourne Upper and fed into the rumor mills. I knew the place well from the days when Angelo was the arts minister and I dabbled in the cultural mysteries.

"Tell Lyndal I'm looking forward to seeing her again," I said.

"Put it back in your pants, Murray," joked Ayisha. "Or I'll have you arrested."

"Too late for that," I said. "I'm already planning to surrender myself to the authorities."

Red had just left for a reciprocal sleepover at Geordie's place when I switched on the six o'clock television news. I was only half-listening as I fixed myself a cup of coffee and it took me a moment to register the headline story. Something about the discovery of a body that morning in the cabin of truck on a remote backroad near Warracknabeal, 400 kilometers northwest of Melbourne.

The boiling kettle screaming in my ears, I spun around to face the set. A helicopter shot panned across a truck parked in a stand of she-oaks on the shoulder of a dirt road beside an endless paddock of yellow-flowered canola. A white Kenworth with blue trim. According to the newsreader, the dead man had been identified as Donald Maitland, a fifty-two-year-old truck driver. He had been shot in the head at point-blank range.

I cut the gas beneath the kettle. The words and images struck me like a series of rolling punches.

A reporter with a handheld mike stated that the truck had been there for two days before a local farmer made the grisly discovery. And that a suicide note found in the cabin connected Maitland to the recent high-profile slaying of Darren Stuhl, son of transport magnate, Bob Stuhl. A handgun belonging to Darren Stuhl, missing since his death, had been retrieved from the truck.

A suicide note? Where had that come from? It could only have been extracted under duress. Threats? Torture?

Inspector Voigt appeared, standing near the truck with his tie flapping in the wind. In gratified tones, he told a cluster of reporters that he believed speculation about Darren Stuhl's death would soon be laid to rest. His inference was clear. The police believed that Donny had killed Darren, then blown his own brains out with the dead man's gun.

By the time the bulletin moved to the next item, I was punching Donny's number into the phone. The line was busy. I called at five-minute intervals for the next hour with the same result. The seven o'clock news brought no additional information. Same story, same spin.

I tried again to reach Jacinta or Heather but either the phone was off the hook or they were under siege. Family, friends, the media, whoever. I called police headquarters and asked for Inspector Voigt, hoping that the homicide chief was back in town. My name was taken and I was put on hold. After a long wait, Noel Webb came on the line. "What do you want, Whelan?"

"To talk to one of the grown-ups."

"About what?"

"About this story you're feeding the media. Donny Maitland would never top himself. It's just not plausible."

"Gun in one hand, suicide note in the other," said Webb. "Looks pretty plausible to us."

"And very convenient, too. Gives you a result in the Stuhl case. I saw Donny just a few days ago and he definitely wasn't suicidal."

"Always the expert, aren't you?"

"I know Donny."

"And do you also happen to know what Darren Stuhl looked like when they scraped him off the ground? What a man looks like after the rear wheels of a ten-ton truck have rolled over him? Try to picture it in your tiny mind, Whelan. Try to imagine doing that to another human being. Think what it'd be like to see that image every night when you close your eyes. Then tell me it mightn't start to eat at you."

"I don't believe that Donny killed Darren Stuhl and I don't believe he killed himself."

"Believe what you like. Us dumb coppers, we believe the evidence. Maitland was aggrieved at being sacked by Stuhl Holdings. Stuhl junior threatened him with a gun. He had the motive, the opportunity and the means."

"What means?"

"Any blunt object, plenty of which were readily to hand. Anyway, it's all academic now. He left a handwritten confession. Said he couldn't live with himself any more, after what he'd done."

"It must have been coerced out of him."

"I know he was a mate of yours," said Webb, "but face facts. Ever since Darren Stuhl's death, Maitland's been acting in a highly erratic, unstable manner. He concealed information. He was an uncooperative witness. Last week, a building he was leasing burned down. A cigarette, he said. Petrol, according to the fire brigade. He claimed his union had colluded with Stuhl Holdings to get him sacked. The real cause was drinking on the job. His body, by the way, was found with elevated blood-alcohol levels. You want me to go on?"

What could I say? That I could provide different explanations for all of those events, mostly based on information I'd concealed from the police?

"Perhaps if you'd been more forthcoming about your own relationship with Maitland, things might've turned out different," said Webb.

"What do you mean?"

"You seem to think we've been sitting around here for the past three weeks with our thumbs up our quoits. Maitland's bank records show he received money from the transport ministry, funds that you authorized immediately after the events at the market. Nobody else in there knows anything about it, only that you wanted it done urgently."

Again, there was nothing I could say. So I didn't say it.

"If you want to go down this road, Whelan, be my guest. I'll put you through to the chief. But I doubt very much if he's going to reopen the case on your say-so."

"You haven't heard the last about this," I said.

"I won't hold my breath," said Webb.

I hung up and stood staring down at the phone, sick to the core. Donny Maitland had paid too high a price for his mistakes. And now the only eyewitness to Darren's killing was dead. Any attempt I made to set the record right would be dismissed as the hearsay testimony of a self-interested party.

Conjecture about Donny's last moments flooded my brain. By what vile means had the confession been extracted? Had he begged for his life? In his position, I would've gone down on my hands and knees and blubbered like a baby.

But outrage and indignation were not the only emotions washing over me. I also felt relief. Bob Stuhl had found his sacrificial victim so I was off the hook. The shotgun men had no reason to return.

And with the relief came guilt. Spider Webb was right. I was not without blame. Donny had given me Darren's gun to throw away. Instead, I'd used it to betray him. And then I'd thrust it back into his hands, to become both the method of his execution and the means to conceal it.

This was all down to Frank Farrell. The prick would be hearing from me. And he wouldn't like what I had to say. First I needed a drink. Opening the kitchen cupboard, I reached for the Jameson's, untouched since Donny and I had broached it together four nights earlier.

The glass touched my lips and I wondered if one drink would be enough.

28

WHEN THE BOTTLE WAS EMPTY, I lurched to the pub on the corner for another, my head spinning in the rush of night air. The stars looked down at me from infinite space. We are tiny, they said, but you are insignificant.

Bob Stuhl, on the other hand, was big. And the CEO of Stuhl Holdings had heavy buffers. Nobody would ever be able to tie him directly to Donny's death. The dirty work had doubtless been done by men who performed tasks for people who arranged things for blokes who did favors for guys who occasionally played golf with friends of a friend of Bob's former chief mechanic's cousin. Probably the same men who had come calling on me.

But Bob's minions had got the wrong man. And, come the dawn, I'd make it my business to find a way to bring that fact to his attention. Then Bob's vengeance would descend on Farrell. In time it might even be possible to make the great panjandrum himself pay for what he'd had done to Donny. In the meantime, I sat in the dark and poured liquor onto the fire blazing in my brain. The fire raged and I danced around it, plotting my revenge. Standing at the lemon tree, I pissed into the hole where the gun that killed Donny had been buried. Had it still been there, I would've dug it up and made my way to a certain French provincial mansion in Toorak.

As I staggered inside it occurred to me that the phone was ringing. "Is that you, Whelan?" said a voice. "It's Frank Farrell here. I just wanted you to know that Bob was very appreciative of your information. He's forgiven you for not coming clean with the cops. Says to tell you it's evens now. Live and let live. He says he's sure you'll understand, being a father and all."

I held the telephone so tight my fist began to tremble. "And what's he gonna say when I tell him that he got the wrong man, that you're the one who killed his son?" I demanded.

A sucking came down the line, a sharp intake of air. "Well, well, well," said Farrell. "I wondered if Maitland told you what he saw. Dumb of him not to tell the cops, wasn't it? But he didn't and that's the main thing. Anything he said is hearsay. And nobody's going to take your word against mine, least of all Bob Stuhl."

"That won't stop me trying," I slurred.

"Get real, Whelan," said Farrell. "Drunk or sober, nobody's going to believe you. You were Maitland's crony. And you were the one uttering threats against Darren. I was the trusty babysitter. I'd been hauling that psychotic bastard out of scraps for years."

My hand found the neck of the whiskey bottle. I poured another slug down my throat. I was scarcely tasting it any more. "Until one day you got fed up, eh?"

Farrell gave a dry chuckle. "You can relate to that, can't you? Darren was riding for a fall. First he stuck his gun in Maitland's face. Then, when I tried to hose him down, he did the same to me. I made my displeasure known. Hit him harder than I intended and accidently put the prick out of his misery."

"Then set Donny up to take the blame."

"You've seen how Bob Stuhl works, so you'll appreciate how keen I was that he didn't find out it was me," he said. "Maitland just happened to be the most likely culprit."

"You arsehole," I fumed. "I don't give a fuck about what you did to Darren Stuhl. But Donny was innocent and he's dead because of you."

"Because of you, too," Farrell reminded me. "Don't forget that. The gun was the clincher. You shouldn't have given it back to him, should you? Get off your high horse, Whelan. It'd be a brave man indeed who decided to make an issue of this. Are you a brave man, Murray?"

Farrell's tone was genial but the note of menace was unambiguous. I held the phone to my ear, listening to his breath, wondering how to answer his question.

"It's the way things are," said Farrell into the silence. "And there's nothing that you can do about it."

He hung up. I was glad he did. I was beginning to see his point of view. We live in a dog-eat-dog world. And sometimes there just aren't enough dogs to go around.

29

I WENT BACK TO THE BOTTLE, mired in the realization that Farrell was so right that he didn't even have to pay me the courtesy of duplicity. He could come right out and rub my nose in it. I had no credibility with the cops. My chances of getting to Bob Stuhl were zero. If I tried, I risked putting myself back in danger. It stuck in my craw to admit it, but there was sweet fuck-all that I could do.

The booze eventually did its job and I crashed out, fully dressed, seething with self-contempt and impotent rage, on top of the bedclothes.

The next voice I heard was not my own. It was Red's. He was ringing from Geordie's place to inform me of his plans for the rest of the day. The gang was going to the movies: *Terminator 2*.

My clock-radio said it was eleven. I dosed myself with caffeine and aspirin, shaved and showered, ironed a shirt and eased myself into my Hugo Boss. At 12:30, wretched but mending, I crept into the restaurant at the National Gallery.

The place was full of Taiwanese tourists bustling about in poly-ester leisurewear. Lyndal and Ayisha were sitting at a table with a view of the sculpture garden, picking at salads. Both were power-dressed. Not the salads, the women. The elegant silk scarf at Ayisha's throat was just bright enough to emphasize her dark Levantine beauty without undercutting her master's degree in public administration. Lyndal was in a plum-colored pants-suit. Her businesslike demeanor reminded me how much I longed for her community welfare services, to fall into her safety net.

I steered my way through the Taipei ramblers and announced my arrival by clearing my throat and straightening my tie. Not the one Red had given me. That was at home, locked in a sound-proof container. I'd chosen my Versace, teal with orange-yellow flecks, in the hope that it might deflect attention from my ravaged eyes.

But there was no fooling Ayisha. "Night on the tiles, Murray?" she said, bouncing her generous eyebrows in a salacious manner.

"I wish," I sighed. "A touch of the flu."

"Poor dear," said Lyndal sweetly. "We can do this later, if you're not up to it. A couple of weeks, say?"

Cute, considering the reason for our meeting was only eight days away. "Angelo would never forgive me," I said, sitting down. "He's paying me very good money to come here and lie to you."

"How much?" said Ayisha eagerly.

She reached for their lunchtime bottle of chardonnay, offering me a glass. I shook my head, not up to it, and turned to signal for a coffee. Failing to get the waiter's attention, I settled for the wine. It couldn't make me feel any worse.

"Let's just say I negotiated a generous redundancy package," I said. "And that for purposes of public consumption, my decision to run came as a complete shock to my employer. Just as your surprise decision, Lyndal, was no doubt prompted by a firm conviction that Melbourne Upper is ready to rally to the feminist standard."

Lyndal speared a cherry tomato. "I wasn't going to sit around forever, waiting for the faction bosses to tap me on the shoulder to tell me, it's your turn now, girlie."

"Particularly since there'll be a party room spill after the election," I said. "And Angelo, one of the old guard, tarred with the brush of failure, will probably be consigned to the backbench.

There's not much kudos in being an opposition backbencher's constituency assistant."

"None at all," agreed Lyndal. "But after we go down in the state election, the national office will start to worry about the next federal poll and begin looking for new blood."

I gave a low, admiring whistle. "A federal seat? You're aiming high."

"And why not? I couldn't do worse than some of the fools already in Canberra. But I'll only get noticed if I make a decent showing in Melbourne Upper. Which I intend to do."

"Coming off a cold start?" I said. "Without factional support? Against an incumbent backed by the machine?"

"The machine's short a cog," interjected Ayisha. "Ange couldn't find Melbourne Upper in the street directory without his electorate officer to tell him the page number. You of all people ought to know that."

"The fact that Lyndal's job is vacant is a plus for Angelo, not a minus," I pointed out. "He can put it up for auction, dangle it in front of twenty different interest groups in exchange for their support. What can you offer?"

"Not enough to buy me the seat, I admit," said Lyndal. "But that's not my objective. All I want is a creditable performance and a decent second-placing. Show some form and I might qualify for a better starting position in a higher stakes race."

Now we were getting down to it. "So what do you reckon you'll get in the first round of votes?" I plucked a figure from the air, testing her confidence level. "Thirty percent?"

"About that," she shrugged nonchalantly. Meaning she was thinking higher. And straw-polling was her professional specialty. So maybe closer to 40 percent. "And you'll get, what, ten percent?"

"Fifteen," I said. My current guesstimate was closer to eight.

She looked at me skeptically. "Okay, so there's your fifteen, plus my thirty, plus the Save Our Trains three. That's forty-eight percent. Angelo gets the other fifty-two. And since a majority of the central panel is already committed to him, he's over the line in the first ballot. Even taking into account shrinkage, slippage, leakage and drift."

God, this was great. Lyndal talked numbers like some women talked dirty.

"First ballot, second ballot, whichever way you slice it," I said. "Angelo's going to win."

Of course these projections were so rubbery they could be dribbled like a basketball and shot through any hoop in sight. The entire system was constructed so that a voter could look at least two candidates in the eye and truthfully swear to have voted for him. Or, less often, her.

Ayisha pounced. "You're saying that Angelo doesn't really need your preferences. So why not sling them to Lyndal. Long as Ange wins, your conscience'll be clear."

"What's my conscience got to do with it?" I said. It was a strange word to hear on the lips of a member of the Labor Party. "I've got a clear-cut deal with Angelo. What can you offer that would induce me to break it?"

"Ayisha," said Lyndal, "would you mind waiting for me outside?"

Ayisha smirked knowingly, drained her glass and stood up. "I'll be in the gift shop," she said.

We waited until she'd gone, eyeing each other with wary amusement. "Your campaign manager's very keen," I said.

"And capable. She'd make a good member of parliament, don't you think?" It sounded like the girls were laying some pipe.

"You too," I said. "If I hadn't already made a commitment to Angelo . . ."

"Yeah, yeah," she laughed. "That's what they all say." She scrutinized my face. Despite my tie, the effects of recent events must have been evident. "Are you okay?"

I cocked my head towards the door. "If you think I look bad, you haven't seen the abstract expressionists."

We went into the gallery proper and strolled among the pictures, side by side. As we warmed ourselves in front of a Rothko, she slipped her arm through mine. "We both know you didn't come here today to propose a preference swap," she said. "So why are you here?"

"I think you know that," I said.

"You want to frot me in a telephone booth?"

"You were tempted. Don't deny it."

"A girl likes to be romanced. Not have her bones jumped when she's half-tanked and keying herself up to quit her job."

"Is that why you agreed to meet? So you could tell me that another try wouldn't be unwelcome?"

"Possibly," she said. "Depends how it's done."

"So I shouldn't shove you against that Jasper Johns and stick my tongue down your throat?"

"Not unless you fancy a swift kick in the Jackson Pollocks."

"So it's dinner at Florentino's, candlelight, champagne?"

"That'd do for a start. Not until after the ballot, of course."

"What if I can't wait that long?"

"Do what you usually do."

"The popcorn girl at the Wangaratta drive-in?"

"Don't push it, buster."

She handed me one of her business cards, the electorate officer stuff crossed out and her phone numbers handwritten on the back, home and mobile. "I hope you're feeling better soon."

"I hope I'm feeling you soon."

"That depends on how you play your cards," she said.

Turning on her heels, she proceeded briskly towards the gift shop. As I watched her go, I noticed a large painting in the contemporary Australian section. It depicted a red-eyed man with his hands sunk into the pockets of his coat. He was standing on a blasted plain beside a burning city while brimstone rained from the sky. A sturdy and independent dog was his only companion.

I knew how he felt.

30

ALL MY CONTACTS, all my skills, were useless. Donny's death cast a pall, but it was one in whose shadow I had no choice but to keep living. Like some poor fucking Bulgarian in a polluted shithole of an industrial town, I trudged each day to the coalface knowing no other way of life. In my case, the mineshaft was a card table and my pick was a telephone. And it was the press that spewed out the degraded crap that sustained the commerce of our city.

Two days after my meeting with Lyndal, the *Sun* led with one of its perennial stories about factional brawling in the Labor Party. Although the editorial line was predictable, certain facts resonated with whispers I'd been hearing on the grapevine. I spent the day on the dog and bone and found nothing but confirmation of the story. The tectonic plates were shifting, ructions were brewing, long-forged alliances were going weak at the welds. Factional deals were coming unglued faster than discount-store furniture.

Mid-afternoon I got a call from Angelo's secretary. "He said same time, same place, usual arrangements," she said. "Whatever that means."

It meant the Gardenview Mews. Angelo prowled the motel room like a caged lion as he grilled me about my progress with Lyndal on the preference swap offer.

"She's taking it under advisement," I told him. "But I'm optimistic. I think my chances are good."

It was what he wanted to hear. I moved the topic to the situation at the center. "Heavy seas," he said, making it sound more like a meteorological phenomenon than a committee of union bosses and party apparatchiks. "Although I think I can ride out the storm."

So much for the shipping news. I left him sitting on the edge of the bed, running up my phone bill. He could call Brazil for all I cared. My easy-money termination pay had finally appeared in the electronic coffers of my bank account.

I walked home and cooked dinner for Red. Grilled steak and baked vegetables. I didn't have much of an appetite but Red was happy to take up the slack. In little more than a week, I told him, my current work arrangements would be at an end. It was time to equip the corporate headquarters of Murray Whelan & Associates.

The next morning, Saturday, we went shopping. My deputy director of Technical Support recommended a 386 with one meg of ram. "State of the art," he assured me. "Fully upgradable."

While we were at it, we bought a printer, a pile of games discs and a book called *DOS for Idiots*. The computer set-up cost me almost three grand. A fax machine set me back another nine hundred dollars. Inevitably, I'd have to get myself a mobile phone, join the wankers. But I wasn't quite ready for that yet. The 99-memory Motorola was priced at twelve hundred dollars. The more memory the better, I figured. Preferably something with a spanner-gripping facility.

But a four-grand outlay in a single shopping expedition was my personal limit so I put the mobile on hold. "I'd need a handbag to carry it around in," I told Red. "Let's wait until they start making them small enough to fit into a man's pocket without it looking like he's got a canoe in his pants."

We took our infrastructure home and set it up in Red's bedroom for convenience. Convenient for him, since he promptly invited Tarquin around to test its game-play capabilities.

I wangled enough access on Sunday to write a brief circular, "What Murray Whelan Can Bring to Melbourne Upper," then spent most of the afternoon pecking it out with two fingers and playing around with fonts. Red, meanwhile, was also enmeshed in paperwork, rushing to finish neglected assignments in time for his return to school. Fortunately, we both finished our chores in time to watch *The Blues Brothers* on television.

Monday morning, after Red went back to school, I took my flyer to Qwik Print, then spent the rest of the day stuffing and addressing 800 envelopes. By the time I'd mailed them and spent a couple of hours calling names on the Melbourne Upper register, the news was out. Predicated on Labor's loss of the next election, a new faction had emerged, an alliance between the hard-left, the medium-right and the double-adaptors. Suddenly all bets were off in the dozens of preselection contests currently in progress.

Tuesday was Donny's funeral. I drove out to the crematorium chapel at Fawkner cemetery and took a pew at the back beside a contingent of his old workmates from the brewery. For the requiem of a murderer-suicide, the numbers were respectable, about forty of us, all up. Some of the faces were familiar from parties of the left, both the boozy and political varieties. There were enough old flames in evidence to do credit to the deceased's memory as a lover.

Jacinta sat in the front row, ashen-faced under a black mantilla. She looked like she hadn't slept a wink since the discovery of the body. She and Donny had been together for little more than a year, so her status as official widow was somewhat tenuous. Meg Taylor, to whom he'd been legally married for most of the seventies, didn't appear eager to contest the title. She was sitting further back, paired with a woman in her mid-twenties that I took to be Ellie, the little daughter she'd taken into the relationship.

Donny's brother Rodney sat across the aisle beside a couple in their seventies who could only have been the parents. The mother was withered and shrunken, her claw-like fingers hooked over a walking stick. The father was more robust. From time to time during the service, he glanced disapprovingly back over his shoulder, as if those assembled were the bad company he'd warned his son against, the ones who'd led him to a sticky end. Heather was sitting beside him and she didn't need to look around for me to know she agreed.

In accordance with the known wishes of the deceased, there was no god-bothering and the bare minimum of ceremony. A civil celebrant conducted the proceedings, possibly an employee of the funeral company. Reading from notes, he summarized Donny's life in tones of anodyne sincerity that conveyed the man's biography but none of his essence. The only allusion to the circumstances of Donny's death lay in the use of the words "tragic" and "untimely."

Donny perished a paid-up member of the union, so the Haulers sent the customary wreath. It was one of a number, including mine, that sat atop the Eureka flag that draped the coffin, half buried in the individual long-stemmed red carnations that we were each handed as we arrived. A pair of drumsticks lay there, too, placed by the bass player from Over the Limit, who tiptoed with awkward reverence up the aisle in his cowboy boots. Roscoe and Len, Donny's putative running mates, turned away shamefaced when I looked their way.

The only surprise, to me at least, was provided by a large-boned, soft-spoken woman in her early thirties who got up after Rodney had done his brotherly recollection bit. Hesitantly, she introduced herself as Donny's daughter, born without his knowledge and adopted by an Adelaide couple. When she recently contacted him, after careful consideration, she said, Donny had expressed surprise and delight to find that he had a long-lost child. The two of them had spoken on the phone several times and planned to meet at Christmas during her annual leave. Although that encounter would now never take place, and she had never actually met her birth-father, she wanted to add her farewells to those of his legitimate family.

For some reason, this brief and barely audible announcement, delivered by a diffident stranger, struck me as providing the most compelling argument yet that Donny had not killed himself.

As the remains rolled slowly through the portals of immolation, the John Lennon version of "Stand By Me" came over the PA.

Somebody was doing their best to lend occasion to the occasion. It succeeded only in sounding cheesy. In the silence that followed, an off-key voice began to sing "Solidarity Forever." We battened onto the familiar anthem with collective gusto but began to falter when we got to the verse about nothing being weaker than the feeble strength of one. After the first chorus we took it no further.

Afterwards, as the crowd dispersed into the overcast afternoon, I approached Jacinta. We shook hands and shared our bereavement in a moment of mutual silence. If Donny had discussed our last conversation with her, she gave no sign of it. When I turned to go, she touched my arm.

"You have my vote," she said.

"Excuse me?"

"For preselection. You have my vote."

"You're a member of the Labor Party?"

"You sound surprised. Did you think I was a mail-order bride? I used to work for the Textile Workers Union. That's how I met Donny, trying to organize a ban on the transport of garments made by out-source workers."

"I didn't know," I said. Hardly a novel phenomenon when it came to the multitudinous facets of Donny's life.

"Twenty of us Filipinas are members of the Reservoir branch," she said. "I'll make sure the others vote for you, too."

I thanked her, somewhat disconcerted that my bullshit activities had raised their head at such a time.

"Donny would've wanted it," she said. "You were a true friend."

Others hovered, waiting their turn. I kissed Jacinta on the cheek and went out into the leaden afternoon, thinking about truth and friendship. And about their obligations.

31

THREE DAYS BEFORE the preselection poll an item arrived in the mail. Bearing only a franking stamp and a printed address label, it gave no external clue as to its sender. Inside was a printed flyer headed "Why Angelo Agnelli Is Unfit to Represent Melbourne Upper."

Because, it stated, he was an oppressor of women. A sexual harasser and serial sleazebag. Instead of putting his hand to the tiller of state, he'd been sticking it up every skirt in sight. Or words to that effect. The overall tone was a melange of lesbian separatism, pop psychology and fundamentalist moralizing. The spelling was appalling. No examples were cited, no names named, no evidence presented. This, the communiqué claimed, was out of respect for the privacy of the women who had been so shamefully used by the "contempteble predater Agnelli."

There is only one alternative, concluded the document. SEND THE CHAUVANIST PACKING — VOTE FOR LYNDAL LUSCOMBE.

For the benefit of readers from non-English-speaking backgrounds, these charges were repeated on the obverse in all the main food groups — Greek, Italian, Turkish and Arabic.

Since I'd been sent one, it was reasonable to assume that everyone else on the Melbourne Upper party roll had also received a copy. I took Lyndal's card from my wallet and started dialing. It took some trying, but eventually I got through. She was not a happy camper. In between taking calls she'd tried to call me, unable to raise an answer because the phone was unplugged.

"It wasn't me," she said.

"I didn't think so," I assured her. "Your spelling's better than that."

"This isn't funny, Murray. It's a dirty trick. Whoever did this has really screwed my credibility. Makes me look like a complete bitch."

"Doesn't exactly make Angelo look great," I said.

"An anonymous shit-sheet? Malicious, unsubstantiated allegations, barely literate. He doesn't even need to dignify it with a reply. Meanwhile, I look like I'm peddling half-baked slander. This sort of thing is a male nightmare. Not only will it cost me support in Melbourne Upper, it'll frighten the horses in Canberra. God, I wish I knew who was responsible. I'd strangle them with my bare hands."

"Issue a statement refuting it," I said. "Disavow all knowledge, say that you've been set up, your name used without your permission or approval."

"And add fuel to the fire? It'll look like I'm having a two-way bet, running with the hares and hunting with the hounds."

"If you don't want to put out a statement, then I will," I proposed. "I can deplore it as both an attempt to blacken Angelo and a bid to discredit you. Try to minimize the damage all round."

"And make yourself look terrific in the process."

"That's unfair," I said.

"Probably. Right now I think my only option might be to withdraw from the ballot. Demonstrate my good faith with an act of self-sacrifice, try to cut my potential losses with the boys in the national back room."

"Might be a better idea to find out who's responsible first," I suggested. "See if you can expose the source."

"Spend the last couple of days of the race running around interrogating people, come across as a complete paranoid? No thanks. Face it, Murray, there's only one person who really stands to benefit. And I never dreamed he'd stoop to something like this."

I wasn't going to ask who she meant. I might not have liked her answer. Leaving her pondering her options, I called Angelo. He took some tracking down, but I ran him to ground at party headquarters.

"Of course I've seen it," he said. "And naturally I don't like it, leaves a bad taste in the mouth and there's always a risk that a little bit of the shit might stick. But for a man like me, a public figure, this sort of thing is an occupational hazard. And, on the up side, our Ms. Luscombe has really shot herself in the foot this time."

"You don't actually think she's responsible, do you?"

"Probably one of her rabid femo-nazi supporters," he said. "Whoever did it, it's a potential windfall for us. If I react, I'll look defensive. But you can capitalize on the opportunity. Put out a statement. Independent non-aligned candidate deplores the use of underhanded tactics. Parliamentary aspirants should be able to keep their more extreme supporters in line. Unwarranted attack on a man of unimpeachable character. So on and so forth. Criticize the policies, not the man. Perhaps not that bit. I'll leave the exact wording to you. I've got my hands full maintaining my outright majority on the public office selection committee, so I need a thundering endorsement from the branches. We've got to wipe the floor with this woman. Get cracking and I'll see you on Friday, usual time and place."

Mumbling something about him being the boss, I hung up and made myself a sandwich. Angelo was entitled to his money's worth; however, a declaration like that wouldn't do anything for my stocks with Lyndal. Better to drag my feet, see which way the cards fell. I thought about who might have been behind the letter. The potential beneficiaries, as Lyndal so pointedly pointed out, were limited. Just how desperate was Angelo getting?

I got my answer late the next morning as I was making out a grocery list. It came via a phone call from the deputy secretary of the United Haulage Workers, the ferret-faced Mike McGrath.

"Heard the news?" he said. "Lyndal Luscombe has tapped the mat. Withdrew her nomination half an hour ago. Decided that shit-letter wouldn't look very good on her resume."

"You were behind it?" I said. "You arsehole. Why do something like that, just for the sake of a bit of gratuitous slander? Just can't help yourselves, can you?"

"Don't be like that," he said. "Your time has come, my friend. I'm calling with a proposition."

"What proposition?"

"Bag Agnelli. Attack his competence as transport minister. Come out with a public statement as his former long-time advisor, say he isn't up to the job."

"Why would I do that?"

"Because we want him out of the portfolio. There's still a year to run before the end of the government's term, don't forget."

"That's your motive, McGrath," I said. "What's mine?"

"Bit slow on the uptake this morning, Murray. A safe seat in parliament, that's what. If you can pick up enough of the lovely Lus-combe's stray sheep to get even twenty-five percent of the branch vote, I can deliver the support of our allies on the central panel. The nomination will be yours. How's that for motivation?"

"Let me get this right," I said. "All I have to do is shaft Angelo, change my allegiances, conceal my secret backers and get into bed with you."

"Don't be prissy. Haven't you heard, flexibility's the name of the game at the moment. I'm offering you the chance of a lifetime."

He was right. I thought about it. Long and hard. For about five seconds. "Get fucked, McGrath," I said.

"You're a bigger fool than I thought, Whelan."

"Yes, but I'm my own fool, not yours."

"You'll come crawling," he said.

"Go fuck your mother, McGrath." I hung up, added mouth-wash to my shopping list, and dialed Lyndal's mobile number. She answered in a coffee shop, judging by the background noise. Either that or a steam laundry.

"It's Murray," I said. "I found out who sent the letter. McGrath at the Haulers. It's all part of their destabilize-Agnelli strategy."

"Makes sense," said Lyndal. "I suspected I'd been caught in somebody's crossfire. I appreciate your efforts, Murray, I really do, but I've bailed. My best bet was to get out while the going was good. Sorry, I can't talk now, I'm breaking the news to a coven of my supporters, but give me a call next week. We'll talk about it over dinner and whatnot."

I liked the idea of the whatnot. "I'll call you Monday."

"Make it Tuesday. I don't want you to think I'm easy."

As distinct from hard. That would be my part. If I passed the audition. I felt my credentials firming, so I hung up and reviewed my immediate priorities.

Where does a man go who has just passed up an offer of a safe seat in parliament? On the balance of probabilities, all things considered, I figured that my best bet was Safeway in Carlton. Free undercover parking with every purchase over five dollars. The amount of food Red was going through, I'd spend that much, easy. And the way the rain was pissing down, undercover parking was an inducement too good to refuse.

I was turning the Honda into Brunswick Street, wipers slapping, the condensation on the inside of the windshield thinning in the warm-air blast of the demister, when suddenly the word "Foodbank" materialized. It was stenciled onto the tailgate of the Bedford truck in front of me.

As we inched along, the traffic thicker than a National Party voter, I recalled that Foodbank was a charity that collected perishable foodstuffs for distribution to worthy causes. I remembered, too, where I had learned that fact.

In an instant I was transported back to the wholesale fruit and vegetable market, to the interior of Donny's Kenworth. Okay, so my zucchini wasn't tangled in the panty elastic between Heather Maitland's alabaster thighs. But I could clearly recall the occluded view through the smeared mist of the rear window. I could see the Foodbank truck parked beside us. Like a film projected onto my windshield, a scene unfolded before me.

Head down, I was sprinting through the rain towards Donny's truck. As I rounded the tailgate of the Foodbank Bedford, I slammed head-on into Frank Farrell. The impact of our collision knocked his mobile to the ground.

Then Farrell was scooping up his phone, casting an appreciative eye over the spanner in my hand and continuing on his way. A few moments later, I glimpsed him again as he ambled into the market, jeans tight around his backside, hands thrust into his jacket. His gray leather jacket with its cinched waist and narrow slit pockets. Pockets suitable for a pair of sunglasses, but far too small to contain a bulky mobile phone.

So where was it? One moment it was in his hand, the next it was gone. No more than fifteen seconds had elapsed since our collision. At some point during that time, he must have ditched it. But why toss away a thousand dollars' worth of communications equipment? And where?

When the Foodbank truck took a left at the lights, I stayed behind it.

32

THE TRAFFIC WAS CRAWLING. My mind was racing.

Spider Webb described the murder weapon as a blunt object, of which there were plenty "readily to hand." And if you happen to be holding one, what could be more readily to hand than a mobile phone?

When I'd called Farrell at the Haulers, ten days after Darren's death, I was given a number for his mobile. The new number. If he had a *new* number, surely that meant he had a new phone. So what happened to the old one? Was it possible that Farrell had tossed it into the load on a parked truck? Might Foodbank have driven away from the market that morning with more on board than just a consignment of on-the-turn vegetables?

We turned into Victoria Parade, four lanes wide. The traffic thinned and the Bedford picked up speed. I stayed with it, tracking it past the edge of the central business district. I hunched over the steering wheel, my eyes glued to the words on the tailgate in front of me. A desperate hope had begun to take root in my mind.

The only eyewitness to Darren Stuhl's killing was dead. But if Farrell's phone could be found, and if it could be shown to be the murder weapon, then the police would be forced to reconsider the case. Once that happened, Farrell's whole fabric of deceit would begin to unravel. It was even conceivable that Bob Stuhl's role in Donny's alleged suicide might come to light.

Whoa, I told myself. You're drawing a very long bow here, Murray. As an object to clutch, the idea didn't even amount to a soggy straw.

By the time we reached the workshops and warehouses of North Melbourne, reality had begun to shine its cold light on my fantasies. For all I knew, the Foodbank truck was bound for Perth or Darwin or Dar-es-Salaam. Even if I followed it to the ends of the earth, what were my chances of finding Farrell's mobile phone when I got there?

I broke off the chase, dropped back and flipped on my indicator, angling for a break in the traffic. At that moment, the Bedford turned down a side street and vanished into a warehouse between a radiator replacement joint and an air-freight dispatch center. The sign above the entrance read FOODBANK CENTRAL DEPOT.

Doubling back, I pulled into the curb in front of the building. Through the slap of the windshield wipers, I watched a station wagon emerge, slow to check for oncoming traffic, then drive away. The driver was a man in a Salvation Army uniform. He was a big bloke, one of gentle Jesus's burlier devotees. He probably believed in miracles. I didn't, but I got out of the Honda anyway.

Foodbank was a drive-through operation, a medium-sized warehouse with a roller door at each end. Down the center ran a row of metal racks containing trays of bread and baked goods. Styrofoam cases of fruit and vegetables were stacked against the walls. A coolroom opened to one side, curtained with heavy strips of clear plastic. A woman in a tracksuit was helping herself to the fruit, loading her choices into a transit van with the words "Street Kids Mission" on the door. Three men in dustcoats were carrying crates of fruit juice from the back of the truck into the coolroom, working efficiently but with no great sense of urgency.

They had about them the fate-buffeted air of individuals who might once have been on the receiving end of the charity they now helped to dispense, who lifted and toted but harbored no illusions about the redemptive value of physical labor. I thought I recognized one of them from the market parking lot, a scrawny old lag, one of the first arrivals at the scene of Darren's pulping.

If Farrell had tossed his phone into the Foodbank truck, then it was possible that this man had found it. It was also possible that the police had already covered this territory as part of their general inquiries. Since I was there, I decided to find out.

The man paused in his work as I approached, leaned against the Bedford's mudguard and pulled out a tobacco pouch. "Help you?" he said, a cigarette paper stuck to his bottom lip.

I opted for the direct approach. "You were at the wholesale market the morning that bloke got killed, weren't you?"

He tilted his head to one side, fingers working at the makings. "You a reporter? Bit slow off the mark, aren't you, mate?"

I took the opening. "I'm doing a bit of follow-up. Progress of the investigation, that sort of thing. Tracking down some of the people who spoke with the cops."

He parked a thin rollie in the corner of his mouth. "Who says I talked to the police?"

I tapped the side of my nose. "Can't disclose my sources, mate."

"Well you'd better get more reliable ones," he said, an aggressive edge creeping into his voice. "I didn't say nothing to the cops. And that's because I didn't see nothing. End of story."

The shutters were coming down fast. I shrugged helplessly. "Looks like I've had a wasted trip, then."

"Looks like it."

Time for a different approach. I nodded apologetically and made as if to leave, then turned back. "While I'm here, I might as well make a contribution." I took out my wallet and offered him a twenty-dollar bill.

He picked a shred of tobacco off his bottom lip and shot a glance over his shoulder. "Can't give you a receipt, mate. We're not set up for cash donations."

"Don't worry about the paperwork." I folded the bill and slipped it into the breast pocket of his dustcoat. "I'm on expenses."

He lit his cigarette and inhaled hard, waiting.

"You didn't happen to find anything unusual in your load that morning, did you?" I said.

He sucked his cancer stick and meditated upon the matter. "Found a python once, in a load of bananas. And a rusty hand grenade in a bag of spuds." He rubbed his stubbled chin. "Can't say I found anything that morning."

That was it, then. I had my answer. "Thanks anyway, mate." I shrugged and started to go, for real this time.

"But then I didn't do the unloading that morning," he added, almost as an afterthought. "We had a couple of young blokes at the time, some sort of youth training program. Anything turned up worth keeping, they'd've kept it. Anything else would've got chucked in the lost and found." He twitched his cigarette towards a large cardboard carton at the end of the vegetable bins.

I nodded thanks, went over to the box and fished among the accumulated odds and sods. These consisted of a dirty check apron with the strings missing, an ancient football jersey with the sleeves torn off and a baseball cap that appeared to have been fed through a hay-baling machine. Some heavier items had settled on the bottom. I tipped the box over and dumped its contents onto the concrete floor. Out tumbled a lidless lunchbox, a fractured thermos flask, a John Deere tractor badge and a black mobile phone.

33

MY MOUTH WENT DRY and my pulse went through the roof. I squeezed my eyes closed and counted to ten. When I opened them the phone was still there.

Before it melted into thin air, I crouched down on my haunches and prodded it with a pen. Its casing was intact, the display panel cracked and the antenna bent. When and where this happened was impossible to tell. It seemed reasonable to assume that it was kaput when it arrived at Foodbank or it would have been snaffled by the youthful trainees.

There was no doubt in my mind that this was Frank Farrell's phone. And that it had been used to deck the despicable Darren. Problem was, would anyone else believe it?

To my dismay, no convenient clumps of reddish hair adhered to the casing. No clots of blood were visible in the crevices of the keypad. But Donny had talked about a bloody big gash and Farrell had disposed of the object in haste, so there must have been at least some prospect that evidence remained of its lethal use. I was no expert, but I'd watched enough police shows on television to know that every contact leaves its traces.

If my discovery was to lead anywhere, I would have to find those traces. Only after that would there be any chance that the police would take me seriously. And since I had no forensic facilities at my disposal, my only hope was to trust to luck and try to wing it.

Taking care not to touch it, I bundled my find into plastic wrapping from a package of date-expired Danish pastries and carried it briskly out of the building. My dustcoated informant made a conspicuous show of not noticing me leave. Our conversation, I understood, had never taken place.

Once back in the car, I resumed my trip to the supermarket. As well as toothpaste, tinned tuna and enough cereal to feed a team of draught horses, I purchased a pair of tight-fitting rubber dishwashing gloves. At the office-supplies store on Elgin Street I bought a magnifying glass.

Back home, I restocked the refrigerator and the pantry, moved my reading light to the kitchen table, snapped on the rubbers and set to work.

Gingerly tweezering the phone between thumb and forefinger, I examined it closely with the magnifying glass. No fingerprints were visible. But a fine seam, I discovered, ran along the plastic molding above the earpiece. This was the most likely point of impact if the phone had been used to strike a blow. Running the tip of a safety pin along the crack, I extracted a minute quantity of dark-brown crud.

Which told me exactly nothing.

I transferred the gunk to the rim of a saucer and turned my attention to the keypad. There were twelve number keys, eight function keys, * and #. From the gaps around these I extracted more tiny samples of muck. What I needed was an electron spectrographic crudometer.

Or the nearest equivalent. I went into Red's room and dusted off the microscope that had been languishing on top of his wardrobe since a week after his tenth birthday. It wasn't the most sophisticated piece of scientific equipment in the world, yet it was more than just a toy. I set it up on the kitchen table and adjusted the mirror until the lens revealed a luminous white circle. Then I sorted through the glass slides and eliminated those labeled Angora Rabbit Hair, Butterfly Scale and Fowl Feather.

Science had never been my strongest suit at school but I'd studied biology until my final year. If any of the stuff I was dredging from the nooks and crannies of the phone was blood, I'd need a sample with which to compare it. I pricked the tip of my middle finger with the safety pin and smeared a drop of blood on a clean slide. I laid another on top and took a squiz. What I saw looked pink and bubbly, like the froth on a strawberry milkshake.

Laying aside the control slide, I proceeded to scrutinize the various bits of detritus I'd dredged from the phone's clefts and crevices, first mixing them to a slurry with a droplet of water. I got the Mekong Delta, mosquito diarrhea and the hide pattern of a Friesian cow. Nothing remotely resembled my specimen of blood.

This was getting me nowhere. I turned the phone over and tried the other side. Releasing the latch button, I removed the battery. A layer of soft residue caked the seam. I smeared some of it on a slide and squinted through the lens. What I saw was caramel rather than strawberry but its bubbly cellular structure was almost identical to my self-sourced sample.

If that's not blood, I thought, I'm Louis Pasteur.

The more I squinted through the eyepiece, the more convinced I became that I had uncovered an item of evidence capable of nailing Frank Farrell for Darren Stuhl's homicide. And thus of putting paid to the canard of Donny Maitland's suicide. Possibly even triggering an investigation that might even reveal Bob Stuhl's role in Donny's death.

Unless, on the other hand, it wasn't Darren's blood. Or Farrell's phone. These were matters that could only be determined by the police. Proper scientific scrutiny might also find fragments of Farrell's fingerprints and further bits and pieces Darren's biology. His hypochondrial DNA or whatever it was called.

But Inspector Voigt would not respond well, I imagined, to the suggestion that an amateur sleuth had discovered more in three hours than his crack team of Spider Webbs had brought to light in a month of flatfooted fossicking. Persuading the coppers would be a substantial job. It would take a substantial man.

I put Red's gunkoscope away, then went into my bedroom and began looking among my papers for One-Stop O'Shannessy's number. The phone rang. It was Ayisha Celik.

"News from the battlefront," she lilted. "With Lyndal out of contention, you are now the thinking woman's candidate of choice. Not that there's much choice. So if you want to reconsider your deal with Angelo, I reckon I can swing a fair few of Lyndal's votes your way."

"Angelo's a done deal," I said. "The money's in the bank."

Ayisha was undeterred. In an attempt to swing me across, she launched into an exhaustive analysis of the current factional fluctuations, with particular reference to the role of the rank and file.

"It's Thursday," I reminded her when I finally got a word in. "Two days before the vote. Even if I reneged on him, Angelo would still have it in the bag. But thanks for the offer."

As soon as I hung up, the phone rang again. It was Agnelli's secretary, Trish, calling to confirm our regular Friday meeting at the Gardenview Mews. I didn't see much point, considering that Angelo's only genuine competition was now out of the race. Still, it was typical of Angelo to want his full pound of flesh. Only when the poll was declared on Monday would I be truly free of him. "Tell him I'll be there," I said wearily. "Same time as usual."

I hung up and dialed One-Stop's number. It was busy so I headed down the hall to my kitchen table crim-lab, wondering if I had a zip-lock bag large enough to hold the mobile. It occurred to me that Red would be home from school any minute.

Too late. He already was. And the moment I saw him, a chill ran up my spine.

Red was crouched over the kitchen table, his baseball cap reversed, spraying Farrell's phone with window cleaner and rubbing it furiously with a tissue. I rushed forward and snatched it from his grasp.

"I've cleaned off all the crap," he said brightly. "But the battery needs recharging. If you want my opinion, you haven't got a hope in hell of making this thing work."

I thrust the phone into the beam of the reading light and stared at it. Farrell's Motorola was spotless. Not an iota remained of Darren's protoplasm.

"Why are you wearing rubber gloves, Dad?" asked Mister Helpful.

"So I can strangle you," I cried, lunging for his throat.

34

RED SCOOTED AWAY, warily eyeing the flecks of white foam that had appeared on his father's lips. "It's not my fault," he pleaded. "Whatever it is."

I counted to ten. He was right. If a lad comes home from school and finds an item of gadgetry semi-disassembled on the kitchen table, the impulse to tinker is bound to be irresistible. "Sorry," I groveled. "I'm a bit premenstrual."

Red got out from behind the couch. "It's the testosterone, Dad. You've really got to find an outlet for your male needs."

I fed him a line about the phone being on loan from a friend, how I'd accidentally dropped it down a drain. Then I stashed it in my laundry basket, slunk down to Brunswick Street and sulked in a coffee shop, smoking cigarette after filthy cigarette. My thoughts tangled in the smoke. For a fleeting moment I'd held in my hand the Achilles heel capable of unlocking the tangled ball of wax that had led to Donny's murder. The missing link that would unravel the house of cards and blow the lid off the hidden hand of Bob Stuhl. But the possibilities that fate had dangled before me had been cruelly snatched away by the fruit of my own loins. Chagrin gnawed at my vitals.

Jesus, was I pissed off.

Nevertheless, the serendipitous discovery of Farrell's phone had raised hopes that could no longer be suppressed. The worm had turned and it was rearing up on its hind legs. If I couldn't use the fucking thing in the way I had intended, perhaps it might yet serve a useful purpose. But what?

I remembered One-Stop O'Shannessy's advice after my little chinwag with the cops at Citywest. No witness, no evidence, no admission, no case, he'd said.

The witness was dead, the evidence was disinfected, so all that remained was the possibility of an admission. Farrell had candidly admitted to killing Darren in our phone conversation on the night that I learned of Donny's death. Perhaps he could be induced to repeat the performance.

But Frankie-boy hadn't been trading idle banter that night. His candor served a purpose. It cowed me into silence. If I wanted him to discuss the subject again, I'd need to provide some pretext. Some bait.

The phone was cactus as evidence, but Farrell didn't know that. Until the fix firmed on Donny, he must have been shitting himself that it would turn up. Well, now it had. Better late than never. I decided to call him. We'd bat the breeze about dear departed Darren. And I'd keep some record of the occasion for posterity. For the police. And for the moment when I told him I'd found his phone.

Now I was thinking fast. Farrell would wonder about my motive in drawing his attention to my discovery. What if I offered to trade the phone for something? Something a dickless pen-pusher like me would really be hot for, that would convince him I'd come to terms with what he'd done. Something suggesting a form of petty revenge to stroke my pomposity. Something plausible.

By the time I ran out of cigarettes, all this had begun to formulate itself into the inkling of a scheme. I paid the black-garbed waiter for my coffees and walked home to mend my fences with Red. The rain had cleared, the pavements were drying and the only clouds that remained in the sky were smeared in glorious technicolor across the western horizon. Shot with the beams of the lowering sun, they glowed yellow, purple and orange like crumbs from some gargantuan marble-cake. The boy will be wanting his dinner soon, I thought.

I found him with a mouthful of clarinet, his weapon of choice in the junior school band. While I made tuna casserole and encouraging remarks, he practiced the first three bars of the Pink Panther theme. Over and over again. "Enough with the dead ants," I screamed after half an hour. "Or I'll go back into strangulation mode."

"Shut up," he retorted. "Or you'll damage my self-esteem."

My bedroom ceiling copped a lot of staring that night. But when sleep finally came my scheme had firmed to a plan.

After Red left for school the next morning, I called the Haulers' office to check that Farrell was in town. No show without Punch. He was at the Mobil refinery, I was told, on a picket line of striking tanker drivers. He'd probably be there all day. But if the matter was pressing he could be contacted on his mobile.

"I think I've got his number," I said.

At ten o'clock, I strolled up the slope to the Carlton shops. It was a good day for it, fine and clear with a forecast high of sixty-four degrees. Young mothers in skin-tight jeans and tattoos emerged from the Housing Commission flats to smoke cigarettes and push their offspring around in strollers. Blossoms were turning to mush on the gutters. Spring had truly sprung. There was no turning back.

My first stop was the office-supplies store in Elgin Street where I'd picked up the magnifying glass. This time, I bought a palm-sized microcassette recorder, batteries and a box of tapes. I only needed one tape, but they didn't sell them singly. I consoled myself with the thought that even if things didn't work out as I planned, the purchase was tax deductible for a man in the consultancy racket.

I stuffed the surplus tapes into my pocket, put the batteries in the recorder and walked back down to Rathdowne Street. As I went, I dictated to myself, getting the hang of the gizmo. Just after eleven, I arrived at the Gardenview Mews. The desk clerk, a thick-set young man with work-out shoulders and the cocky deference of a recent hospitality studies graduate, recognized me from my previous two check-ins.

"We have your reservation, Mr. Whelan," he said. "But you're a little earlier than usual. I'm afraid you'll have to wait for a room to be made up."

This meant that the place was fully occupied. Which was just the way I wanted it. I asked for the room I'd first had, if possible. The one at the end of the ground-floor walkway, right next to the ice machine. "Sentimental reasons," I explained.

The clerk consulted his keyboard. "No worries, sir," he confirmed. "Room twenty-three. It'll be yours in a jiffy."

During the jiffy I went into the parking quadrangle, soaked up some rays and admired the way the wisteria drooped from the cast-iron lacework around the balconies. Guests arrived and departed. Cars came and went. A tired-looking housemaid dragged her trolley along the walkway, unlocked Room 23 and set to work. At a rough count, her arrival was visible from the doors of at least thirty other rooms. Excellent.

I was thinking about the set-up for the swap-meet. No clever-clever stuff this time, I'd decided. No Ferris wheels. No guns. Just a well planned, cautious exchange. That's what Farrell would expect and that's what I'd give him. And while we were swapping, we'd chat.

Taking the tape recorder from my pocket, I pushed the record button and laid the device on top of the ice machine. It didn't stand out a mile. It didn't stand out at all. "One, two, three," I said, stepping out the paces to the open door of Room 23. "The time has come, the walrus said, to speak of many things."

The housemaid looked up from her bed-making. "Can I help you, sir?"

"Just thinking out loud," I said. "Thank you very much."

I pocketed the tape recorder and walked up the steps to the balcony rooms. At the first landing, I replayed the tape. It wasn't going to win an Emmy, but every word came back at me crisp and clear. When I got back downstairs, the housemaid had trundled away. I collected my key, walked home through the gardens, made myself a cheese and pickle sandwich and rehearsed what I'd say to Farrell.

I imagined the picket at the gate of the Mobil refinery. Twenty or thirty shuffling tanker drivers. Hand-lettered signs flapping on the mesh fence. Shoulders hunched into windbreakers. A fire burning in a forty-four-gallon drum. A radio turned up loud. Thermos flasks and cut lunches. Boredom the main enemy. Frank Farrell prowling the perimeter, on stand-by in case of rough stuff. Or maybe sitting in a folding chair, awaiting developments, his phone in his lap.

Just after 2:30, I crossed my fingers and made the call.

"The mobile telephone you are calling is switched off," announced a Telecom robot. "Please try again later."

Shit. I was ready to rock'n'roll. Farrell was being inconsiderate, fucking with my schedule. I mopped the kitchen floor, watched it dry, then tried again. Same message. I vacuumed the living room, then went into the backyard and smoked a cigarette. Somehow I was back up to twenty a day. Not in the house, of course. I tried Farrell's number again and got a busy signal. Progress. I started working the redial function.

Twenty minutes later I got the ringing tone. Then Farrell barked his name.

"It's Murray Whelan," I said. "How are things at the barricades?"

"All quiet on the western front," he said. "What is it this time, Whelan?"

"The same matter as we last discussed, Frank. Seems you mislaid your mobile phone that morning. After you decked Darren with it, I mean. Anyway, I thought you'd like to know that I've managed to lay my hands on it."

"You're breaking up," he said. The signal was crystal clear. "Give me your number, I'll call you back on a land line."

I recited my number and hung up. So far, so good. Since he was taking precautions against eavesdropping, I'd definitely found his frequency. I went into the backyard and stared up at the wild blue yonder. That was where I was headed, flying solo. Flapping my arms and hoping I didn't fall. Flap, flap. Ring, ring.

I went back inside and picked up, hoping nobody else had chosen this exact moment to call. Farrell's breathing was labored and traffic roared in the background. Now I could see him in a payphone beside an arterial road, rigs whizzing past, phone pressed to his ear.

"What are you crapping on about, Whelan?" he said. "I didn't mislay any mobile phone."

"Suit yourself," I said. "My mistake. Sorry to disturb you."

I hung up and started counting. I got to nine. This time, Farrell's voice had a steely edge. "This phone you reckon you've got," he said. "Where'd you get it?"

"I saw you throw it away," I said. "Lucky for you it took me so long to put the pieces together. You took a big risk tossing it away like that. Darren's blood in its tiny crevices. A quick wipe with a hankie just doesn't do the job in the face of modern forensics, Frank. You must've been feeling pretty confident, I guess."

A long silence came down the line. It did not sound like a denial. I swung into the pitch. "Naturally my first impulse was to go to the police," I said. "Good citizenship and all that. My credibility might be shaky on the hearsay front but physical evidence cuts a lot of ice. Particularly if it happens to be the murder weapon. But dealing with the cops can be very time-consuming. And as you know, they're not always as fast off the mark as they should be. On top of which, once the wallopers get in on the act, who knows what other sleeping dog might get woken up, eh? So I've decided to offer you first option."

Farrell didn't say anything. I gave him all the time he needed not to say it. "Go on," he grunted, eventually.

"I've taken on board what you told me last time we spoke," I said. "What's done is done. Let the dead bury the dead. I've come around to your point of view, Frank. I don't like what you did, but I don't think that should stop us doing business."

"What sort of business?"

"A trade," I said. "It so happens that I'm in urgent need of a job at the moment. And you're just the man to help me get one."

"You want me to find you a job?"

"In a manner of speaking, Frank. Like you once told me, something can always be found for a friend. This is what I'm thinking. If I was able to provide Angelo Agnelli with some sort of ammunition to use against the Haulers, he'd be very well disposed to finding me a cushy position on the government payroll. Maybe even an overseas posting. You supply that ammunition and I'll give you back your mobile. It's a win-win situation, Frank. So what do you say? You want your mobile back, or should I take it to the cops?"

"What do you mean by ammunition?" he said.

"Nothing more than a piece of paper," I said. "If you want in, go to the Haulers' office. I'll call you there in half an hour. If you don't answer straight away, I'll assume you're not interested. Getting you sent up for killing Darren will take time. And there'll be nothing in it for me from a personal point of view. But I don't have anything better to do at the moment. Not having a job and all."

Farrell did a little contemplative breathing. "Yeah, all right," he said. "I'll be there."

"By the way," I added, "I've got the trade item in a safe place. So don't get any clever ideas about dropping around to pick it up."

I hung up. Farrell was cagey, but he was sniffing the bait. I thought I'd hit just the right note of venality. My lunch-hour gruyere sandwich didn't agree. It was trying to work its way back up my gullet. There were ants in my pants. Not dead ones, either.

Fifteen minutes later, Red lolloped through the back door, home from school with a bunch of the guys in tow around 4 P.M. I drew him aside, told him I had a commitment for the next few hours and suggested he try to wangle an invitation to dinner at Tarquin's place.

"Hot date?" he said.

I most sincerely hoped not.

35

I'D BUDGETED TO MEET FARRELL before my six o'clock confab with Angelo. Thanks to the delay in getting through to him, we'd now have to meet afterwards. This meant keeping him in cold storage for a couple of hours.

Joggers thundered past me in damp T-shirts as I headed back to the Gardenview Mews. I was wearing a lightweight spray jacket over a polo shirt and jeans. Farrell's mobile was under my arm in a family-size zip-lock freezer bag. I walked through the archway, nodded hello to a bloke in a well-cut suit getting into a rental car in the motor court, checked that the ice machine wasn't vibrating and let myself into Room 23.

I put the mobile and the tape recorder on the dresser, hung my spray jacket over the back of a chair and took a miniature of scotch out of the minibar. I thinned it with tap-water and sipped very slowly, getting my full six dollars' worth. And keeping Frank Farrell waiting a half-hour longer than the specified time. At 5:30, I called the United Haulage Workers.

A machine started to tell me the office was closed, then Farrell cut in. "Is that you, Whelan?"

"Personing the desk yourself?" I said.

"What do you expect, this hour on a Friday?" he said. "They've all gone home. So what's this piece of paper you want?"

"Go to the stationery cupboard," I said. "Get yourself some union letterhead. Write me a statement that you witnessed Howard Sharpe and Mike McGrath concocting a false and slanderous letter accusing the Minister for Transport of sexual misconduct."

Farrell snorted derisively. "Fuck off," he said. "Agnelli starts flashing something like that around, I'll be run out of here on a rail."

"Would you prefer to be taking suicide-note dictation from Bob Stuhl's death squad?"

Farrell made a noise like oatmeal going cold. "Like that is it, eh? You want to have your bit of flesh as well. Make you feel better, does it?"

"I'm helping you get away with murder, Frank," I reminded him. "Your job at the Haulers is a small price to pay. A man of your talents can always find work. If he's not in jail, that is. Or dead."

"Okay, you'll get your ammunition," he said. "When do I get the other thing?"

"Start writing," I said. "Keep it simple. Nothing too fancy. I'll leave the wording up to you. I'll call back shortly and tell you where to bring it."

I hung up, cracked another miniature, lay back on the bed, stared at my shoes and thought about Donny Maitland.

I thought about the time we'd stood in a crowded kitchen at a loud party. We were drinking flagon claret and arguing about whether Ho Chi Minh was a communist or a nationalist. To the best of my recollection, the only conclusion was a terrible hangover. I remembered, too, that I still had his copy of *The Unbearable Lightness of Being*. And how he'd brushed me aside in his haste to rescue Red from the burning site office. How it was exactly three weeks since our last conversation. And how his last words to me were an apology.

This rigmarole with Frank Farrell, I reminded myself, was just the first step. Maybe I was tilting at windmills, but one day Bob Stuhl would pay for what he'd done to Donny. At five to six, I swung my feet onto the floor and dialed the Haulers' number. "Written it?" I said.

"I've done what you told me," he said. "What now?"

"Be in the lounge bar of the Southern Cross Hotel at seven o'clock," I said. "Bring the statement. You can read it to me there. And you won't need your phone or any other weapon. Come alone."

I hung up, wrapped Farrell's mobile and the tape recorder in my jacket and put it on the luggage rack. Then I opened the door and stood in my shirtsleeves on the walkway and waited for Angelo to arrive. Dusk was beginning to fall and the floodlights had been turned on in the quadrangle. Doors were opening and shutting on the balconies. An elderly couple with Queensland accents bickered their way cheerfully down the stairs and into a station wagon. He hadn't, he told her, driven all this bloody way to eat bloody Eye-talian.

A couple of minutes later, Angelo strode through the archway. For a man whose nomination was now assured, he looked less than entirely gruntled.

"How's Lothario this evening?" I asked.

"That bloody sexual predator letter," he scowled, slinking disconsolately into the room. "The press have got hold of it. Under normal circumstances, it wouldn't merit a second glance. But now that there's blood in the water, they're trying to dig up dirt on everybody in sight, discredit the entire government. Some hack from the *Sun*'s been trying to corner me all day. I only just managed to give him the slip."

"Stop bleating." I followed him inside and shut the door. "And quit pacing about. You're giving me claustrophobia. Sit down and shut up."

He did as he was told, shedding his suit jacket and sinking into the sofa. I took a half-bottle of champagne from the minibar and filled two plastic tumblers. "To your imminent renomination, Comrade Shoo-in," I toasted. "And the end of our long association."

Ange raised his glass. "You don't know how much help you've been to me, Murray," he said, adopting his most sincere expression.

For an awful moment I thought he was going to get sentimental. "And I hope you never find out."

We bumped our plastic cups together and sipped. By this small gesture, it was mutually acknowledged that my obligations to Angelo were now fully acquitted. My hand-holding days were over.

"Remember the time you invested the party election funds in that dodgy company?" I said. "Every last cent. On the day before it went bankrupt."

Ange unbuttoned his waistcoat, loosened his tie and levered his shoes off. "You were nothing when I found you," he said. "I made you what you are today."

"Unemployed?" I said.

"And I think I can truthfully claim," continued Ange, "that I've taken you as far as you can take me."

In other circumstances my departure from Angelo's employment might have been marked by a small gathering in the office and a farewell card signed by my co-workers. Instead, the two of us lolled in a motel room and exchanged low-level insults over a dribble of South Australian brut and an overpriced bag of chips. Before long, Ange's eyes were drifting towards the phone on the bedside table.

"Just a couple of quick calls," he said. "Won't be long. No need for you to stick around."

Angelo's idea of a couple of quick calls meant factoring at least another half-hour into the time I'd need to keep Farrell dangling. I gave a resigned shrug and left him to it, engaged in conspiracies about which I no longer gave a twopenny toss. Before I left, I pocketed the room key. I took my bundled-up spray jacket with me, donning it on the walkway outside the door. Farrell's mobile and the tape recorder fitted easily into its large pockets.

It had just gone 6:30. A cobbled lane ran behind the motel and I followed it towards Lygon Street, my footsteps echoing up the narrow alley. If Farrell was obeying my instructions, he was somewhere between the Haulers' office in South Melbourne and the Southern Cross Hotel.

Lygon Street throbbed with life. Low-slung cars cruised, motors throbbing, music pulsing behind their tinted windows. The sidewalk tables were filling fast and the aroma of tomato paste and oregano hung heavy in the air as prospective diners window-shopped for tagliatelle con vongole and fritto misto.

I strolled the length of the street to the Astor Hotel, an old-style pub with tiled walls the color of a lung disease, and drank a whiskey at the bar. Then I walked back the way I'd come. Dusk had given way to night and the floodlit cupola of the Exhibition Building glowed above the dark treetops of the gardens. At a phone booth on Rathdowne Street, I called the Southern Cross, had Frank Farrell paged and waited an anxious five minutes for him to pick up the house phone.

"Slight change of plans," I said.

"You wouldn't be fucking me around, by any chance?" he growled.

"Do exactly as I say and you'll have what you want very soon."

The Southern Cross was only four blocks away. I gave Farrell directions to the Gardenview Mews, told him to enter through the archway to the parking quadrangle and said I'd be waiting for him there in exactly fifteen minutes.

Traffic hummed along Rathdowne Street, the theater and cinema crowd streaming into town, late commuters heading the other way. A black BMW turned from the northbound lane and drove through the archway into the motel. I recognized the driver as the leggy press secretary to the deputy leader of the opposition. What was she up to, I wondered?

I didn't wonder for long. I confronted more compelling questions. Would I be able to get Farrell to talk? Would my little tape-machine trick succeed?

I had a ten-minute start. I used three of them to smoke a cigarette and stare across the road at the sign on the back entrance of the Exhibition Building. THE NATIONAL BOAT AND FISHING SHOW, it read. I had the bait in one pocket and the hook in the other. All that remained was to land the catch. I ground my butt underfoot and went into the motel quadrangle.

The black BMW was nose-in to the walkway, two doors away from Room 23. Its driver was nowhere in sight but there was a healthy degree of coming and going along the upper balconies. So far, so good. A public place, but not too noisy for recording purposes. We'd be out in the open, so Farrell would be unlikely to attempt to overpower me and snatch the phone. The most important thing was that he should believe that the swap was the main game. All the while, the tape would be running.

I went along the walkway to Room 23 and tested the handle, assuring myself that Ange had left the room locked when he left. I stripped off my jacket and stuffed it behind the ice machine. Goosebumps rose on my bare arms but I wanted Farrell to see that I wasn't wired. Every possible suspicion was to be allayed.

Pressing the record button, I placed the microcassette on top of the ice machine. Then, clutching the clear plastic bag that contained the mobile, I stood in front of Room 23 and waited.

Thirty seconds later Farrell prowled through the archway.

36

HE WAS WEARING A DENIM JACKET, a denim shirt and crotch-hugging jeans. At fifty meters, his eyes were caverns of impenetrable darkness. But when he tilted his head back to scan the scene, the light caught the tautness of the skin over his cheekbones, the hardness of his face.

Until that moment I hadn't really thought of him as a physical threat. Not to me, at least. Perhaps I should've made provision for the possibility. It was too late for that now. I was so far out on a limb I could've got a job as a ring-tailed possum.

I waited until he saw me, then dangled the bait and beckoned. He stalked forward warily, scoping the set-up, eyes darting from side to side. When he was four steps away, I signaled for him to stop. The tape recorder was a meter beyond his right shoulder. I willed myself not to look at it.

"We'll do it here." I nodded towards Room 23. "When I tell you, shove the statement under the door."

He raised his eyebrows. "Think I'll try to snatch it back once I've got what I want?"

"Absolutely," I said. "You can hardly blame me for not trusting you, Frank. You're a devious bastard and you've got a terrible temper.

Look what you did to poor Darren Stuhl. Analogued him off. Would that be the right expression?"

Farrell didn't rise to the topic. He took a folded sheet of paper out of his breast pocket and extended it into the space between us. In response, I took the phone from its bag and lay it on the ground at my feet. One swift kick and it would be under a car, out of reach. The zip-lock bag went into my back pocket, a crumpled ball.

"Read it to me," I said.

Farrell read quickly and without expression, like a courtroom clerk speeding through the ticket. For recording purposes, however, his volume and diction were perfect.

"I, Frank Farrell," he read, "an official of the United Haulage Workers, do hereby state that I was present when Howard Sharpe and Mike McGrath, respectively state secretary and deputy secretary of the aforesaid union, did maliciously conspire to fabricate and disseminate a libelous letter alleging sexual misbehavior on the part of the Minister for Transport, Angelo Agnelli. Signed and dated."

"A bit bush-lawyerish," I nodded. "But it'll do."

Not that I gave a stuff what it said. It was just a stage prop. A rubbery little tentacle designed to conceal the hook. What I needed now was a tongue-loosener, something to get the dialogue flowing.

"Pity you killed Darren before I filed my dental-damage compensation claim," I said. "Maybe I'm selling myself short here."

Farrell jerked the statement back and scowled. "You want money, too?"

"The thought occurred to me," I said. "But things tend to get messy when money's involved. So I'll settle for a bit of personal satisfaction. Like you said, Darren Stuhl had it coming. Tell me what it was like when you killed the prick."

Farrell raked me with a look of disgust. "It didn't feel like anything," he said. "He wouldn't put his gun away, so I hit him. He went down. End of story."

Beautiful, I thought. Come in spinner. Gimme more. "You think there was any chance he was still alive when you shoved him under Maitland's truck?"

"He was stone dead, you sick fuck." He nodded down at my feet. "Are we going to do this or not?"

I had what I wanted. All that remained was to finish the charade, bring down the curtain and see him off. "Okay," I said. "Slide the statement under the door."

He crouched, reaching out with his free hand as he fed the paper through the gap. As it disappeared, I kicked the mobile forward. Farrell grabbed it and came back upright.

Now that the evidence was in his grasp, he wasn't taking any more chances. He whipped a can of lighter fluid from his hip pocket, doused the phone and set it alight with his slim gold cigarette lighter.

Grab, squirt, flick, whoomph.

He dropped it to the ground and squirted it again as it burned between his feet, a smokeless ball of blue flame. Frank was a man who liked a fire.

"What about Maitland?" I said. "No remorse about feeding him to Bob Stuhl's wolves?"

The phone was shrinking to a molten blob. Farrell prodded it with the scuffed toe of his elastic-sided boot, hurrying it along. "You just don't get it, do you?" he said.

"Get what?"

He put a hand to his groin, made a hissing noise through his teeth and pretended to piss on the fire. Then he directed the stream from his invisible dick in my direction.

The scales fell from my eyes, washed away by a blast of imaginary urine. "You were the guy who pissed on me?" I said. "But why?"

Not just the pissing. I meant the entire exercise.

Farrell shrugged. No skin off his nose if I knew the truth. He had what he wanted. I prayed the tape was picking this up.

"Things weren't moving along quite as briskly as I hoped," he said. "The cops were taking their time buying the Maitland frame-up. So I thought I'd give the process a nudge. Rounded up an old army mate, told him we were doing a favor for Bob Stuhl. Coached him on his lines, of course. Didn't want you recognizing my voice. That was a very busy night, believe me. We'd just finished winding you up when I got the call about the cars being vandalized. Had to rush off and attend to union matters, put Maitland out of the election business."

"So Bob Stuhl was just a smokescreen?"

"And you bought it," said Farrell. "Lock, stock and shotgun barrel."

Holy Christ, I thought. I am a fucking moron. If Stuhl hadn't sent the pantyhose twins, did that mean he hadn't had Donny killed either? A band of steel closed around my chest. Farrell smirked and twisted the knife.

"If you'd done as you were told," he said, "Maitland would currently be awaiting trial on a murder charge. Manslaughter, even. Improper disposal of a body. Six or seven years, tops. But you had to get all hairy-arsed and start waving that gun around, didn't you? Forced my hand. After that, the only way I could be sure the fix would stick was to kill him. The pig-headed bastard. It took some considerable effort to get him to write that suicide note."

I felt sick to my soul. Farrell had wound me up, all right. He'd played me like a Stradivarius. But that was nothing compared with what he'd done to Donny. I wished I had a gun so I could shoot him on the spot like the mad dog that he was. My eye darted to the cassette recorder.

Farrell didn't notice. He was stomping the remains of the phone beneath his boot. When he'd pulverized it, he kicked it aside. Then he turned and slammed his heel into the door of Room 23. As it flew back on its hinges, he reached down and snatched up his statement. "You didn't really think I was going to let you keep it, did you?" he sneered. It flared briefly, then disintegrated into ashes.

A startled yelp came from inside the room. Our heads turned.

A woman was kneeling on the bed. She wore nothing but a studded dog collar and a leather harness. She held a riding crop in one hand and was straddling an albino sea-lion.

For a bizarre moment I thought it was a Helmut Newton photo-shoot. Except Helmut's people hadn't been in touch to ask if he could use my motel room. And the woman wasn't a model but the press secretary of the deputy leader of the opposition, the driver of the black BMW. She stared back at us in alarm, her arm shooting up to cover her naked breasts. They were okay but her legs were better.

"Very juicy," said Farrell. "Nothing like a bit of bondage."

Golden showers were more his preference, I thought. Along with bashing, torture and cold-blooded murder.

"No way," cried the woman, leaping off the sea-lion and scooping an armful of clothes off the floor. "I'll go along with dress-ups and a little light spanking, but I draw the line at groups. This is too weird for me."

Farrell's palm slammed into my chest and I reeled backwards. "So long, sucker," he crowed, and took off across the quadrangle.

"Baby doll," gasped the sea-lion. "Where are you going?"

Grabbing the tape recorder off the ice machine, I dashed into the stairwell. As I hit the rewind button, Madame Lash erupted from Room 23, a loose bundle of clothing pressed to her bosom. Her other attractions were now swathed in the voluminous folds of a man's shirt. It flapped around her knees as she wrenched open the door of her BMW.

I hit the play button and heard Farrell's voice: ". . . sexual misbehavior on the part of . . ."

Angelo Agnelli burst out onto the walkway tucking a towel around his expansive waist. The black beamer roared into life and backed away, tires screeching. "Wait," begged Ange. "You've got my pants."

"You sick fuck," said the tape recorder.

The desk clerk emerged from the reception area and started along the walkway, preceded by his out-thrust jaw. I ejected the tape, slipped it into my pants pocket and backed deeper into the obscurity of the stairwell.

Angelo hurled himself at the BMW, signaling wildly and pleading for his pants. But the dominatrix was a woman without pity. She spun the wheel, laid rubber and sped away. Propelled by his own desperate momentum, Angelo lurched after her for a dozen futile steps. Then he pulled up short and abandoned the chase.

He stood there in the middle of the floodlit quadrangle, clad in nothing but a bath towel and a gorilla mat of chest hair. Suddenly a screech of brakes resounded through the archway from the direction of the street. This was followed by the loud crump of an automotive collision. Then another, then another, then another. Then came the blare of a horn. The insistent, unremitting wail of a jammed horn.

Doors flew open all around the quadrangle. Inquisitive faces appeared on the balconies and peered downwards. Angelo was center stage. Firming his towel around his midriff, he adopted the insouciant air of a man who had lost his way while looking for the swimming pool. There was no swimming pool.

"Hey, you," shouted the desk clerk. He bounded towards Angelo, blocking his way back to the room. "What have you done to my door?"

The horn continued to shred the air. More people emerged. The manager advanced. Panic swept the face of the Minister for Transport. Clearly baffled by the sudden turn of events, he knew only one thing for sure. Explicability-wise, he was in a very vulnerable situation. Casting about for an escape route, he spied the only one available. Taking a firm hold of his loincloth, he beat a hasty retreat through the archway to the street.

It was a popular destination. Others were also headed that way, drawn by the incessant bleat of the horn. I joined them.

The pile-up was impressive. A six-vehicle fender-bender. Drivers, passengers and busybody onlookers were milling around, surveying the damage, yelling and gesticulating. The driver of the lead car, a dark gray Mercedes, was remonstrating with a cluster of people. Occupants of vehicles further down the line, judging by the way they were rounding on him.

"A black BMW," he said, gesturing helplessly up the street. "It shot out in front of me, so I hit the brakes. What else could I do?"

"You should've been paying attention," accused a bystander. "Instead of yapping on your mobile phone."

The blaring horn was coming from the last vehicle, an orange transit van with the words "Stuhl Couriers" along the side. It hadn't connected with the other cars. Swerving to avoid the pile-up, it had mounted the curb and slammed into a wall. A young man in a long ponytail and a Stuhl Holdings shirt was standing at the point of impact. He was wringing his hands and staring with stricken disbelief at a body which was pinned between the wall and the front bumper of his van.

"Somebody call an ambulance, man," he kept repeating. "For Chrissake, man, somebody call an ambulance."

It was too late for an ambulance. You didn't need to be a Fellow of the Royal Australasian College of Surgeons to see that much. The eyes of the hapless pedestrian were wide open, staring lifelessly ahead. Blood trickled from the corners of his mouth. One minute he was walking along the footpath, the next he was winging his way to eternity.

It was Frank Farrell. He didn't look quite so pleased with himself any more.

Traffic was building up. Cars in the southbound lane were slowing to a crawl as the occupants craned for a look. Spectators were converging from all directions. Across the road in the gardens, a pale ghost was flitting from tree to tree, thighs flapping, disappearing into the night.

37

THE RIDE WAS COMING TO AN END. Three men were dead. One good, one bad and one capable of very nasty behavior while drunk in a nightclub. It was time to hang up the Superman costume, crawl back down the limb and renew my trust in the due process of the law.

I went back into the motel, retrieved my jacket from behind the ice machine and ducked into Room 23. The bed was ravaged, underwear lay scattered across the floor and the atmosphere was pungent with the tang of body fluids and leather-care products.

Clearly, Farrell wasn't the only one who thought I belonged in a sheltered workshop. Ange had been playing me for a sucker, too. Our hush-hush pow-wows were simply a cover for his surreptitious rumpy-pumpy. To add insult to injury, he'd contrived to have me pay for the room. And his behavior was even more scandalous than alleged in the shit-letter. Fooling around might be forgivable. Kinky is a matter of taste. But doing it with a member of the Liberal Party was beyond the pale.

I slumped on the edge of the bed, called the Curnows' place and fixed it so Red could spend the night. "I had a meeting and things got out of hand," I told Faye. "You know what it's like."

Back out in the street, barriers were going up, ambulance and police lights flashing. I stood in the red-blue stroboscopic flare and watched as Farrell's body was strapped onto a gurney and whoop-whooped away. Then I sidled up to one of the cops and told him I had information pertaining to the deceased pedestrian. And to related matters of probable interest to the Criminal Investigation Branch.

By the time the uniforms passed me up the line and the dicks at headquarters had done listening to the tape, it was past midnight. Detective Senior Sergeant Noel Webb joined the team at that point, not pleased to have been summoned from some Friday-night piss-up. "If being a fuckwit was an indictable offense, Whelan," he told me, "you would've spent most of your life behind bars."

The coppers would have liked to arrested me, they made it plain, but couldn't think of a charge. Professional jealousy, I decided. Like me, they could hardly be expected to greet with delight the revelation that they'd been given the right royal runaround. With the tape in the hands of the authorities, however, the burden of responsibility at last moved back to where it belonged.

When I was shown the door of the cop shop, it was two in the morning and I was as spent as yesterday's lunch-money. I hailed a cab, gave the driver my address and sat numbly in the back. As the convent of Mary Immaculate flashed past, I offered up a silent prayer for Donny's repose. Not that there was anyone to hear it. Or that Donny would've looked kindly on such a lapse. At least his killer had not escaped retribution. The dead mightn't care, but the living take consolation from such things. I did, at least.

I stared into the gardens, too, as we drove by, and wondered what had become of Angelo. That question was answered the next morning, after I was dragged from my slumbers by a brief and enigmatic phone call from Lyndal Luscombe.

"Seen the *Sun*?" she asked eagerly.

"Huh?" I snuffled. "Is there an eclipse or something?"

"Quick," she ordered. "Take a look."

I tugged at the curtains, squinted at the cirrus-streaked sky and realized she meant the newspaper not the celestial orb. So I pulled on some track pants, padded down to the corner shop and bought a copy.

Ange was plastered across the front page. The photograph showed him with one hand raised in an unsuccessful attempt to shield his face while the other gripped his trusty Gardenview Mews towel. Flanked by two Parliament House stewards, he looked like a Roman senator being arrested at the baths by a detachment of the Praetorian Guard.

SEX CLAIM MINISTER IN NUDE ROMP declared the headline.

According to the report, the Minister for Transport had been disturbed the previous evening by parliamentary staff while trying to slip into his office in a state of undress. Not immediately recognizing him, they had given chase. In an attempt to elude his pursuers, the government leader in the Upper House had taken a wrong turn and crossed the floor of the chamber during a debate on the deficit. The incident was witnessed by a *Sun* reporter, who was waiting for an opportunity to seek the minister's comments on allegations of inappropriate sexual behavior circulating in his electorate.

Claiming he had been robbed of his clothes while taking a stroll in the nearby gardens, the minister lunged at a press photographer and attempted to destroy his camera.

The menials of Murdoch had struck paydirt and they mined it for all it was worth. Further pictures appeared on the inside pages, along with reports that a near-naked man had earlier been observed in the vicinity.

Poor Angelo. Timing is all in politics, and this was far from the ideal moment to go streaking through the corridors of power. By late morning, Ange's allies on the public office selection committee had hung him out to dry. Finding himself a faction of one, he was compelled to review his priorities. Citing stress, he submitted his resignation as minister and announced his intention to retire from parliament at the next election.

That left just me and Save Our Trains at the starting gate. On the following Monday, when the result of the preselection poll was declared, I became the endorsed Labor candidate for Melbourne Upper.

The state election was held almost exactly twelve months later. The result was a landslide that buried Labor so deep it might be the next century before we tunnel our way out. As always, Melbourne Upper remained solid and I was duly elected as its representative in the Legislative Council. I sit there now, one of a tiny rump of Labor members.

Unfortunately for my constituents, vengeance is the watchword of the new regime and my days in parliament are spent ineffectually voting against legislation that appears specifically designed to punish safe Labor seats for their traditional loyalties. Banished to the wilderness, the party has directed its energies into squabbling over the spoils of defeat.

Bob Stuhl is bigger than ever. According to Faye, he is diversifying into the telecommunications sector. Australia has one of the highest take-up rates of mobile phones in the world and Bob is positioning himself to capture a significant share of the traffic they are expected to generate. The size and cost of cell phones is shrinking before our very eyes and it will soon be difficult to believe that a fit young man could once have been beaten to death with one. I myself have finally succumbed. Twice. One for me for work-related purposes, the other for Red. He needs it, I feel, since he travels so far to and from school every day.

One of the first acts of the incoming Liberal government was to close two hundred government schools, Fitzroy High among them. Somewhere else had to be found for Red. Reluctantly, after considerable soul-searching, I decided to enroll him in a private school. To be frank, his academic performance at Fitzroy was disappointing and Wendy's ceaseless telephone tirades were beginning to wear me down. On top of which, sending your children to government schools is contrary to established practice for Labor members of parliament.

Red still thinks the purple blazer makes him look like a twat, but he's finally settled down to the two-hour daily commute. At least he doesn't have to wear a boater. He still sees Tarquin socially, of course.

What with the annual school fees, the mobile phone and the mandatory laptop computer, I'd probably be feeling the strain if it wasn't for my parliamentary salary. My interim year as a consultant was not as financially rewarding as I'd hoped and there wasn't much left of my lump-sum pay-out by the time the election rolled around. Angelo's spectacular fall from grace tended to tarnish me by association, despite the fact that our connection had been formally terminated three weeks prior to his self-immolation.

Angelo has returned to the law, where a tendency to lewd behavior is a professional asset and a reputation for misogyny is a recommendation for appointment to the bench. His wife, Stephanie, stuck with him steadfastly in the aftermath of his ordeal. They were divorced, however, soon after his parliamentary term expired. She got the lion's share of his superannuation.

Howard Sharpe continues to rule the Haulers' roost, having been re-elected without opposition for his seventh successive four-year term. Soon he'll be looking for a new sidekick. There's a federal election coming up and Mike McGrath made the cut for the Senate ticket, so he's Canberra-bound. He'll doubtless find many kindred spirits in the national capital, particularly among those visiting from Sydney.

Miss Leatherette of the Liberals, by the way, is currently in charge of the new state government's prison privatization program. Word has it that she's very close to the marketing director of the global corrections corporation, Wackanut Inc.

As arranged, Lyndal and I had dinner together on the Tuesday evening after the preselection poll. What with one thing and another, I didn't feel like Italian, so it wasn't candlelight and champagne at Florentino's. Instead, we settled on sake and tonkatsu in a shoji-screened alcove at Kenzan, the Japanese restaurant at the Regent Hotel.

"I'm keen to come to grips with that issue you raised prior to the closure of nominations," she told me.

"And I remain curious about your preferences," I said.

"Perhaps we can go upstairs afterwards and assess each other's credentials," she suggested, taking a hotel key out of her purse.

"Waiter," I called.

Soon after, she landed a job with the Department of Human Services, reviewing its needs-based service-delivery performance. I gave her an excellent reference, based on a personal assessment of her capabilities. She continues to harbor long-term ambitions for a federal seat. After almost eighteen months she and I are still bedding down the central plank in her platform.

Red approves of our relationship. "She reminds me a bit of Mum," he told me. I have no idea what he means.

The lad will be fifteen soon and Wendy has finally conceded defeat on the custody front. My status as a member of parliament makes it a tad difficult for her to cast me as a complete incompetent, although it hasn't stopped her from trying. I'm reluctantly forced to agree with her on one point, however. Being an opposition member in the Upper House of an Australian provincial parliament is hardly the most high-powered job in the world.

Still, it meets my modest requirements. It keeps the bank at bay and the refrigerator stocked. I have time to devote to the tasks of fatherhood. I do what I can for my constituents. And I have absolutely no reason to visit the Melbourne Wholesale Fruit and Vegetable Market at four o'clock in the morning in the middle of winter.

Anyway, that's the story of how I became a member of parliament. Whether you believe it or not is entirely up to you.

It's a big ask, I know.